awakening
shadows

The Navarre Chronicles Book One

Kristiana,
Never stop reaching
for the stars!

Sydney♡

awakening shadows

Awakening Shadows

Copyright © 2020 by Lilac Daggers Press LLC

Trigger Warning : Contains scenes of mild violence, nudity, and mild language

For information contact :

Lilac Daggers Press LLC

9429 Monticello Drive

Twinsburg, OH 44087

www.worldofsydneyhawthorn.com

Cover design by CelinGraphics

Map design by Lizard Ink Maps

ISBN: 978-1-7349004-0-8

First Edition: September 2020

10 9 8 7 6 5 4 3 2 1

To Nana, for giving me the courage to reach for my first dream and fueling my endless imagination to pursue it.

one

The effort not to breathe was unbearable as he fought to swim toward the surface. The water engulfed him, almost blinding. His energy slowly ebbed away as the movements became more difficult. He shook, his legs beating against the vicious current struggling to pull him back, to suck him down into her frigid blackness. One more second, and he would be free. If he could just break through the darkness...

Quinn's eyes shot open, but he couldn't move. His lungs struggling for air as he lay waiting for the sensation to fade. The dreams were always paralyzing no matter how many times they played within his subconscious.

After a moment, a groan escaped his lips and the thin pile of old quilts slipped to the floor as he sat upright. Sparrows chirped outside the shuttered window.

Voices sounded from the hallway.

With another groan, he wiped a hand over the layer of scruff covering his jaw and yawned. He leaned against the wall, wood cold against his back as he stretched his arms above his head, his eyes shifting toward the door when it opened.

Jenson poked his head into the room, dark eyes playful. "So," he said, slipping through the door. "He's awake after all. I thought I

1

heard you grumbling to yourself."

Quinn swung long legs over the edge of the bed, rolling his eyes as he strode toward the wash basin near the window. Splashing icy water into his face, he removed one of several daggers from a belt draped over the chair before him, the blade cool against his cheek as it scraped along the dark stubble coating his jawline.

Jenson huffed out a breath, running a hand through onyx hair. "Oh, come on, smile. I'm teasing."

The sharp steel froze mid-shave as Quinn replied without turning to his friend. "Isn't that all you ever do?"

A chuckle. "Usually." Jenson straightened his tunic, the leather overvest creaking from the movement. "But I shouldn't jest today. The Waeshorn Princess rides in her name-day procession this morning."

"I know." Quinn's voice was flat as he fiddled with the aquamarine pendant against his chest, shifting his blade to the other cheek. "You let me sleep."

Jenson shrugged, leaning against the dresser beside the door. "You needed it. You've been exhausting yourself in Fallon's absence."

Quinn frowned. "So maybe I have."

"Quinn."

He raised an eyebrow. "Jens."

"You always do that, single yourself out. You don't have to do everything alone. Maya and I are here to—"

"Fallon is returning from The Redlands today. I can't afford to spend all morning resting. Every one of us knows that he expects the princess to remain unharmed without him here."

Sighing, Jenson pursed his lips. "It's hard to forget how he is about details." His pleasant tenor voice sounded almost bitter. "But details are vital. The Order of Kynire's existence is built to protect Navarre."

"It's more than that. Without the assurance of Princess Joseline's safety, there would be no stopping Aeron's return." Finished shaving, Quinn sheathed the dagger, then pulled the dark gray cotton tunic over broad shoulders and adjusted the dagger belt around his hips. The leather vest, fitted to his broad shoulders perfectly, pulled taut when he secured the laces at his chest.

"I don't even want to think about that alternative. If Aeron rose again, the city would be in chaos." Jenson shuddered.

Quinn's expression was stone as he fastened on two thick leather wrist guards, testing the dagger hidden against his left forearm. "Never mind the city, Jenson. The realm would be in chaos."

Maya's voice echoed from the door. "Well then, we'll just have to make sure that doesn't happen, won't we, gentlemen?"

Both men turned to where she leaned against the frame, honey blonde hair bobbing against her chin. Her green eyes were piercing as she smiled, the slight gap between her front teeth barely noticeable. "You two weren't planning to chatter away up here like old hags all day, were you? There's work to be done."

Jenson's jaw dropped, his eyes widening. "Work to be done? You don't say, Maya."

Quinn rolled his eyes, lips tightening into a firm line. "I am aware."

Within seconds she was behind him, eyes playful as she smiled sweetly, a dagger pressed against his throat despite the height difference between them.

"I know you are, dearest Quinn," she whispered. "But if you forget, well, you won't be here to explain the tale of your disobedience. Besides, I'm not the one who was snoring loud enough for The Twelve and all their enemies to hear."

Jenson snorted, muttering, "I thought Quinn was in charge during Fallon's absence."

"So did I," Quinn growled.

Maya stepped away, sheathing the dagger at her thigh. "He is in charge. I'm just making it clear there are things we will not fail at this morning, that's all."

Quinn huffed out a breath, running his fingers through his hair. "Gods, Maya, when did you get so demanding?"

Maya shrugged. "Someone has to be, right?" Before he could respond, she winked and left the room, swaying narrow hips.

Quinn shook his head, reaching for the thick wool cloak draped over the chair. "Is it brisk this morning, Jens?"

"I'm not sure, why do you ask?"

Quinn checked to make sure his window was locked as his friend spoke, sealing the shutters using a magic enchantment, his power tingling his flesh as it ebbed from his palms. "Just wondering if I should add a layer," he said, pausing to slip on worn leather boots before the two men stepped into the hallway.

"I knew you two would come out sooner or later," Maya said from further down the narrow hall. Quinn glared at her.

"Maya," Jenson said. "It's been two blasted minutes."

"Besides, did you really think we were going to let you take all the credit for this?" Quinn added. "What sort of brotherly figures would we be if we let the youngest have all the attention?"

Maya laughed. "The best kind, but I know you both better than that. This is the moment we've been—"

Trumpets sounded in the distance and Quinn took off down the hallway at a jog, Jenson and Maya at his heels. The hallway ended in a narrowed spiral staircase. Quinn jumped two steps at a time with catlike stealth and grace, his boots hardly touching the wood beneath his feet.

The staircase let out into a small living area—the only decorative items a single couch and a matching chair, a low, wooden table, and a worn, peach-colored rug crowded at its center. A kitchen wrapped around to the right near the door to the stables.

Jenson scanned the empty room. "The others are already out in the streets?"

Quinn raised an eyebrow. "They should be, or my orders were disobeyed." He glanced around the room one final time before they put their hoods up and slipped into the alleyway, running into the gathering crowd.

Quinn kept his face blank while his companions dispersed amongst the peasants. The crowd lined the streets and alleyways, chattering with excitement and anticipation as they awaited the arrival of the royal procession.

Today was the name-day of the Rathal Princess, Her Royal

Highness Joseline Marie Waeshorn. The young maiden who had never once in eighteen years shown her face to her city, whose life and safety encompassed the reason for The Order of Kynire's existence, for *his* existence.

Quinn slipped unnoticed into the crowd, his blue-green eyes wandering the shadows.

two

Joseline Marie took a deep breath as she watched the outer castle wall draw nearer and nearer.

Freedom.

The past eighteen years her life had been spent confined, dictated, and observed by her ever-hovering mother, her free time—if you could call it that—consumed by young courtiers and suitors fighting for her attention. Smothered by a life she often wanted no part of and trapped within the palace meant to ensure her safety and the continuation of the kingdom's peace.

But today was the day she had longed for, the day her overprotective mother had agreed to let her step foot outside the castle confines. It took all she had to sit up straight in her saddle, her body shaking with nervous energy as her mind raced. Starlia was calm beneath her as she stroked the mare's white mane with a gentle hand.

Before her rode her mother and father. Queen Talia, narrow framed with pleasant curves accented by a tight bun of black hair, was a mere shadow to her tall, burly husband. King Nathaniel sat proud in his saddle, eyes dancing, chin high, his hand resting on the long sword strapped to his side. His fiery hair and beard blew in the soft breeze as he turned to her, flashing a confident smile that crinkled his almond-shaped eyes.

Joseline returned the gesture, her own smile weak as she toyed with the burnt crimson ringlet framing her narrow face.

She recognized most of their entourage from the endless council meetings her mother insisted she attend. At least two dozen people rode with them—important clergymen, advisors, and nobles from neighboring cities surrounded by several dozen Jade Cloaks all dressed in heavy armor engraved with the Waeshorn crest. Kellen, the young Captain of the Guard and her personal man-at-arms, rode to her right, armor gleaming, jade cloak billowing in the breeze. The castle's head healer, Mikenna, rode on her left. Joseline adored the healer, much preferring the solace of her workroom or the library to attending court sessions.

Joseline stared at the road ahead, her heart racing with excitement.

"Your Highness." Kellen's deep voice broke Joseline's focus. She blinked at him, short sandy blond hair blowing across his tanned forehead. "Are you nervous?"

"Nervous? Don't be absurd, of course not."

Kellen's smile always soothed her nerves. He looked around before leaning toward her. "Your Highness, please. I can read you better than that. Your eyes are dancing."

Joseline's nostrils flared. "They most certainly are not, Sir Kellen. That would be childish."

The captain winked at her but didn't argue, his own hazel eyes playful. "Well, I don't know much, but I heard rumors from several merchants that the magic folk are all on edge for some inexplicable reason. Few have just up and left, but others...well, they're talking of staying to fight whatever it is that's stirring up trouble."

Joseline's eyes lit up. "Oh, do tell me more, Kellen. You know I am so fond of the stories you hear!"

Mikenna clicked her tongue sharply, glaring at the young knight with firm authority before he could continue. "Now Kellen, you know how the Queen feels about you fillin' that girl's head with those nonsense stories of the city folk. No more of that. The princess has other things to worry about today. Better to encourage her actin' like a young woman rather than a child."

Joseline rolled her eyes, but said nothing, huffing out a loud breath as she faced forward. Knowing it would cause an argument with her mother, she thought better of sending the healer a smart reply. As if sensing her irritation, Kellen reached over and squeezed her hand. Joseline gave him a weak smile before facing forward once more.

The light breeze blew toward her from Mikenna's direction. Joseline smiled, the healer's scent of pine and frankincense as soothing as her workshop always was.

The outer palace wall towered thirty feet above them, the width of thick stone littered with heavily-armored palace guards. The sturdy iron gate yawned, revealing the steep descent into Rathal's capital city, Corae. The Princess leaned forward in her saddle, all previous annoyances forgotten.

She'd never been this close to the outer gate before. Her mother insisted even while out riding she stay close to the Citadel; behind the inner wall. Now, all her restrictions lifted away, blowing into the breeze with flightless grace.

Her large eyes widened at the city, her city, growing before her. A crowd gathered at the base of the hill to greet them where the uneven gravel leveled to firm ground once more.

The city wall, infused with protective magic centuries ago by the mystical Fae King, was a faint dark smudge in her vision. Holding back a childish giggle, Joseline's head darted from side to side, afraid she might miss something if her attention lingered in one spot too long.

Buildings towered above her on either side, apartments and shops reaching into the bright morning sky. Clothes hung between open windows high above, drying in the soft breeze. Peasants vanished from upper level balconies only to reappear at doorsteps, and merchants squinted through sunlight from the shade of wheeled carts.

The townsfolk stared at her with awe. Children sat on father's shoulders, waving, while mothers, still wearing cooking aprons smeared with batter from breakfast, grinned. Joseline beamed, fighting the urge to leap from her saddle as she waved her hand with fluid grace.

"Long live the Waeshorn heir, long live Princess Joseline!" someone shouted when she passed.

The crowd cheered as they rode deeper into the tangled streets of Corae. Joseline took in a deep breath of air as if she could somehow savor this moment forever, the frustrations of her ever-hovering mother and lonely life melting away. The late spring breeze was refreshing, the smell of spices and fresh fruits tickling her nose.

Corae was just as she imagined—small, quaint, beautiful...

Chaos erupted without warning.

The city streets exploded with frantic people from some unknown source.

Screams and children's cries filled the air, panicked villagers running about in a frenzy to return to the safety of their homes, knocking over anything in their path. Some, unable to get out of the way of merchants' bucking mounts, were tossed to the ground, ducking to prevent being trampled beneath looming hooves. The dusty earth puffed up clouds of debris and dirt from the road, blinding amidst the surrounding panic.

Confused and scared, Joseline searched for the terror's source. Her heart drummed in violent thumps against her chest.

Scattered among the townsfolk, hooded figures moved toward the royal procession from the twisted alleyways lining the main road. Some wore a deep gray while some wore black, etched with a strange symbol she'd never seen before. Dark shadows swirled at the black cloaked figures' feet, swallowing the sunshine in their path.

Joseline froze. Fear gripped her stomach as thick clouds pushed the figures forward, consuming the light. The stench rolling off them made her gag, vomit sour in her throat. She couldn't move, paralyzed with fear.

"Your Highness!" Kellen's voice broke through the trance. He raced toward her, shield up as he drew his sword. "Stay near your parents." He pointed to the group of Jade Cloaks circling her mother and father.

She nodded, giving Starlia's reins a sharp tug. But her mount reared as if whipped from behind, charging into the mass of people and clouding dust. Joseline shrieked, fighting to stay in the saddle as Starlia galloped down a narrow alleyway branching off the main road.

Kellen's deep voice boomed behind her, followed by the shouting responses of several other knights, but she couldn't make out the distant words.

Joseline tried to calm the frantic mare, but she charged deeper into the back streets of the city. Scarlet curls whipped about her face, stinging her cheeks as she clung to Starlia's mane. It was all Joseline could do to remain in the saddle.

Daring to glance behind her, Joseline prayed she would see Kellen and the other guards, but she was greeted by dark, empty streets. The madness of the outbreak was nothing more than a faint whisper in the distance.

At last, her snowy-colored mare began to slow. Gulping down breaths, Joseline brought Starlia to a walk. The alley was too narrow to turn around, but it opened into a small space behind one of the many stone buildings ahead of her.

She tugged on the reins, urging Starlia to turn around, but her mare lurched forward, her front legs giving out as she stumbled to the ground. Joseline shrieked again, the sound barely leaving her throat as she flew through the air and slammed into the brick, landing with a motionless thud on the ground.

Quinn dropped into the alley from a low-hanging rooftop, his grey cloak billowing around him when he landed.

Removing his thick hood, he crouched beside the mare. She nickered hesitantly as he approached, trying to stand on the injured front leg, but calmed beneath Quinn's gentle touch. He glanced toward the wide dip in the dirt leading back into the alley, clicking his tongue as he stroked her mane and urged her to her feet.

"Poor girl, you must have taken a nasty stumble to send your mistress flying like that." Reaching into his wool cloak, he produced a fresh apple.

The horse's ears perked up and she lunged for the fruit, but Quinn pulled his hand out of reach.

The horse met his eyes, almost narrowing them.

"Tell you what. If you come with me, I promise I'll see to that leg of yours." He tossed the apple into the air, catching it smoothly with the other hand, blue-green eyes flickering to her injured ankle. "And I'll give you this."

The horse nickered, taking a step toward him. As promised, he tossed her the fruit and walked over to where the princess lay.

He touched her neck with two fingers, relieved to feel the light thump of a pulse. Gently, he lifted the young girl into his arms, cradling her against his chest. Dirt smeared her silk gown and freckled ivory cheeks.

She was tiny; at least a foot shorter than him, and she felt so small, so fragile for a woman of eighteen.

"Just what do you think you're doing, commoner?" The deep voice behind him was male.

Quinn set the princess down, fighting the growl rising in his throat. "I had hoped it would take you a bit longer to find her."

"You have no business laying your hands on Her Royal Highness. Leave, and I promise you will not be harmed."

A half-laugh escaped his lips as he turned to face the speaker, his eyes narrowing instantly. "Sir Kellen." Quinn folded his arms across his broad chest, keeping himself between the princess and her knight. "I'm surprised you weren't riding at her side. Quite lousy of a protector, if you ask me."

Kellen stepped forward, holding his long sword up toward Quinn's throat and forcing him to step aside in the process. "Well, I'm here now. So, if you don't mind, I'll return the princess to the castle." Kellen tried to push him back again.

This time, he didn't move. "Now why is it that I don't trust you?"

Kellen smirked, leather creaking beneath his hand as it tightened around his sword's hilt. "Maybe you shouldn't."

The princess shifted beside them, a small groan escaping her lips. "Kellen?"

Before she could open her eyes, Kellen knelt, thumping her against the temple with the pommel of his sword hilt.

She didn't move again, her head falling to one side.

Quinn took a step toward the captain, eyes feral. When he spoke, his voice was a low growl. "You aren't taking the princess to safety."

Kellen hesitated only slightly, but Quinn caught it. He also caught the black ink marking Kellen's inner wrist—an encircled X beneath crossed scythes: the demon king's symbol.

His body went rigid. *Aeron.*

"The princess isn't going anywhere with you."

Kellen grinned. "I have strict orders to ensure her safety."

Not waiting for Kellen to stand and challenge him, his hand jabbed the pressure point along the throat—a heel simultaneously slamming into Kellen's ribs as he struck with inhuman speed. The captain collapsed with a grunt.

"As do I, Sir. I don't plan to abandon them for the likes of you." Blue-green light swirled around Quinn's fingertips as he spoke, dancing along the princess's temple. The light shimmered softly, then faded into her flesh as the sleeping enchantment took hold of her body. He lifted the princess, cradling her to his chest once more, and motioned for the mare to follow. The animal obeyed, leaving the unconscious captain in the alley behind them.

thRee

The distant bell chimed a third time, marking the hour. Sweat stung Quinn's eyes. He longed to set the princess down and wipe his face but didn't want to risk waking her. Mercifully, she had remained unconscious thanks to the sleeping enchantment.

She was tiny, but after walking for over an hour in the blinding sun with her weight against his chest, he regretted taking the less traveled route. Quinn didn't need to glance at the limping mare behind him to know it was the smarter choice. However, the exhaustion and lack of sleep were catching up to him; the dull ache of a migraine spread across his temples.

They were so close, the rundown two-story building not even a block ahead. Quinn bit his lip, quickening his pace.

The stables were attached to the eastern side of the building, dull and ordinary to any passers-by. Quinn kicked at the olive-colored barn doors, cursing as the princess almost slipped from his arms.

"Who's there?" a young voice cracked.

"Reive, open the damned door."

A young boy poked his head out. "Yes, Sir. Sorry, Sir. I didn't know it was you, Sir," Reive mumbled without meeting his eyes.

"Find a stall for the horse. I'll be back to look at her leg later." He walked toward the main building. "And lock that door again before you forget."

"Yes, Sir. Of course, Sir."

Inside the living room, Jenson lounged in the armchair, lean and cat-like, one leg draped over the side. Maya paced before him, every so often glancing out the window near the main door.

"I have been giving him time!" she wailed. "I just wish Fallon didn't always ask him to do the dangerous assignments."

Jenson met Quinn's eyes and grinned. "I know he can be difficult, trust me. But he knows what he's doing. Try not to concern yourself."

Quinn kicked the door shut and Maya's head snapped toward the sound. "Quinn! Thank the Gods." She rushed to him, but Quinn shook his head. Maya walked to the small kitchen without another word, her expression hardening.

Jenson eyed him, taking a casual sip from the mug in his hands.

"There are castle guards all over the city," Quinn said. "I had to take back streets."

He laid the princess on the couch, careful not to wake her. Sweat dripped down her temple, her head lolling to one side, but she didn't move.

"Where was she?" Maya returned with a water skin, handing it to him.

Quinn took several deep gulps and wiped his mouth along the back of his hand before he replied, "Behind Swan Lagoon. Her mare stumbled, and she hit her head. She'll have a bruise on her temple and a few scratches."

Jenson stood, moving to pull the blinds halfway across the window as a group of Jade Cloaks rushed by. "Good. It's not what we planned, but Fallon will still be pleased."

Quinn nodded, his eyes lingering on the guards as they vanished. "I'm going to cloak the house." Both Maya and Jenson gave him an inquisitive look. He never used magic unless there was a good reason. "The streets are swarming with palace guards." *Or worse, Aeron spies,* he thought. "I don't want to take any chances."

14

"I'll stay with her." Jenson jerked his head toward the princess.

Quinn ignored Maya padding up the spiraling stairs behind him. Only when he reached the landing did he turn to face her. "Magic is dangerous. I don't need you in the way."

She rolled her eyes. "I'll be fine."

Quinn struggled to keep the snarl from his voice, the headache making him cross. "You aren't coming. I don't have the time to argue about this."

"So don't argue." Maya stepped toward him, a flash of sensitivity she always fought to hide flickering in her eyes. "Please, Quinn, I worried about you. You always make me worried sick."

"You worry for nothing. You know I always come back." Quinn's voice softened. "So, try not to fret, Yaya."

Her cheeks reddened at the childhood nickname.

"You know you're the only one who still calls me that?" She smiled. "I just can't help but worry, Quinn. If something happened to you..."

Quinn forced himself to make the smile genuine. "You know I'm always careful."

Without warning, she gripped his tunic and pulled his face down to hers. Quinn had no time to object as her lips touched his cheek. Quinn knew he was glaring at her, but she met his eyes evenly.

"I...go. I'm sorry." She brushed past him, vanishing into one of the rooms on the left side of the narrow hall.

Quinn shook his head as he opened the door to his study. He cracked his knuckles, glancing around without success for the jar of ginger root. Gods, his head was pounding. Willing the headache to ease, he stepped into the intricate circle etched along the wooden floor.

His body relaxed, filling with a state of blank contemplation. Quinn reached inside himself, searching for the slumbering well of magic power. The pool of blue-green fire grew as he touched it with his mind, seeping through his skin. Slowly, he drew out the flame until it shimmered visibly in his palm, the swirling tattoo covering his left side giving off a faint glow. Quinn swirled the magic around his body, testing it, willing it to grow. His thoughts slipped away, his mind nothing but a void of focused tranquility.

When the fire filled both his fists, he closed his eyes, mentally demanding his power bend to his request. Moments later he opened his eyes; a faint blue-green glow flickered outside the shutters. Quinn whispered his thanks to The Twelve, breaking the bond, and the flames vanished, retreating within him once more. He stepped out of the circle.

Closing the door to his study, he hesitated, glancing sideways at the bathing room across the hall. A long, steamy bath would do wonders to ease the resurfacing headache. But raised voices echoed from the main room downstairs: Jenson's calmness counteracting the second, fear-laced tone.

With a sigh, he jogged toward the stairs, pulling at the tie holding thick hair away from his face. Once on the main level he leaned against the wooden railing, gnawing on his lower lip, arms folded across his chest.

The princess sat upright and alert. Her freckled nose wrinkled in anger, large forest-green eyes blazed, and she held a wet rag against the greenish-purple bruise forming on her temple where Kellen struck her.

"You won't—" she caught sight of Quinn and stopped mid-sentence.

He strolled over to the armchair where Jenson lounged once more. "You seem distraught. Is something wrong?"

Her voice was no more than a whisper. "You're spies. Who do you work for?"

"Spy is a filthy word," Quinn said. "I'm no spy, I merely collect information."

She ignored him. "I would know your face anywhere. All the young palace spies do is swoon over you, and you're the talk of all my father's council meetings. It's Quinn, correct?" She was shaking, fists clenched in her lap, but her soft voice remained calm.

She hides her fear well, he thought. *That's a good start, I suppose.*

"Pleased to meet you," he said, trying not to let his exhaustion fuel his sarcasm. "Although you misunderstand. We don't want to harm you. Those are Aeron's intentions."

The princess's face paled. "Aeron?" she whispered. "He doesn't exist. He's a nightmare made to scare children who won't stay in bed at night."

"Is he?"

She opened her mouth to reply but said nothing.

"We mean only to protect you," Quinn continued. "Like our organization, Aeron has spies everywhere. Nowhere is safe. He infiltrated the castle years ago. So rather than complaining, you could start with a thank you."

"A thank you?" Her eyes brimmed with ice. "You have no right to tell me where I am or am not safe. How do I know I can trust you? You have quite the reputation. Seduction and lies are hardly the proper way to get information regardless of who you work for."

Jenson's laugh went unnoticed.

Quinn stood, inches from her face in a single stride. He towered over her, but her eyes didn't falter as they met his. "My dear, that's just business. Business required of me to avoid any harm befalling you. Besides," he leaned forward, "I'm an honest man."

Her throat bobbed, though her stare never faltered. Quinn almost raised an eyebrow as she stood, her expression defiant. "That's Your Highness to you, and something tells me there's no such thing as an honest man in your line of work."

Quinn's smile was feral as he stepped back, teeth flashing. "Oh, but there is, *Your Highness*. An honest man takes only what they need. A dishonest man, well, they will take more than they need and stab you in the back while you sleep to keep you from discovering the truth."

Jenson's foot bounced against the side of the chair. "That's the sort of men Aeron collects, the men we mean to keep you away from. Quinn's never done anything besides attain information we might use to protect you."

Her pretty voice dripped with sarcasm. "I guess I should thank you."

"Yes, you should." All three heads turned toward the stairwell to see Maya perched on the edge of the wide railing. "What these lovely gentlemen are taking forever to say is, we want you here no more than you want to be here. But your safety has been our focus for years. We have no interest in seeing Aeron rise to power."

"Stopping Aeron? You realize how ridiculous that sounds, do you not?" The princess shook her head. "I can't help you."

"But you can," Jenson said.

Maya jumped to the ground, blonde hair bouncing about her chin. "It is foretold that were royal blood of any race to set foot on the soils of Raenya and drink the waters of the Amber Falls, their soul would be forever blessed and protected against Aeron's shadow magic. They say the Goddess created the country as a safe haven for her Demi-Fae children by removing a piece of her soul and placing it at the country's heart. She dwelled there in mortal form, and over time the sacred waters eroded at it—fueling the country's magic and beauty. The Amber Falls still flow with her power."

"But that has nothing to do with me!" the princess protested.

"As far as anyone knows, you are the only remaining heir to the four royal houses of Navarre," Maya said. "All other royal children were slaughtered by Aeron's demons a hundred years ago or haven't been heard from since."

The princess huffed, delicate brows knitting together in frustration, but Jenson added, "Each moment you fight the truth, his chances to completely break the seal containing him increase. You are the only hope left for this realm, the only one alive who could stop him. There are prophecies passed down through generations, speaking of the promised heir to unite the people should Aeron rise again. Those prophecies are talking about you."

"This is insane!" Joseline cried. "I know the stories of Aeron. My nursemaid whispered them at night to scare my sister Julia. They're just *stories*. It's been centuries since Aeron threatened Navarre, and my parents stopped believing in fables and myths years ago. I refuse to—"

Quinn cleared his throat, interrupting her.

"And he, dark and immortal,
shall rise thrice from the shadows to thrive;
his eternal glory and power unleashed once more.
Mortals shall slave for him, Gods shall fear him.
Pain, torture, and destruction in his wake.
But she, the blessed mortal, who resembles the darkest embers of the
sun shall be his purity and imprisoner;
the last of three to be the key.
For she holds in her soul the capacity to feed him or destroy him,
her bloodline his everlasting salvation.
With diligence and patience, she may learn,
guided by great warriors to achieve her royal fate.
The slumbering waters of light bend to her will, the warriors follow her
command, the first of six united in the elements of power.
And only she may command the supremacy
to push the shadows back into their dungeon of eternal darkness."

four

The silence following was deadly.

The princess glared at Quinn. Her eyes glowed with fiery golden flecks, small fists clenching and unclenching in her lap.

Nobody moved.

When Quinn spoke, he refused to let the building annoyance show. "That prophecy is about you, *Your Highness*. I don't give a damn what you believe. You can believe whatever you'd like. But I've spent my entire life training for your safety. The world needs you, yet you chose to be a whimpering child and leave your people to suffer."

The contact of Joseline's hand against Quinn's cheek resonated throughout the room.

Her nose wrinkled in a scowl, nostrils flaring with anger. "How *dare* you speak to me that way. I don't know who you think you are, *Sir*, but I am your princess and heir to your kingdom's throne. Keep your thoughts to yourself if they are unpleasant."

The throbbing pulse along his temple did nothing to ease his growing anger. "Why, because I'm speaking the truth? You're a woman now, best time as ever to start making your own choices. Unless that isn't something a spoiled, insufferable princess can manage."

She slapped him again.

Quinn closed his eyes, gnawing on an already raw bottom lip to settle his nerves. "Look, *Your Highness*, I don't want to argue. I apologize."

"We meant no offense." Jenson's light tenor voice was even more pleasant than usual.

Joseline gave a half-laugh. "Meant no offense? Yet you drag me here while I'm unconscious and ramble on about some ancient myth you call a prophecy. Oh, and did I mention, I'm going to save the realm from the demon king who wants my soul?" Her face reddened with anger. "You must take me for a fool. I may be young and naive, but I most certainly am *not* a fool."

Quinn fought to keep a rein on his temper even as hers flared. He had no intention of causing problems, but she was being so damned difficult. "Princess, forgive me. I've angered you."

The remark came out more sarcastic than he wanted.

Joseline pulled at the pins holding up fiery curls, the scarlet waves falling to frame her thin face. Her lips tightened in a firm line, the breath shuddering through her.

"This is absurd." She moved toward the door. Jenson and Maya cut her off, swift as shadows. She spun around, nearly colliding with Quinn.

"We can't let you leave, Your Highness." Jenson gave her a weak smile as Joseline attempted to dash for the stable door. Quinn blocked her with ease, an arm around her waist guiding her back toward the room's center.

"I beg your pardon. That is no way to handle a lady!" She struggled to control the shaking, arms folded across her chest gripping the teal silk of her dress with white knuckles. "You've all given your souls to Sauda if you think I'm some savior who's going to rescue Navarre from ancient demons. Now if you'll excuse me, I would like to leave. You've got no right to keep me here."

"Whether you choose to accept it or not, Aeron is coming for you. Stepping out that door now is suicide." There was pity in Jenson's voice.

"Oh, stop, both of you. Can't you see how frightened the girl is?"

Maya gave Jenson's arm a light slap.

The princess straightened her dress, her shaking defying her words. "I am *not* frightened."

Maya gave her a weak smile. "We're only trying to protect you from those who want to harm you."

"By doing what, kidnapping me?" she cried.

"Yes, damn it. If that's what you must call it, yes," Quinn growled. "Your return to the castle is neither safe nor wise. Aeron has spies watching you."

Joseline let out an exasperated sigh, her eyes flicking to the door again.

"You can hate it all you want, but if we let you go, your soul is as good as his." Maya took a cautious step toward her. "You're lucky Quinn found you first."

Concern flashed in her eyes seconds before the hatred returned. "When I was thrown, I woke for a moment." She turned her gaze to Quinn. "What did you do to Kellen?"

"Who?" Quinn rubbed a hand around the back of his neck.

"You know who. My guard, Kellen. Stop treating me like a child."

"There was no one else there." *She has no idea who he truly is,* he thought. *Not a clue that the man responsible for guarding her life is now trying to end it. I could have ended his life if I didn't have her to worry about.*

He walked to the window, her glare burning into his spine. His eyes glazed over, the headache making his vision blur.

When Joseline spoke again, the change in her tone was drastic. "Can you promise me something?"

Quinn turned to her, frowning. He fought to keep his own expression neutral at the smooth, otherworldly fluctuation in her previously sweet voice. The voice she spoke with now could have belonged to someone else entirely—calm, wise, sincere—the determined gleam in her eyes contrasting the prior concern as if she knew exactly what she was agreeing to, all her fears and hesitations forgotten. Her eye color shifted from forest green to a dancing, swirling gold, but he disregarded that change until he could focus on

22

it later.

"No, Your Highness, I can promise you nothing."

She nodded, her gaze unblinking. "Hypothetically speaking, if I agree to help you, can you guarantee that my city and my people will be safe from harm?" The strange tone lingered. Even her posture changed; her hands folded neatly at her waist, her movements less timid, more graceful and regal.

Almost godly.

Quinn's pulse quickened, but still he ignored the shift in the princess, keeping his own voice even. "To the best of my power. I would die to save the people of this city, to save you. It is my fate. As it is yours to learn what you must to defeat Aeron."

Joseline turned to Maya and Jenson, her head tilting curiously to the side, eyes still demanding and flecked with gold. "You two can say the same?"

"Quinn has never led us astray. I trust him with my life. I would follow him to the demon realm and back if he thought it in our best interests," Jenson replied solemnly.

"As would I," Maya agreed.

If either of them noticed the change in her demeanor, they didn't show it.

The princess brushed off the dusty satin skirts, releasing a shuddered breath. She hesitated before speaking, though the presence that had overcome her body remained. The power awakening within her seemed to turn her from naïve fear to royal acceptance and determination. "As the future Queen of Rathal, it is first and foremost my responsibility to make decisions that will keep my people safe despite my own fears. Aeron plans to harm them. So, it would seem my duty aligns with this fate you speak of."

Quinn held his reply, breath hitching at her sudden agreement.

She opened and closed her mouth several times. Her nose flared slightly, as if she fought whatever controlled her, but still she continued, "Furthermore, you seem to care for the people of my city as much as I do. You are not only willing to sacrifice your safety for theirs, but you saved my life."

23

"So, what does that mean?" Quinn asked, tasting blood where the skin of his lip had broken.

"It means I am in your debt. I don't like that, and I don't believe you, but if my people's lives are in danger…I must be a strong ruler before anything else, before my own fears. How can I hope to rule justly if I cower in terror and leave my people to suffer? Aeron threatens them, he threatens my family, so I must find a way to stop him, for their sakes." She gave a close-lipped smile. Her expression returned to normal, the gold vanishing from her eyes, and her shoulders trembled, though her posture remained near-perfect.

Quinn walked to her, half expecting her to take back everything she'd just said, but she only watched him, waiting for him to speak. "Your Highness, we would be honored to serve and protect you."

Maya rolled her eyes. "Leave her be. I'm sure she would like to change."

Joseline was silent for a moment more before she glanced down at the torn and dirtied satin, the ivory lace trim along her chest, upper arms, and waist now an unpleasant brown, and gave a small laugh. "I suppose that would be nice."

"It's the least I can do," Maya said, starting toward the stairs.

Tugging on scarlet curls, Joseline murmured, "I don't suppose I could borrow a bath as well?"

The two women disappeared up the spiraling stairs, the warning bells still echoing through the streets outside.

Quinn released the breath he'd been holding. "Well, I was expecting worse."

He undid the clasp of his cloak and laid it over the couch on his way into the open kitchen. Filling a mug to the brim with golden-brown ale, Quinn took a long swig. The bitter taste settled his shaking nerves, but the headache remained.

"You always expect the worst." Jenson was a silent shadow beside him.

"Which is why I have a *seilapora* who expects the best," he mused. "Kindred souls are meant to balance one another after all. You're meant to see the things that I can never find, isn't that what

Fallon always says?"

Jenson smiled at that. "Please, at least tell me I'm not the only one who saw that power awakening within her."

Quinn took another long swig. "You aren't." He let out a low whistle. "The Goddess blessed princess. I wasn't expecting the Great Mother's power to impact her like that. It was like her consciousness shifted to influence her decision but when she regained control she didn't fight the statement. It was interesting."

"I don't think any of us knows what to expect," Jenson said. "How can we? Queen Maren was the last Waeshorn ruler to have the Goddess's strength and she died in the Second Demon Wars. Not to mention this is probably the first time the power has awakened within Joseline at all."

Draining the mug, Quinn set it on the counter. "Regardless of how the power affects her, I don't think she comprehends the danger she's in. Despite her own beliefs, she wants to help her people, to protect them."

"She shows potential to be a great ruler." Jenson braced his elbows against the counter, leaning back.

Quinn sighed. "Part of me wishes we didn't have to drag her into all this."

"There is no one else."

The stable door opened again.

Fallon, all lean muscles and silvery flowing hair, strode into the room, Reyes and Resa, the dark-haired twins, at his heels.

Quinn dipped his head in a swift bow. "All went well, I assume?"

Fallon ignored him. His voice, smooth and demanding, was steady as he met Quinn's eyes. "Princess Joseline?"

"Safe with Maya. Her mare is in the stables. Building and barn are under a cloaking enchantment."

"I noticed."

"I didn't want to take any chances."

The aged scar running from Fallon's lower lip to his chin was accented by his thin smile. "Have you talked to her?"

Quinn nodded. "She thinks Aeron is a children's story, but she's going to help for her people." He gnawed on his lip again. "The Goddess power awoke and made the decision for her, but as long as we reach the end goal, right?"

Fallon patted Quinn's shoulder. "That's my boy."

"One problem," Resa said from the window.

"What would that be?" Jenson asked.

"The palace sent out guards lookin' for the girl," Reyes replied, with a quick glance at his sister. "Not only the Jade Cloaks, but there's other strange creatures. The darkness trailing behind 'em makes me uneasy."

"Yes, they attacked during the procession. I've never seen demons of that kind before." Fallon glanced to Quinn. "We need to get her out of Rathal, start toward Raenya. We can take care of training on the way. If we make haste, we can reach Rekiv before Kyaos ends, do most of the traveling while the days are longer."

"That's two months of traveling," Jenson murmured, eyeing the window as several guards rushed by. "Do you expect it will take that long to reach Rekiv?"

Fallon nodded. "At least. I'll try to contact the other legions of Kynire once we leave the capital. We should be able to contact the branch in Ebondenn once we reach the Rekiv border. We haven't spoken in years, but they will come when we need them. The assassins in the Redlands, they'll come as well."

Quinn watched Fallon as he spoke. He looked older now than he once had. The silvery shoulder-length hair remained the same, as did the firm, lean muscle beneath his tunic, and the ageless beauty of his expression, but his bright eyes were tired.

"I'll finish my preparations to leave." Quinn turned to Reyes. "There's a pure white mare in the stables. Could you go take care of her? I know it won't be wise to take her with us, but she took a stumble. I think her leg is alright, but you're the expert."

Reyes slipped through the side door before Quinn finished speaking.

"You can't expect to get out of the city now with the princess." Resa's tone was sharper than usual. "I know Reyes and I are to remain here with Rieve when you go, and the others are already starting to settle in Swan Lagoon as we arranged, but I thought the rest of you agreed to wait till things calm down a bit."

Fallon gave Quinn a sideways glance, the unspoken question of his opinion lingering. Quinn cleared his throat. "I agree. Aeron could have spies anywhere. We need to be more cautious with who we trust. He's been watching her. The captain of the guard, Kellen, he had Aeron's mark."

"We shall wait." Fallon' voice was firm and touched with authority. "I do not want you straining before we leave, Quinn. It's going to be a long enough journey without exhausting ourselves."

"Quinn is already exhausted. He's been straining himself for days." They turned to see Maya standing in the arch of the stairwell.

"You left the princess alone?" Jenson asked.

"I gave her the decency of dressing in private." Jenson went to open his mouth, but Maya continued, putting a hand on her hip, "Don't worry, she won't run. The thought of what could happen to her city and her people if we don't stop Aeron horrifies her. She's a sweet thing. Naïve, but sweet. It's surprising what you can get out of someone when you aren't trying to get slapped."

Maya winked at Jenson, stepping into the room with a knowing smirk.

Quinn's blank stare brimmed with ice, a growl rising from his throat. "What was that for?"

"We all know where your desires lie." Her voice, though teasing, was laced with jealousy.

The growl in his throat deepened with the pain in his head. "You're being ridiculous. She's impertinent."

Maya wiggled her eyebrows. "Oh, I don't think so."

"No," Jenson shook his head, nudging Quinn with a shoulder. "You got it all wrong, Maya. He just desires all women that way." They both laughed.

Resa snickered from the window, turning to Fallon. "It would seem his reputation precedes him."

Fallon's smile didn't reach his eyes. "We lay low for the time

27

being unless something changes. Begin preparations for when we move out."

Resa nodded and left.

"Where are we going?"

Quinn shifted his attention to the delicate voice. The simplicity of the townsfolk suited her well.

Short leather boots scrunched around her ankles, matching the black leather stretching over slim thighs and hips. The jade tunic, laced along her chest and held in place by a thin black belt, stopped mid-thigh. The heavy wool cloak kissed the floor, her scarlet curls tumbling in little ringlets, bouncing about her waist when she walked.

Quinn frowned as he met her inquisitive stare. "We were discussing our plans to leave the city."

Inquisition turned to fiery distrust. "I see, and what did you decide? It might help me trust you a little better if you include me in conversations about my well-being."

Fallon stepped forward. "Your Highness. Allow me to introduce myself." He held out a hand, and she shook it briefly. "I am leader of The Order of Kynire. I understand you've met my second, Quinn. I apologize for our manner of getting you here, but many thanks in your cooperation." Fallon's bow was diplomatic. He always had a royal way of carrying himself. "Your help is most appreciated."

The princess gave a weak smile. "I must admit, I am helping you only for my people and because..." her voice trailed off and she paused slightly, shaking her head. "Their safety has always been my primary concern. I'm not sure how much of your myths I believe." She gave Quinn another fiery glare. "Or how much I trust you."

"If we can help it, you will learn the skills to protect yourself. Suspending your disbelief will be one of the hardest parts." Jenson picked a handful of nuts from the bowl decorating the table and tossed them into his mouth. "When you're kept sheltered away from anything magical and told it's nothing more than myth, seeing its evil shoved into your face can be difficult to comprehend."

She moved to the couch, crossing her ankles. "It isn't that though. I can't explain it. What you've told me defies all my lessons regarding magic or myth. Part of me still wants to feel terrified, but somehow I know I'm safe and I can trust you." The golden shimmer flashed in her eyes again but didn't remain. "It's as if I've always known, even before I knew you. It's strange."

If the color change in her eyes surprised Fallon, he concealed it well. "That is the way we want you to feel after all."

Joseline smiled, the action more genuine than before. She twirled a curl around her finger, glancing about the room. "So, when are we leaving?"

"A few days," Quinn said, using the excuse to leave. "I'm going to pack my herbs."

He didn't wait for a reply before heading toward the stairs. His head pulsed with sharp throbs, blinding his vision again. He was halfway to his study before he paused in acknowledgement of the princess following him.

"I...I'm sorry."

Quinn shrugged, gritting his teeth. "I'm not used to having someone clonk around after me. Try not to stomp when you walk." He turned just as the blush faded from her cheeks.

"I know we didn't get off on the best foot. I still don't trust you, but I feel the need to apologize. I wanted to see your herbs."

The comment was unexpected. "Why?"

She blushed again. "I find them interesting, alright? I like learning how to use them."

Quinn continued walking without dismissing her. "I've never met a girl from a non-healer family interested in such things. It isn't a common hobby for non-magic wielders." She said nothing as he pushed the door open.

Quinn rummaged through several chests near his worktable, at last finding the jar of ginger root. Opening it, he grabbed a shaved sliver and threw it into his mouth, reaching for the water skin hanging over the chair as a hot sensation exploded along his tongue. A moment later, the headache eased slightly.

The princess knelt before the circle, gasping in awe at the symbols etched into the wooden floor. Tribal swirls sprouted from the center; the Goddess carved into a blooming lotus blossom tree—a tree of life. Her slender arms enveloped her chest, birds, lotus flowers, and tiny Faeries dancing about her form.

"This is incredible," she breathed.

Only half-listening, Quinn eyed the towering cedarwood shelves on the wall near the door. Ancient, thick, and sturdy, they supported a never-ending stock of herbs both dried and fresh, flower petals, oils, and roots. Clay bowls, mortar and pestles, clean rags, bandages, and salves occupied the shelves closest to the door.

"You must have been gathering all this for years." She turned to him, eyes shimmering with curiosity. "How old are you?"

"Twenty-four. This was Fallon's collection. He doesn't use magic much now, but when he discovered I possessed the gift, he taught me."

"Is Fallon your father?"

"No, he found me when I was a boy. He always said my mother was a healer. I never knew her. I was only four when she passed into the Nightlands."

"I'm sorry to hear that."

He shrugged. "I don't remember. I blocked it out."

She still twisted her damp curls around a finger. "Could you teach me? Magic, I mean."

Quinn laughed outright before he could stop himself. He didn't need to look at her to feel the fire radiating toward him. "It's impossible to teach someone who doesn't already possess the ability to wield magic. I could try, but I doubt it would do much."

"You are my warrior, aren't you?"

Quinn narrowed his eyes. "Excuse me?"

"From the prophecy. You, Jenson, Maya, and the others are my warriors, correct?" He folded his arms across his chest, raising an eyebrow. "So, you have to do as I say. I want you to try. I want to learn."

"I understand what you're asking, but I'm not sure *you* understand—"

"I'm not asking." Her sweet voice was surprisingly firm.

Quinn held back the snarl in his throat. "You are a feisty one, aren't you? Figures I'd get stuck teaching a feisty one." Joseline tapped her foot. "Alright, *fine*. I'll consider it. But I decide when, and your safety always comes first."

She held out a hand. Quinn rolled his eyes at the formality but shook it, his hand consuming her small one as she said, "We have ourselves a deal."

"See all the small bottles?" He pointed to the shelves she could reach, handing her a bag with compartments and clasps lining the inside. "Put them in here, and for the Goddess' sake make sure you wrap them in rags or secure them."

Joseline worked with an ease as if she'd handled such things before. He almost forgot she was with him until she spoke.

"This is lavender, correct?" She held up a dark tinted bottle, a sprig of lavender tucked under the rope around its neck.

"Smell it and tell me," he challenged.

Without breaking their stare, she uncorked the bottle and sniffed, wrinkling her freckled nose in disgust. Quinn raised an eyebrow.

"Definitely lavender." Replacing the cork, she asked, "Why so much?"

It helps me sleep, keeps the nightmares away, he almost said. But instead replied, "It's useful when dealing with a number of things. Fatigue, insomnia, headaches, menstrual cramps..." he thought he saw her blush.

"I most certainly did *not* need to hear that from you."

"Your womanhood is nothing to be ashamed of. It isn't something you can control. Maya swears by the stuff in her tea, that's the main reason I have so much."

The blush deepened. "That doesn't mean I have to like it."

"It's also a good natural sedative," he said.

She strapped the jar into the satchel. "Do all your oils and herbs have so many uses?"

"Most have at least two. Fallon taught me the benefits of having multiple options for healing."

"I'll keep that in mind, for when I'm an expert." Quinn stifled a chuckle. "Is that funny to you?"

"The princess who wants to be an expert on anything other than dancing and courtship? Yes."

Joseline glared at him. "Aren't you the one who is going to teach me self-defense so I might stop a demon king?"

He had no answer to that.

She shoved the satchel into his arms and marched from the room, making sure to slam the door behind her.

Quinn rolled his eyes. *Spoiled brat.*

It was well past dusk before Quinn finished packing. He bathed until the steaming water turned cold, nearly passing out in the herb-filled bath from sheer exhaustion, and slipped into his room, the towel still hanging from his hips.

The nightmares were getting worse. The flickering dreams tormented his mind every waking moment.

A woodland cottage that smelled of herbs and fresh bread.

A young girl with silver hair.

A monster, reaching in the darkness.

Nothing constant, nothing concrete.

He hadn't had more than five good nights of sleep a month. He glanced at the useless twig of lavender hanging from the wall, a second twig barely visible beneath his pillow. *Worthless, and ineffective.* He tossed the dirty clothes and damp towel toward the growing pile near the wash basin and pulling on a clean tunic and pair of pants before collapsing into bed. An owl hooted outside, the steady sound calming. Quinn closed his eyes, praying tonight would bring him rest from the tormenting dreams at last.

five

The distant bell tower struck midnight before Joseline sat up, pulling her knees into her chest. Despite all efforts to sleep, her mind wouldn't relax.

Aeron, one of her most feared childhood terrors, was real. The palace she had thought of as both prison and sanctuary her whole life was no longer safe. Quinn, the most mysterious and sought-after man in the capital, belonged to a secret organization of warriors and was risking his life to protect her from a legion of demons.

In one afternoon, a world she'd thought so concrete had shattered.

It was confusing yet exhilarating all at once. She didn't know how to feel or what to think about any of it.

Then there was the matter of the strange, irrepressible power that stirred inside her.

She couldn't explain it.

An almost ancient feeling awakened in Quinn's presence that used her voice and her mind, urging her to give them her trust, as if it knew, for her own safety and the safety of her people, she must. It was otherworldly, uncontrollable—like the Goddess herself had reached into Joseline's soul and spoken through her.

She imagined the look on Julia's face, her younger sister's

innocent fascination with ancient myths making her lips twitch into a small smile. But the emotion was short-lived as she thought of how little Julia would react to the procession returning home without her. She would be terrified for Joseline's safety, and there was nothing Joseline could do to comfort her.

With a sigh, her head fell into her hands.

"Can't sleep either?"

Joseline gripped the edge of the couch to keep from falling to the ground. She hadn't even heard him come downstairs. Her cheeks heated at the sound of Quinn's chuckle.

"Sorry," she mumbled. "I'm just feeling a bit jumpy."

"You have every right to be." It took her eyes a moment to find him in the dark. He leaned against the arch of the stairwell, arms folded across his broad chest. "Tea?"

Before she could respond, he was walking toward the kitchen. She followed, pinching a curl between her fingers.

He moved like a large cat, his steps silent and graceful despite his towering height. Once the water boiled, he added a few pinches of dried rose petals and another unfamiliar herb to steep. She watched him, her eyes drawn to the dark, swirling ink of a tattoo peeking from the collar of his tunic and along his left forearm. She hadn't noticed it before.

Seeing it now, made him seem all the more dangerous.

"Lemon balm and rose is quite soothing. It should help settle those nerves." He didn't look at her when he spoke.

"Anya, my wet nurse, would give me green tea as a child when I couldn't sleep."

"Not the best choice for helping one sleep." Quinn turned, nearly colliding with her. He swore. "Don't do that."

"Do what?"

"Surprise me like that." His eyes were guarded when they met hers.

She gulped. "You're the one who told me to be lighter on my feet."

The look softened, then hardened again. "I didn't expect you to

34

pick up on it so fast."

"Kellen always said I was a quick learner," she said.

At the mention of her guard's name, Joseline could have sworn Quinn flinched, but it passed. He turned back to strain the tea. "Honey?"

She nodded, her eyes shifting to the crystal pendant resting against his chest. "What sort of stone is that? It's beautiful."

Quinn followed her eyes, as if unsure what she was referring to. "Oh, this? It's aquamarine."

She almost reached for it, but stopped herself.

"Does it have any significance?"

He shrugged, touching the leather cord absently. "I don't notice it's there half the time, I always keep it with me. It's just been there for as long as I can remember." Dismissing the subject, Quinn handed her a mug and walked to the couch. She followed, unable to stop staring at the tattoo.

"Why are you doing this?"

Quinn took a sip from the steaming liquid, raising an eyebrow. "What do you mean?"

"How do you know this is your fate? I'm sure your family must be worried sick about—"

"You're very forgetful."

Joseline frowned. "I beg your pardon?"

"I don't have a family, remember? Just Fallon. Well, Fallon, Jenson, and Maya."

She still fumbled for the words. "I mean, why protect me? What is it to you?" Steam tickled her nose as she took a careful sip. She swore, pulling her lips away as the heat scalded the tip of her tongue.

"I told you before, I've trained with Fallon since I was a boy. This has been Kynire's entire purpose since it first came into existence hundreds of years ago: the protection of the promised princess."

She took another longer sip, blowing away the steam this time. It was soothing just as Quinn promised. She covered an unexpected yawn with the back of her hand. "Everything is so confusing..." Another yawn. Her eyelids grew heavy. "That tea sure is something..."

35

Quinn took the mug from her hand and set it on the table, scooting away from her. "It'll help ease your nerves so you can sleep. You need your rest, Your Highness."

She couldn't fight the sleep, nor did she want to. Her head fell against the side of the couch, curls sprawling around her in a fiery tangle. "Just don't let anything happen to me," she mumbled. The trust in her words shocked her but she ignored them, the uncanny pull of the Goddess noticeable in the back of her mind.

"I won't, I promise." His voice was melodic.

She smiled, and slept.

The eminent bong of the warning bell echoed through the empty streets. Joseline bolted upright, Quinn doing the same.

"What is—" His hand shot toward her mouth and he shook his head.

Fallon raced down the stairs, followed by the others. "We leave, now." An authoritative command.

"Why, what's going on?" Joseline muttered against Quinn's palm.

"There's no time to explain, Princess." Fallon nodded to the twins. "Resa, Reyes, go saddle the horses. You know what's expected of you in our absence." They slipped away without a word.

Quinn peeled Joseline's fingers off his bicep, his tunic wrinkled where she'd gripped the cloth too tight. "This way."

"Quinn, here." Maya handed him the satchel packed with herbs and another, bigger bag clinking with concealed steel, then his leather vest, and cloak, and a thick leather guard he strapped to his forearm. He flicked his wrist back and a small blade shot free along his palm, glistening in the dim light.

Nodding, he swung the bags over his shoulder and flicked his wrist again, sheathing the dagger once more. The concealing spring mechanism gave a soft click within the leather as the blade retracted.

He led Joseline to a door near the kitchen. "Where are we going?" she asked.

"The stables."

Jenson spoke from behind them. "Reyes said the western expanse of the city wall is crawling with thick darkness."

Like the shadows swirling around the legs of those shadow figures, she shuddered.

The low, constant sound of the bell made the dim barn even more eerie.

Starlia nickered as they passed her by for a beautiful chestnut mare. "This is Bellona."

A twinge of sadness gripped Joseline's chest. "But—"

"We can't, she's too obvious."

Tears stung her cheeks and she ran toward Starlia, throwing her arms around the mare's neck. "I won't forget you," she whispered. "I have to go now. I'll come back for you, if I can."

Collecting herself, she mounted Bellona. The chestnut mare was calm beneath her.

"You don't have any skill with a weapon, do you?" Quinn asked from atop a black stallion.

Joseline shook her head. "I wanted to learn, but my mother said it wasn't becoming of a future queen to spend her time toying with weapons. She didn't even want me to ride, but my father had other plans."

Quinn frowned. "Remind me to teach you how to at least use a dagger or shoot. As far as riding—"

"I'll be able to keep up, if you're worried." She flashed a smile.

"We stay together," Fallon said as Reyes and Resa opened the sliding doors.

"Princess, stay in front of me, understand?" Quinn's voice was stern, commanding—a man used to his orders being followed. She nodded as the barn doors creaked.

Dawn light covered the sleeping city in shades of orange and red, dark clouds blocking out the color in some spots. A raindrop splashed her nose, lightning flashing in the distance.

Joseline tugged on the black wool slipping off her shoulder, jumping at Quinn's voice. "Pull your hood over your face more. I don't know many commoners with fire-kissed hair."

She jerked the hood down over her eyes, her pulse hammering rapidly. There was no sign of the shadows Reyes spoke of, but it was well past dawn, and the market streets were almost abandoned.

"Something doesn't feel right," Maya whispered.

Fallon sent her a warning glance.

Joseline caught herself checking the alleys, staring up at opened windows and tall rooftops expecting to find the shadowy figures trailing behind them. The further they rode from the city center, the more people they encountered. Whispers she couldn't quite make out flowed on the breeze.

A crowd grew, fearful eyes watching the swirling dark clouds now visibly creeping up the ancient, sturdy wall. They clutched the stone, digging in with invisible claws.

Joseline kept her eyes on Bellona's mane, the shadows sending a chill down her spine. Only a bit further, and they would be out of Corae, away from the ominous darkness. Quinn's stallion nickered behind her as they pressed on, guiding their mounts through the congested streets toward the northwest gate.

A crackling boom filled the air, drowning out even the dull gong. Civilians shrieked, running past them to the security of the inner city. Joseline gripped Bellona's mane to keep from falling as she stared at their reason for alarm.

The ancient stone wall had loomed over the capital city of Corae for centuries. It matched the palace walls in height, reaching over thirty feet into the air. Nadie used to tell her and Julia stories of the Fae King Reul who had enchanted it to protect them for any future evil and infused it with the magical strength and eternal light of the Fae people.

Now that great wall, proud and strong for centuries, was *collapsing*.

SIX

The ground rattled. Dark shadows churned, spanning across the aged stone for miles, those invisible claws raking, gouging deep in the thick barrier. Snake-like, inky tendrils erupted from the earth as massive chunks of rock crumbled from above, crushing anything in their path. Fireless smoky curls brought to life oozed from the darkness, branching into the sky to capture hovering rainclouds.

Joseline's skin crawled with pure terror. *No. No, that's not possible.*

"Great Mother and The Twelve, grant us your strength and guidance," Quinn whispered.

Citizens streaked past them, shrieking. One young man was unlucky enough to stumble, a heavy slab of stone looming above him. Joseline covered her mouth to hold back the scream as his body vanished with a sickening crunch. The fireless smoke thickened and spread, reaching the inner streets on the heels of fleeing people.

Joseline coughed, her eyes watering as she fought to see the road. She could barely make out Maya's gelding a foot before her.

A deep rumble hissed from the shadows. Joseline feared at any moment the earth would split, city and palace alike falling into the nothingness below.

She turned to Quinn, hoping to find some reassurance, but his eyes were blank. He stared at the wall, at the dark swirling shadows, at Fallon. Something unspoken passed between them.

"Your Highness, it's time to see how fast you can ride," was all he said before nudging his stallion into a gallop.

Joseline fought to keep her gaze from the wall reaching for her attention. The world around them blurred into nothing but screams, the bell, and the flashes of lightning promising the storm that awaited them.

She tried but couldn't ignore the yearning hiss. Her eyes wandered to the mass of shadows molding into the gap they'd created.

They whispered to her, called to her, pulling her mind and soul into the swirling depths. Joseline was oblivious, dazed, even as Bellona slowed, her eyes focused on the figure forming in the darkness.

"Joseline..." it hummed. "Joseline, my dear, come to me...come to me..."

It was a horrid voice, ugly and twisted and evil.

But it soothed her, calmed her. She smiled, the sound relaxing the fear racing through her mind.

"Your Highness!"

The trance broke. The figure vanished.

Bellona stood inches from the darkness.

Quinn tugged at the reins, pulling her away, even as the swirling black tendrils reached for her, attempting to draw her in once more. "Gods above, don't do that again."

"Hmm?" she murmured, head still a bit groggy.

"What happened? One minute you're beside me and the next you're handing your soul to him." Quinn's expression was blank, but his vibrant eyes were feral, his voice shaking with anger.

She said nothing as they approached the northwestern gate. The gears, damaged from the eruption and the tremors, were trapped, useless beneath a heap of heavy rock. But the wall beside the gate had crumbled as well, the gap wide enough for the horses to pass through. Fallon motioned for the others to follow him.

"Is everything alright, Your Highness?" he asked.

She rubbed at the growing throb along her temple.

"Your Highness."

"Yes, I'm alright." She hoped her voice sounded stronger than she felt. *What was that figure? Was it...* "I think he spoke to me."

She couldn't bring herself to say his name.

To her relief, misty clouds of darkness hovered over the outskirts of town now, the thick smoke from within dispersed, at least for the time being. But her head still rang with the eerie, haunting echo.

"We need to keep moving. The more distance between us and those shadows, the better." Quinn brought up the rear, the melodic sound of his voice soothing.

With a nod from Fallon, they started up the northern road, entering the cover of Farowa Forest. A cloud of restlessness hung over the group, and Joseline dreaded the approaching storm. The heavy underbrush and trees lining the road would be useless against the rain, but she tried not to think about it, focusing on regaining her breath. Her headache eased the further they rode from Corae.

A few hours later the storm broke, rain pouring down through the canopy when the city was no longer visible. Joseline gasped at the unexpected chill of the water. Yet somehow it cleansed her, cleared her mind of that horrid, unnerving voice.

He knew my name, she thought. *I know nothing, and he knew my name. I walked right to him.*

"Your Highness."

Quinn broke the trance again.

Joseline sniffed, her nose starting to run as the water droplets slithered down her face. She wiped at her mouth with the back of her hand, but it was useless. The wetness soaked into her bones.

I need them. I would have been dead back there. It was a hard realization.

The world was saturated with the storm. The horses trudged on even as thunder shook the ground. Quinn returned her stare, his eyes a piercing turquoise. His face was still a mask of stone, but for a moment Joseline could have sworn she saw those eyes smile. She couldn't help but smile back, as if that would be enough to thank him for saving her life a second time, for pulling her from the darkness.

He frowned. "Is everything alright?"

She nodded, focusing once more on the road. "No, but it will be. I hope."

seven

The blood red moon cast eerie shadows across the rocky wasteland.

The moonlight was always red here.

Evalyn gritted her teeth till they ached, lugging the dirty burlap satchel of heavy, dark stone over her shoulder. It hit her bruised spine, but she swallowed the cry of pain, biting her lower lip until it bled as she approached the warehouse.

Each movement stung.

The iron binding her wrists and ankles gnawed at dirt-stained skin beneath with invisible fangs.

It was always the same. Wake at dawn and mine till dusk. Step out of line and the foreman's whip would sting more than the binding chains. She cursed them all, the hatred and rage swelling within her.

One day, she would be free. And when she was, she would paint the cavern walls with their blood.

She'd been telling herself that for eighteen years, though she knew she could never bring herself to make good on the threat.

Eighteen long, agonizing, fearful years of wondering if she would live to see another day. But she had to keep going. She had to stay strong, stay angry. Without her anger the fear would take hold, and she would have nothing left to keep the darkness from swallowing her.

The Dwarf boy in front of her stumbled, threatening to fall. Evalyn caught his elbow, pushing him to his feet before the foreman could glance in their direction. The boy offered a grateful smile.

The stone fortress loomed before them, high turrets reaching like vicious, uneven talons into the scarlet sky. The towers were sturdy, though stone crumbled in several places, the larger, taller ones connected by bridges in an effort to keep their ancient peaks from collapsing. Ash puffed up clouds of grey dust along the ground as rusted iron gates swung open in an uninviting embrace.

The lines moved in weak shuffles, slaves laying the sacks of stone outside the overflowing warehouse. The harvest of foul rock was never ending.

She cursed her grumbling stomach as they were led through the massive archway beneath the fortress and into the winding tunnels of dead volcanic rock. Sturdy cells lined the walls despite the cracked and broken exterior, each filled with one to four prisoners. Some wore thick iron chains at ankle and wrist, while others were bound from head to toe, preventing the use of whatever magic they might be capable of.

There was no light in their eyes, no hope.

The gentle part of her, the soft, foolish part, longed to comfort them, to tell them everything would be fine. But it was useless. There was no hope here, only death and darkness.

At last they reached the end of the hall. The foreman, a stout, ugly man, paused to open the remaining two cells before shoving her to one side and the Dwarf boy to the other.

The man sneered at her, spitting through crooked and broken yellow teeth, then retreated down the hall, his heavy boots thumping against aged stone. Evalyn shuddered as the door slammed shut.

"Thank you, for earlier," the Dwarf boy across the hall said.

Evalyn turned away from him, resisting the growl that rose in her throat. She knew she should be more cordial, but she was too hungry for pleasantry. "No need to thank me. Don't be stupid next time."

The door at the end of the hall opened again, this time one of the pirate wenches bearing a cart of food. If you could even call the stale bread and mush they served from the kitchens edible.

Evalyn scarfed it down anyway, not bothering to glance at the extra scraps Captain Dax left in her cell again. She longed to see the man who had saved her life, to insist he stop treating her like a lost child, but didn't dare seek him out for fear of letting the snarky exterior she showed her captors slip. She would eat those later.

"You've been looking out for me ever since I got here. You don't have to." Again, the boy from across the hall.

Evalyn knelt on the ground, pushing through the exhaustion to take her body through the exercises she completed daily. Her arms shook as she pushed herself off the ground and sank back down, the muscles outlined against dirt-stained skin.

One hundred. With several breaks, she was able to do one hundred now.

Six years ago, she could barely do one.

Sweat rolled off her nose and splashed onto the cold floor as she collapsed, her shoulders aching. She wiped her forearm at the long silver hair that had slipped free from her braid, clinging to her neck and face. The once shimmering color was a knotted mess caked with dirt, ash, and sweat.

"Oh," she panted, sitting with her back against wall to catch her breath. "Well in that case, maybe I should stop."

"No, Gods, no."

She could smell the fear on him. The whole Goddess-cursed mountain smelled of fear.

She let out a sarcastic laugh. "I was just like you once, years ago. Paralyzed by the fear."

He gripped the bars, pressing his forehead to the metal. "What stopped you from fearing everything?"

Evalyn grunted, lying on her back. The rags she wore slipped down her leg, exposing well past her thighs. She ignored it, and curled her shoulders upward, relishing in the burn it brought her stomach. "I stopped giving a damn." She gritted her teeth as she spoke.

"What else?"

45

After several minutes she sat up, crossing her legs, and faced him. Her grin was wicked. "I told myself I wouldn't be afraid anymore. I wouldn't let the fear control me. I promised myself I wouldn't, that I'd be brave."

She paused, leaning toward him as she whispered, "I promised that one day I'd splatter them all against the walls like the weaklings they are. I'm going to break out of here and show them they can't tame me, and then, I'm going to burn this damned fortress to the ground."

eight

Julia spent the past two days watching the expanse of shadows cover the capital from any vacant window she could find. Two days of waiting for one of the search parties to return, sweeping Joseline through the outer gates and into the safety of the Citadel, away from the darkness chilling her bones. Cries echoed from the city day and night, Jade Cloaks rotating their posts atop the battlements every hour.

The first day came and went. No one spoke to her. Everything was fine, they claimed, despite the chaotic atmosphere that filled the confines of the inner grounds and the Keep. King Nathaniel had gone from furious fits of bellowing orders to frantic spurts of anger that first afternoon, Sir Kellen doing his best to ensure the patrols were doubled, the injured tended to, and the shadows prevented from destroying the inner city. Queen Talia hadn't stopped crying.

Julia watched it all, the fear in her chest increasing by the hour as the shadows grew and spread. The crumbled expanse of the great wall left a stain on the earth, a warning, some whispered, that Aeron's return to power was upon them. An outburst—that the human race could no longer exist within their naïve fantasy of the past three hundred years.

Aeron, the long-forgotten demon king.

Anya, her previous nursemaid, used to tell her and Josie stories of the horrors from the Second Demon Wars, and the banished demon king who fought to rule Navarre with pain and fear. How the four royal houses had come together to seal him away through immense sacrifice, protecting the realm as long as the bloodlines remained pure on their thrones. Should the bloodlines weaken, the seal would break, Aeron rising to power once more.

But as the years went on, the truths became myth. The great races of Navarre returned to their own countries, rarely leaving their borders. The peace held, and the stories faltered with each generation until Aeron was no more than a name to elicit fear in the hearts of those who whispered it in the dark. A nightmare to keep children in their beds at night.

Only now, the reality of those stories was surfacing before her eyes.

Even so, everyone fought to protect her from the truth she didn't want to ignore. Nobody but Nadie had spoken to her in over a day, brushing her questions aside as a silly child's curiosity. But the moment the procession returned from Corae in a panicked frenzy, *without Joseline*, she knew everything they told her was lies, knew that Aeron was in fact a real threat to the world she held so dear.

Each day that passed with no sign of Joseline continued the never-ending nightmare she couldn't escape from.

Even now, the air in her parents' private dining chambers was heavy, dull—hopeless. Almost as hopeless as the day's failed search parties.

Julia couldn't believe it. Couldn't believe Sir Kellen or her parents would just let Josie vanish in thin air. They'd taken three dozen Jade Cloaks with them into Corae. Three dozen soldiers and Sir Kellen, who never left Joseline's side...it just wasn't possible. Yet here they were, the castle walls a chaotic burst of soldiers and advisors scrambling to search for the missing princess. For her sister.

Julia glanced toward her parents, twirling onyx hair as she shoved roasted potatoes around on her plate. Queen Talia, despite never getting along with her eldest daughter, had continued her crying all day. She clung to her handkerchief, occasionally blowing her nose.

King Nathaniel was a beaten man. This morning, the anger flaring from yesterday was gone, her father nothing more than a hollow shell of his usually boisterous self. Julia had never seen him so distant, so lost. She couldn't tell if he was angry, sad, or in shock. Quite possibly it was a mix of all three.

And still, nobody would tell her anything.

Julia clenched small fists beneath the table. Why wouldn't they tell her anything? She wasn't blind. She could hear the whispers that echoed through servant stairways when they thought no one was listening. They'd said the same thing years ago when Anya and her husband vanished. Even Sir Kellen refused to talk about his parents' disappearance. But she was almost eleven now. If anything, she understood more than she had before.

Julia huffed out a frustrated sigh, resting her chin on her palms.

"Julia, dear, finish your food. You haven't eaten anything." Talia's voice was a harsh whisper, the first words she'd spoken in two days.

Julia frowned, ignoring her mother. "I'm not hungry."

"You haven't eaten anything," Talia repeated.

"I said I'm not hungry."

The Queen was silent.

"Did you even try to find her?" Julia couldn't help the question from slipping out.

Talia blinked. "Julia, why would you say that? Everyone is trying to find her. Sir Kellen has as many guards as he can spare searching the capital."

Julia rolled her eyes. "You don't have to pretend, mother. I know you don't care."

"Sweetheart, of course I care..."

"You've never gotten along with Josie. You've never..." she sniffed, rubbing at the tears threatening to fall. "You've never loved her, not the way Father and I do. How could you have any idea what I'm feeling?" She gestured to her father. He didn't so much as flinch or acknowledge the gesture. "Just look at him!"

A soft knock on the door saved Talia from replying.

Good, Julia thought. *Not like she could say anything anyway.*

There was a moment of silence as her mother waited for Nathaniel to speak. But his forest-green eyes remained distant, glazed over in pain. Talia put a hand on his, a small sigh escaping her lips. Julia's heart clenched.

"Come in," Talia said at last.

The door swung open and Sir Kellen stepped into the room. His armor was in desperate need of cleaning, the usually-polished silver now a dull gleam. The Waeshorn crest was engraved on the plate along his chest—a blossoming white rose behind a downward-facing triangle—his clothes accented by the royal colors of ivory and forest green, a longsword strapped to his side. He was the image of strength and valor, but the sight of him only increased her internal fury.

Kellen closed the door behind him. "Evening, Majesties." He took a step toward the table, adjusting the long sleeves of the tunic he always wore, even during Rathal's hot summer months. He glanced to Talia, then Nathaniel, ignoring Julia completely. "I'm afraid I don't have any positive news to report."

"Hopefully nothing negative either?" Talia asked. Kellen shook his head. "And the city wall?" Her voice was cautious.

"The bigger pieces of debris have been removed from the main roads. Those who were killed or injured are being seen to or prepared for the Forest of Stars by Master Kasia. Several with more serious injuries have been moved to the Citadel, Mikenna's healers are tending to them now. Repairs will begin tomorrow and should be done by the end of Ryneas."

Talia barely concealed her frown beneath the ever-calm composure. "A whole month? That's nearly a third of the summer."

"I understand, Your Majesty." He was quiet for a moment. "No sign of Princess Joseline either. Several patrols have yet to return, but those who have all report the same. I'm running out of places to search within Corae. Perhaps if I took a search party north, searched along the Great Northern Road, I could—"

"This is all your fault," Julia breathed.

Sir Kellen turned to her. "Princess..."

She met his eyes, her own blazing with held-back tears. "It's your fault Josie is gone."

"Julia..." her mother warned.

"If you'd paid more attention, she would be here. Josie would be home!" Nobody spoke. "You're a horrible guard. Why are you here if you can't even protect her?"

"Julia, I've heard enough of this nonsense. Sir Kellen is doing everything he can to find your sister. Accusing everyone of incompetence isn't going to bring her back," Talia said.

Julia banged her fists against the table, shoving her chair to the floor. Her father blinked. "No, he isn't!" She flung shaking hands toward Sir Kellen. "He isn't trying at all!"

"Princess Julia, my men are doing everything they can."

She stalked over to him, fists clenched till they ached at her sides. She barely came up to his chest, but she glared at him, tears leaking down her cheeks. "I hate you!" It was a childish thing to say, but she didn't care. "I hate you!" She shook, the sobs loosening from her throat.

"Julia Sophia, go to your room immediately. I thought you were raised with better manners." Her mother's authoritative demand sounded from behind her.

Something like sorrow flickered across Sir Kellen's face. Julia ignored it, stomping from the room. She could hear her mother apologizing, but she didn't care. He didn't deserve the stupid apology anyway.

Niven, her personal guard and Kellen's second in command, said nothing as she burst into the hall, only bowed, following her in silent understanding with the jade cloak billowing around his dark, muscular frame, a hand resting on the eagle pommel of his longsword. He never questioned her temper tantrums, but the past forty-eight hours he'd been even more sympathetic than usual. He made no comment on her tears, always staying a step behind in case she needed him.

By the time Julia reached her room she was a blubbering mess. The guards posted outside exchanged a look with Niven behind her back, but he shook his head, opening the door for her with a weak smile. Only when it clicked shut did she allow herself to collapse to the floor on trembling knees.

"Miss Julia, is that you?" Nadie's raspy voice echoed from her sitting room.

Julia tried to speak, but just continued to cry. The elderly woman came into view, her usual peasant blouse and skirt soaked with water.

"I miss Anya," Julia whimpered, rubbing at her nose. Nadie concealed the shock on her face quickly and knelt to bring Julia into her arms. Julia fell against her, shaking. "Where did Anya go? Why did she leave? Why is everyone leaving me?"

The nursemaid stroked her hair, rocking her. "What's all this nonsense about people leaving you, sweet one? Nobody is leaving you now. I'm here, you're alright."

"Do you think Anya left because she hated Kellen?" Julia sobbed. "I hate him too, he's stupid."

"Why would you say that? Anya was his mother, she loved him with all her heart."

"But he's stupid. He can't even find Josie."

"Oh, sweet one, he's trying." Nadie squeezed her tighter. "You and Joseline are very close. Such a wonderful sister bond you have."

Julia nodded weakly. "I just want her to come home. I miss her."

"I know, dear." Nadie pushed to her feet, easing Julia up as well. "Your sister is very strong and very stubborn, just like your father. She'll be just fine, you'll see."

Julia rubbed her eyes. "How do you know?"

They walked toward the bathroom, the sound of running water filling her ears. "The Goddess and The Twelve guide us in times of trouble. If Joseline had been..." Nadie paused. "If something happened to her, you would feel it. That I know for certain. A sister's bond, kindled through the purest love, is something sacred, something only death can tear apart."

Julia's lips twitched into a small smile.

Nadie returned the gesture, tapping her nose then removing the pins sweeping dark hair away from her face. "There now, let's get you cleaned up." She tucked the pins into her apron and ushered Julia toward the tub before shutting off the water.

The candlelight illuminated the walls, reflecting against the thick glass window beside the tub. Julia's eyes darted toward the cloudy sky, to the shadows that vanished before she could see them clearly. Her pulse quickened, fear engulfing every fiber of her being for only a moment.

"Everything alright, dear?" Nadie's voice brought her back to reality.

Julia frowned. "Yes, I just thought I saw..." She shook her head. There were no demons here. She was safe within the palace, safe with Niven and Nadie. The darkness cloaking the city and the nightmares within them couldn't harm her here. "It's nothing."

But outside the shadows flickered, a secret acknowledgement of the doubts swarming within her subconscious.

nine

The thin fog coating the obsidian tunnels swirled in malevolent whispers that went on for miles, evil vibrations cloaking the air. Despite the numerous times Kellen had walked the maze below Corae, the atmosphere remained the same. His footsteps echoed against dark stone as he journeyed deeper, his destination drawing nearer with every breath.

King Nathaniel and Queen Talia were terrified and furious over Joseline's disappearance.

The Queen and her oldest daughter had never gotten along, but Joseline was still her daughter and heir. The King, well, it had taken an hour of empty promises and triple the normal sentry guards at every entrance of the Citadel to calm his rage. Julia admired and loved her sister dearly and had spent the past few days mourning as if the girl was dead.

The young princess was being absurd, but he didn't expect less from the ten-year-old. She'd thrown a tantrum the night before, saying it was all his fault Joseline was gone and she hated him. Queen Talia sent the young princess to her room, apologizing for her childish behavior, but Kellen wondered what they would say if they knew Julia was right.

Joseline was far more trouble than he'd ever agreed to.

Nevertheless, he promised to double the search parties for the displeased King and Queen, leading several himself, and tried his best to soothe the grief ridden Julia with presents and sweet smiles. He'd planned for that.

But Kellen wasn't prepared for what terror awaited him now.

Echoes sounded from the tunnels ahead, and his hand tightened on the hilt of his long sword. The stench hit him before the two cloaked figures appeared, Aeron's mark etched into the dark fabric over their hearts. He relaxed.

"He's is waiting for you."

Kellen fell into step with them.

"He isn't happy."

Their voices were all like snakes, hissing and spitting every word. Kellen shivered as they turned the corner. The heavy stone door and the anticipation of what awaited beyond kept the mumbled apologies lodged in his throat as he walked into the dimness.

The moon, covered by clouds, did nothing to brighten the sewer alcove. He could barely make out the faint outlines accenting the wall to his left.

"Kellen." The voice was eerie, deep, and terrifying.

"Yes."

"You are aware you disappointed us. You failed us."

He shuddered a breath. "Yes."

A tall being loomed before him—a being of earth and shadow not fully visible in the darkness. Sharp, talon-like claws seized Kellen's throat, lifting him off the ground. Blood dripped down his neck where claws met flesh, but he knew better than to scream despite the pain consuming his body.

"How dare you fail me. Do you not remember what is at risk for you?"

Kellen's skin prickled at the anger in the wispy, rasped voice behind the creature holding him. He'd expected the monstrous guard dog—the Houzo—but he hadn't anticipated the master's presence; he hadn't thought the master strong enough yet to speak.

The breath knocked from his body as his head hit brick, the

creature tossing him as if he were no more than a feather. "Master, with a bit more time, I'm confident I can—"

"You've had six years to plan this, and you've failed. I need her. She is the key to everything, and you've failed to bring her to me. Do you not recall the leverage I hold over you? Your lack of strength has not only cost me my prize, but now she walks toward my doom with our enemy. Stupid, pathetic mortal. I have no room for failures in my army, *Captain*."

Lightning flashed outside. The monstrous form standing before him hissed at it. The master's beastie: he was the body while the master had none, while he was trapped and broken and could only thrive in the darkness. He needed her blood for his body to be whole again, needed her soul, and the power within it, for his magic to be at its strongest. Only with her sacrifice could he rise from his eternal prison—the Goddess Blessed Princess.

"Master—"

The slap stung his cheek, leaving a scratch he knew would scar. Blood swelled against the wound, dripping down his jaw. Kellen winced.

The clouds outside cleared, allowing some moonlight to seep into the sewer from the sliver of grate above. Along the wall, chained and trembling, were several of Kellen's guards who had been missing since the attack. The Houzo's eyes followed his gaze and he walked to them, those deadly talons gleaming in the moonlight.

"No, wait. Please...they're innocent..." Kellen's plea was almost too quiet to be heard as he fought to maintain his composure.

"This," the master said, "is what we do with failures."

His pet ran a nail along the first guards throat.

The soft skin sliced easily, silently, the blood bubbling and pooling down his body. Kellen watched, paralyzed with fear as the man twitched, his eyes widening. He struggled uselessly to clutch at his throat with hands chained above his head. The struggle didn't last long.

The beast continued down the line, ripping open their flesh delicately and slowly. It grinned with sharp teeth as if it were nothing more than a game. Kellen could only watch, choking back sobs.

When the last man stopped shaking, his life's blood soaking into his clothes and coating the floor, Kellen dared to stare toward the darkness. His eyes burned with tears he refused to let fall.

"You have one final chance to bring the princess to me. Fail, and you know my price. You'll beg for your death before I'm through with you. Is that understood?"

Kellen forced himself to stop trembling. "Yes, Master."

ten

Snarling, red-eyed creatures crawling on all fours, rotting flesh, a dark, evil power...

The sizzling crack of the fire woke him. Quinn swore, scanning the clearing with predatory focus.

The forest was quiet.

He sighed, splashing his face with a handful of water from the skin beside him. The dreams felt so real, so alive, like something he needed to remember but couldn't. Gods, they had to mean something.

A rabbit jumped into the clearing. Half a second later Quinn was on his feet, his dagger sticking from the animal's side. The rabbit squeaked, then lay still. He swore again.

Walking to where the animal lay, Quinn sent a silent apology to the hunting goddess, Era, before removing his blade. He knelt next to the fire, exhaling.

He hated skinning animals. He hated killing animals, for that matter.

But Fallon had broken the weakness quickly.

As a child, Quinn ate poison berries rather than a deer Fallon killed. After that, Fallon swore to whip Quinn every time he refused to harm an animal. Killing them was necessity, his mentor said, and he'd stood by the threat. Quinn's back was littered with scars to prove it.

Fallon had always been hard on him, sometimes more so than the others. But Quinn had been a soft, foolish child, and he'd learned from the lessons.

Blood soaked his hands as he snapped the tiny creature's neck, cutting fur away from the animal's throat and ribs. He swallowed the bitter bile rising in the back of his throat.

"I didn't take you for someone with a weak stomach."

Quinn's eyes shifted to where the princess lay at the sound of her voice. Despite her taunt, her skin was pale, and her gaze remained pointedly on his face. "I'm not." He returned his attention to the rabbit.

Once skinned, he gutted the creature, removing the insides with a disgusted shiver. He clenched his teeth and exhaled, throwing the bloody handful into the flames.

"If you aren't, why do you look like you're going to be sick?"

Quinn glared at her. "Look, Your Highness. If you're going to judge me, you do it." He held the dagger not even an inch from her nose.

She didn't take it. He wiped his forearm on his cheek, blood smearing his flesh.

"I'm not...you just don't look well."

He reached for an arrow from Jenson's quiver, skewered the rabbit along the spine, and placed it over the hot coals to smoke.

"I'm fine," he growled, rubbing his hands together.

"There's no need to get angry, I wasn't making fun of you..."

Quinn clenched his teeth tighter. "Look, I...I don't like killing animals, alright?"

She didn't respond.

He turned to her, and immediately wished he hadn't. The gentle, understanding look in her eyes made him cringe. "What?" he snarled.

"You have a heart after all, Quinn. Here you had me thinking you were just a heartless killer." Her tone was mocking.

Quinn swore and looked away. "Of course I'm not a heartless killer, stupid girl. What do you take me for, a monster?"

Her silence was almost worse than a snarky reply. Quinn bit his lower lip as he wiped the bloody steel in a patch of moss and sheathed it on the inside of his boot. Removing another, smaller dagger, he picked at the dirt beneath his nails with the tip of the blade and waited.

"I know you weren't being honest with me about Kellen," she said at last.

Quinn couldn't help but laugh, the sound cold. "Your precious captain? He was going to kill you."

"You didn't answer my question, peasant."

Quinn narrowed his eyes as he poked the fire with a large stick. "Oh, I'm just a peasant to you now? My most humble apologies for any offence. Here you had me thinking you weren't just a childish royal snob." He paused before adding, "You're welcome, by the way, for saving your life earlier, Your Highness."

"Kellen would never...he swore an oath to protect me!" Her voice cracked as she fought to keep from shouting and waking the others. "I remember hearing him for a moment and then everything went black again."

"You really think he wouldn't harm you, regardless of what he had at stake?"

Her nostrils flared up when she breathed, lips pressed together in a firm line. Her small fists clenched and unclenched in her lap.

"You want to know what happened?" She nodded. "When you started waking up, when you asked for him, he hit you to keep you from waking. *He* hit you, Your Highness."

Her eyes were red as if she wanted to cry, but wouldn't let herself.

"He was, is, a spy. The kind of spy you cannot trust. For how long, I don't know, but he was going to betray you."

Her chin trembled. "You're lying..."

"What reason do I have to lie to you?"

Joseline wiped at her eyes. "I know him..."

"You know him, yet you're unsure if he would harm you? It doesn't sound like you know him at all." She didn't wipe at the tears running down her cheeks this time. "He had Aeron's mark of power

60

on his wrist."

"I don't believe you," she said.

"No, I think the reason you're so upset is you *do* believe me. You just don't want to admit it to yourself."

He wasn't expecting the slap that followed.

He smiled defensively, gnawing at his lip to stop the sting. "Tell me. Did that really upset you, or do you just enjoy hitting me?"

"You have all the answers, don't you?"

His icy laugh clashed with the heat in her tone. "I have none of the answers, Princess, and I don't pretend to. I'm just following orders. You don't have to like me for it."

Joseline glared at him. "Good, because I don't."

Silence followed. Quinn thought she'd fallen back asleep until she spoke. "Would you harm me?" Her voice was so weak he almost didn't catch it despite his keen hearing.

Quinn kept his expression blank. "No. I, too, swore an oath to protect you. I would die before I break that oath." He paused before adding, "Anything else? You should sleep. We have a lot of ground to cover."

When she didn't respond, he glanced toward her. Her eyes fluttered, her head resting on her forearm, scarlet curls sprawled across her freckled face. Her shoulders rose and fell with each breath.

Quinn sighed, taking a swig of water though he longed for something stronger. Gods above, that temper of hers was going to get them nowhere.

A chorus of owls and nightingales sounded from the trees overhead. This time, he didn't jump. He only eyed the clearing around them until the stars above vanished into the dawn light.

"Some guard you are."

Quinn groaned, wiping the groggy feeling from his eyes. "Don't you have anything better to do than whine?"

Maya shoved his shoulder. "Oh, come on, we're leaving."

Quinn opened his eyes, squinting into the sunlight. Eclipse

nickered, placing a slobbery lick along his nose and butting his forehead affectionately. "Alright, alright, I'm up."

He shooed the horse away, standing, then tied his bags to Eclipse's saddle and swung onto his back. Quinn glanced over to where Bellona grazed, his nose itching.

Joseline's eyes darted down to her hands and he held in a smart remark.

"Thanks for breakfast, I was starved," Jenson said, his mouth full of rabbit meat.

Maya snickered, rolling her eyes. "You eat more than any of us."

Quinn laughed in agreement. "You're always starved. It was roasted rabbit."

"Well, it was fresh and cooked. It's better than nothing." Fallon jerked his head toward Joseline, breaking his chestnut stallion into a trot as he spoke. "Make sure she gets some."

The others followed, Quinn taking his place at the rear as Maya offered Joseline a piece of rabbit meat.

She shook her head. "No, thank you."

"I insist. Fallon is right, you need to eat something," Maya said.

"I'm fine, really."

Quinn's temper flashed at her defiance. "Leave her be, Yaya. She can starve if she wants. She's just upset I killed the bunny, that's all."

Maya frowned. She looked first at Quinn, then Joseline, noting the tension between them. But she merely shrugged and urged her gelding forward to ride beside Jenson.

A long silence passed between them before Quinn said, "So, this is how we're going to act?"

Joseline focused on the road. "I don't know what you're talking about."

Damn, she was stubborn.

He rode up beside her, holding out a strip of meat. "Look, you don't have to believe what I told you last night. But you do need your strength. Starving yourself because I'm the one who cooked the cursed thing won't change that. Eat something, please."

"I don't trust you. Kellen wouldn't—"

"Gods, Your Highness, can we talk about anything other than Kellen? I don't know what else to say to you about it. Now quit being stubborn and eat it. You're acting like a child."

"Quinn, she is a child." Maya's voice echoed back on the wind.

Quinn raised an eyebrow at her. "And you're younger than her, so I don't want to hear it from you."

Jenson snickered, shrugging when Maya scowled at him, and they returned to their conversation.

Joseline opened her mouth as if to make a smart reply, then closed it. She grabbed the meat from his hand and bit off a piece. The tension ebbed away as Quinn fell back, bringing up the rear again. He watched her until she chewed and swallowed several more bites.

By the time they stopped for the midday meal, the sunshine was blinding through the thin canopy of trees. Not needing a fire, they didn't bother trekking off the road. Maya, Jenson, and Fallon worked as they always did in silence, Quinn seeing to the horses and keeping a close eye on Joseline.

He wasn't sure when the faint humming started.

At first, he didn't notice it. Tiny voices whispered through the trees, wind carrying them on swirls of air. It was pretty, yet haunting, like violins in a dark alley. Quinn closed his eyes, paralyzed by the melody, but still smiling to himself as he hummed along to the unfamiliar tune.

"Quinn." He shook from the trance at the sound of his name. "Quinn, where's the princess?"

Quinn rubbed his temple. "What?"

"The princess, where is she?" Fallon's voice was touched with concern.

Quinn cocked his head to one side, confused. "She's standing right—" His heart dropped into his stomach at the empty road beside him.

"Where is she."

Quinn's mind raced. How long had he been daydreaming?

Then he heard it again, the beautiful yet eerie melody floating toward him from within the forest, tempting him.

The others didn't seem to hear it. He stepped into the trees, the underbrush crunching beneath his feet.

"Where are you—"

"I'll be right back," he called over his shoulder, taking another step.

"Do you want someone to come with you?" Jenson asked, his voice barely audible.

Quinn shook his head. The melody pulled him, inviting and coaxing, into the trees. But this time he forced his head to remain clear.

eleven

Joseline didn't know how long she'd been walking. It seemed like an eternity yet no time at all. The melody guiding her was alluring and beautiful. She strode along the shore of a small lake, humming absently. Then, as quickly as it started, the song vanished.

Joseline blinked several times, shaking her head. The unfamiliar trees around her resonated with tinkling bells and tiny voices laughing as they dispersed into the woods.

She resisted the urge to panic, slipping on the muddy embankment as a soft yip echoed from across the water. Her eyes darted toward the sound, ignoring mud covered hands and pants.

A small pair of pale blue eyes stared back.

Joseline tilted her head to the side. A pair of silvery pointed ears poked up above the ferns, followed by those same pale blue eyes. The fox staring at her yipped again, louder this time.

Afraid to move and startle the creature, Joseline smiled. The tiny animal mimicked her, one ear flopping to the side before it vanished into the ferns again.

Swearing, she glanced down at her reflection. Without the elegant dresses and curls pulled back from her face, she didn't recognize the young woman who stared back. She scrubbed at several drops of mud splattered against her cheek, tugging on a scarlet ringlet, contemplating how she might find her way back to the others.

Tall ferns shook beside her and her eyes met the pale blue ones of the white fox a second time. She held her fingers out, smiling as it sniffed her hand.

"Hello there, little one." The tiny creature shrank back at the sound of her voice. "It's alright, I won't harm you."

Pale eyes cautious, the fox rubbed soft fur against her hand, its small body vibrating with a faint purr.

Seconds later the animal flattened against the ground, teeth bared.

"I thought they were all extinct."

She jumped at the sound of Quinn's voice behind her. His expression remained neutral, but he crouched to the ground as she did. The fox relaxed, its eyes still fixed on Quinn.

"I've never seen a creature so beautiful," she whispered.

"The Aonani foxes are said to descend from the heavens, born from the stars and moonlight, appearing only to those with the purest of hearts. They are creatures of the Goddess herself, her companions in life and death." He inched forward until he knelt beside her, careful not to startle the fox. "You aren't hurt, are you?" His eyes grazed her face.

Joseline's brow furrowed. "Hurt? Why would I be?"

"The sound you were following…" He shook his head. "As long as you're alright, it doesn't matter. Come on, we should get back to the others." He stood, and the fox dashed into the ferns.

Joseline scowled. "You frightened her."

Quinn held out a hand, but she pushed to her feet alone. "How do you know it was a her? Did she tell you?"

"No, but I could tell." A bird chirped from a branch overhead, finally breaking the silence in the surrounding trees. "Do you know what that music was? I don't recall leaving."

Twigs crunched underfoot as he walked away, shrugging. "If it was what I suspect, nothing good. But as long as you're alright, I wouldn't worry."

Joseline followed Quinn in silence. Pausing, she glanced behind her, hoping to see the white fox one last time, but the clearing around the lake was empty. Sighing, she jogged to catch up.

❦

"You're angry with me."

Quinn stopped. "Why would I be angry?"

"Because I wandered off." She fiddled with a curl of hair.

He furrowed his brows. "I'm not angry with you. They..." Biting his lip, he amended, "Pixies can sway anyone unsuspecting of their presence easily, even me. Besides, I'm sure you wouldn't have been completely helpless."

She didn't smile. "Quinn, you need to train me."

To confirm her point, he snapped his wrist back with a flick, the small, spring-locked dagger snapping free of the leather sheath from the motion. In the same second, he pressed Joseline's back into the nearest tree trunk and held the sharp steel to her throat. It bobbed against the blade.

"That's good," he whispered in her ear. "The first step to improvement is admitting your weaknesses." Snapping his wrist inward, the blade sheathed itself. "Training will begin tomorrow at dawn."

Her eyes widened. "At dawn?"

"Yes."

They walked the remainder of the way in silence. Quinn kept waiting for her to mention his comment on the Pixies, but she never did. They walked back to the main road in silence.

He didn't have to see Fallon's face to know his mentor was furious, his arms crossed against his chest, a foot tapping the ground. Quinn didn't blame him.

Maya saw them first. She all but launched herself at him. "Quinn, thank goodness."

Quinn stiffened at the contact, but patted her back gently, his eyes meeting Fallon's. He opened his mouth, then shut it. Fallon nodded and walked back to the horses. Maya let him go, and the rest of the group followed Fallon's lead.

Quinn swung himself onto his stallion, trotting up to the older man.

"You should be with the princess," Fallon said without looking at him.

"She was following Pixies."

"I thought as much."

"They didn't harm her, and she didn't see them. Something must have chased them off. If I had to guess, they were testing her, little devils." Quinn pulled at the tie holding back his hair.

Fallon faced him. "She still has a lot to learn. Now, assuming you've discussed this with her, return to your post." Quinn nodded but didn't obey. "Well, what else?"

"She saw an Aonani fox."

The older man raised his eyebrows. "Interesting indeed."

Quinn knew the sound of his dismissal. Jenson hung back, wiping a hand around the back of his neck. "Did she wander off on her own?"

Quinn shook his head. "Pixies. I heard them too, that's why I didn't realize she was gone."

Jenson whistled, running a hand through his hair. "Pixies? Troublesome little bastards if you ask me. Pixies are dangerous with their allegiance to Aeron, but there are others amongst the Faerie Folk who could be a positive asset."

"You're right. Looks like we're in for quite the journey."

The group rode on until dusk, stopping to make camp only when it was too dark to go any further. They fell into routine, Quinn crouching near a makeshift fire circle while the others hunted.

"Maybe this will help?" He looked up at Joseline, a collection of various-sized twigs in her hands.

Quinn couldn't quite hide the smile tugging at the corners of his mouth. "Impressive."

Joseline laughed, and Quinn raised an eyebrow. "I didn't collect them, Maya did."

Quinn motioned for her to kneel. "First lesson, how to build a fire."

"I thought we didn't start until dawn?"

"Step one, gather something dry." He ignored her and pointed to the small pile of dried leaves. "Step two, gather the wood and place in the circle."

He took a handful of small branches, arranging them in a square. His fingers brushed against hers as he took twigs from her hands. She jumped at the contact. "Then repeat that step with bigger logs."

He pointed to the pile of thick wood beside her. She handed several to him and he laid them across the other sticks at different angles. "Then you light it." He struck the flint and rock together to demonstrate, then held them toward her.

A horrified look filled her eyes.

Quinn frowned. "Nothing to be scared of, it won't hurt you to try."

Joseline reached for the flint and stone, hesitating slightly. Quinn raised an eyebrow in response, and she gritted her teeth. She struck the rock ten times before managing to cause a single spark. A few minutes later, the leaves caught, and she sat back admiring the flame as it grew, spreading to the smaller twigs. She wiped at the sweat visible on her brow with the back of her hand.

Quinn watched her. *She's probably never sweated so much a day in her life.* Whether he cared to admit it or not, her determination reminded him of himself. "Well done."

Her eyes danced with enthusiasm. "I had a wonderful teacher."

Quinn laughed outright. "I didn't do a damned thing besides tell you how to do it. You're a quick learner."

She tossed scarlet curls over her shoulder. "I know."

Quinn ran a hand through his own hair before meeting her eyes. Joseline blushed, the heat of her breath sweet against his cheek.

He pulled away as someone coughed from behind them. Maya and Jenson leaned against a thick tree several feet away, eyeing them curiously.

He cleared his throat, returning the stare and running his tongue along the inside of his cheek. Maya held up several rabbits, a squirrel, and a pouch full of what he assumed were berries. She threw the

69

animals to the ground at his feet.

Quinn picked up the squirrel by the tail and unsheathed the hunting dagger strapped against his calf.

"I thought you didn't like to skin animals?" Joseline's voice was quiet beside him.

He turned to her. "I don't, but a warrior must do things they don't like to survive." She nodded, fixing him with an intent stare. After he'd skinned and skewered the squirrel and placed it over the fire, he picked up a rabbit. "Would you—"

"Oh no," she protested, holding up a hand. "I'll leave the animal skinning to you."

"As you wish."

Jenson settled himself on the ground between them, taking out his own hunting knife to skin the other rabbit. "Don't let him fool you, Princess," he whispered to her. "Quinn's a big softie."

"I'm not deaf you know," Quinn growled, poking at the fire.

"No, but you are a softie. Try all you want to deny it, you know I'm right." Jenson's tenor voice was teasing.

Maya laughed, popping a berry into her mouth. "He doesn't like to admit he's wrong either," she added. "It must be part of the big macho man façade." She plopped down beside Joseline and winked at her.

Quinn glared at them. "If you two are quite finished—"

"Your Highness." They all fell silent when Fallon entered the clearing. He tossed another pouch to Maya, who pulled out a handful of blackberries. "Today was not your fault. But it stresses the utmost importance of our caution. I know you have already discussed training with Quinn."

"Yes." Joseline sipped at the water skin Jenson handed her but said nothing else.

Giving her a swift nod, Fallon sat, tossing another log onto the fire.

They ate in silence, no one daring to speak after Fallon's unspoken demand for quiet. Mercifully, Joseline remained silent as well while the uneaten meat was stored and bed rolls laid out. Quinn rubbed at his temple, exhaustion at last taking a toll on his body.

"Quinn." Joseline fiddled with the cord at her waist, not meeting his eyes. "I...I'm sorry if I got you in trouble with Fallon."

He let out a breath. Of course she blamed herself. "You didn't get me in trouble. Trust me, he's been angry with me for less. There was nothing you could have done about what happened."

She looked down, mumbling, "It's just...I'm sure Pixies aren't as dangerous as half the creatures we might face and...I don't mean to be useless."

"I know. But we're going to fix that." He wasn't one for reassuring words, but she seemed comforted enough. Soon after, her body rose and fell with the gentleness of sleep.

Quinn watched her. The fire of her hair consumed her entire being. So determined to succeed, so disappointed if she failed, yet the failure only seemed to make her will stronger.

He found himself resisting the urge to touch her, comfort her guilt. Her curls blazed, alive in the firelight. *No*, he frowned, shaking the thought from his mind.

"Quinn, you need to rest." Fallon's voice was firm.

Quinn rubbed his nose, his mind drifting into restless unconsciousness.

twelve

Jenson leaned back, bracing himself on the ground as he watched Maya. "You should talk to her more."

Maya turned to him. "What do you mean?"

The fire crackled, and Quinn turned in his sleep, letting out a soft sigh. Fallon snored loudly.

Jenson rolled his eyes, smiling. "To the princess. She's only a year older, and I think having a friend your age would do you some good."

"I have you, and I have Quinn." She turned back to the fire, poking it with the end of her staff.

Jenson chuckled, scooting closer to her. "Yes, and you always will." He gave her shoulder a shove. "Where would we be without our little sister?" Maya snickered at that. "But you're young."

Maya frowned up at him, green eyes glittering in the firelight. "What does that have to do with anything?"

"Quinn and I are considerably older than you, you should have a friend closer to your age."

She sighed, hugging a knee to her chest. "I'm not good at making friends, not with my past. I'm still surprised I can even call you and Quinn friends."

"Your past doesn't define you, Maya," he whispered, reaching over to squeeze the hand gripping her knee. "Having a hard past only makes the friendships you do create more meaningful. Look at us," he said, winking at her.

Maya's smile didn't quite reach her eyes. "I'd just mess it up, say something stupid."

"Well of course, but that's the fun of making friends."

Maya blinked up at him, the smile more genuine. "Sure," she nodded. "Okay, I'll try."

"That's all I can ask." Jenson tweaked her nose, and she grinned, showing the gap between her front teeth. He took the staff from her. "Get some rest. I'll take this watch."

Without another word, Maya laid down, adjusting her saddlebags into a makeshift-pillow and falling asleep soon after. Jenson smiled, settling back on the ground as the crackling fire illuminated the trees around them.

thirteen

The door at the end of the dark hall creaked slightly when it opened. Evalyn held her breath, not daring to move as her pulse quickened. It wasn't morning yet. Snores and shifting chains echoed through the narrow space as the other slaves moaned and grumbled in their sleep. She released the breath, pinching the bridge of her nose to calm herself.

Get a grip, you're being ridiculous and paranoid. They think you're dead. They can't hurt you anymore.

"You're awake."

Her eyes darted up to the man standing outside her cell.

Dax, the pirate captain. The overlord on this gods-forsaken island. The man who had saved her from drowning eighteen years ago, whose loyalties still confused her.

She gritted her teeth, flashing him a smile as she brought her knees up to her chest. Sometimes, she wished he'd let her drown. "To what do I owe this pleasure?"

He scoffed, kneeling when she didn't stand to meet him. "You're usually asleep when I come at night." Dark hair fell into his eyes and he tucked it behind his ear, the dark navy feather woven into his hair almost invisible.

"Spying on your slaves while they sleep?"

"No, only you." He glanced over his shoulder at the Dwarf snoring across the hall. "Well, you and Elyon."

Evalyn huffed, fighting to keep her temper from flaring, to keep her voice a whisper. "Look, you saved my life. But as much as I appreciate that, I don't need your pity. I don't want your sympathy either."

"I wasn't being sympathetic," he murmured, pulling a piece of bread and a small water skin out of his long jacket and placing it on the ground just inside the bars.

Evalyn bit her lip to stop herself from drooling over the delicious smell and snatching the bread. "Bringing me extra food isn't exactly unsympathetic. I told you to stop unless you have some for everyone else."

Dax laughed softly. "Why do you think I do it at night or when you're in the mines and no one else is watching?"

Evalyn narrowed her eyes at him. "Well stop. It isn't fair to everyone else who's starving for your stupid plans." She wiped her forearm across her nose, sniffing and avoiding his gaze. *To everyone else who I've watched die here,* she couldn't bring herself to say aloud.

"You don't give the orders here." His deep voice was silky, soothing somehow.

Evalyn glared at him. "Unless you're going to bring extra food for everyone else, stop. I'm not special."

"On the contrary, I think you're quite special. I've been sure to keep an eye on you."

She wasn't sure what to make of that response.

A moan sounded from down the hall and Evalyn turned toward the noise, blowing hair out of her face. "You're a pig. If you think flattery is going to win my trust after you imprisoned me to a life of servitude, you're mistaken."

Dax was silent for a long time before he spoke again. His voice was almost too soft to hear in the silence. "Believe it or not, little dove, I'm as much a prisoner here as you are. I can only try to keep you safe in so many ways." He stood then, and though Evalyn could feel his eyes on her, she didn't meet his stare. "There's danger everywhere in the darkness. Even I have to be careful."

With that, he walked back down the hall. This time, the door made no noise when he opened it.

Evalyn wet her lips with a dry tongue, eyeing the gifts. She stared at them for a long time, then sighed, scrambling over to the food and biting into the soft bread. She tried to savor the water sliding over cracked lips, biting back a moan at the flaky crust.

Elyon, the Dwarf boy whose name she never bothered to ask, shifted. "Did you see who it was this time?"

Evalyn blinked, meeting his eyes in the dark. She tossed him a chunk of the bread, then swallowed down the rest of the water and wiped her mouth before breaking their stare, lying on her back to study the ceiling. "No," she said at last. "No, I didn't."

I can only try to keep you safe in so many ways.

Dax's words echoed in her head, but Evalyn shoved them aside. It didn't matter. He didn't care. He *couldn't* care. If he did, he wouldn't have forsaken her to this living nightmare.

fourteen

Joseline bolted upright as freezing water doused her face. With a yelp, she glared up at Quinn. "Of all the ridiculous...it isn't even..." The blank look on his face stopped her.

"It needs to happen. I said training would start at dawn three days ago. Instead, I let you get used to riding. A thank you will do. Fallon never gave me time to adjust."

Joseline hated admitting he was right.

Her entire body throbbed. Already her fingers bled in several places, and her thighs were so raw from riding she was surprised they hadn't blistered yet. She wanted nothing more than to ignore him and go back to sleep, dreaming of the palace's comforts.

But that life was an eternity away, and despite Quinn's rare smiles, she couldn't bring herself to trust him, to believe his accusations about Kellen. He was often so cold, it wouldn't surprise her if the distrust was mutual. Constant fear enveloped her. She was consumed by the dream-world—a living, breathing nightmare she couldn't awaken from.

But her feelings and opinions didn't matter.

It was the future of her sister, her people, her kingdom. A future which Aeron threatened to swallow whole if she didn't ignore her discomfort and let Quinn teach her. If she didn't learn to fight. He was one of the only people who could help her stop the demon king. The strange power within her stirred in agreement.

"Your Highness."

Joseline stood, following him away from the others. "Yes, sorry, just lost in thought I suppose."

He shrugged, and when the smoking embers of last night's fire were no more than a speck in the distance, he stopped to sit cross-legged, tapping the damp earth beside him.

She sat, confused. "I thought you were teaching me to—"

The dagger unsheathed itself like lightning, Quinn's wrist pressed against her throat, like that day by the lake. She couldn't breathe, terror quivering through her core.

She hadn't even seen him move.

His breath was hot against her ear, the responding smile too dark to be completely human. "You aren't ready to learn fighting yet, dear princess." A warning, not quite a challenge.

Silence lingered between them as he leaned back, sheathing the dagger in a fluid motion. His eyes never left hers.

Joseline shivered at the unwavering stare of blue-green piercing through her as if he could see her soul.

"Fallon always told me any well-trained warrior can fight. An exceptional warrior can clear their mind, using the emptiness to hone their skills and strike without hesitation. Emotions, like all weakness, can be a powerful tool of deception for one's enemies if not kept balanced."

She nodded, closing her eyes.

"Good, now take a deep breath."

Joseline sucked in a lungful of air.

"No."

She opened her eyes to glare at him. "No?"

"You aren't focusing."

"I was!" she cried.

"You weren't. Don't force it. Allow yourself to become part of your surroundings. It should be effortless, weightless." Joseline fiddled with her curls. Sensing her hesitation, Quinn closed his eyes.

"Watch me."

A cool wind rustled through the trees, blowing strands of wavy brown across his forehead where his hair slipped from the tie pulling it back. Birds chirped from the branches above, their calls resonating through the leaves rustling on whorls of air. Behind him, a rabbit dashed out of the undergrowth, vanishing behind a thick trunk.

Try as she might, Joseline couldn't stop her eyes from darting toward even the smallest sound. But Quinn remained still, frozen by an unknown force. His eyes fluttered open when Joseline touched his knee, a fascinating serenity shimmering in them. "You didn't flinch once. You *became* the forest."

The hint of a smile tugged on his lips, but it faded. "Now, try again." She focused on his voice. "Don't force the breath, let it flow through you as it pleases. In through the nose, out through the mouth."

Joseline tried not to push the breath from her lungs. The sounds of the forest kissed her skin, goosebumps rising along her flesh from the vibrations. The wind tickled her ears, toying with the curls around her shoulders. She resisted the urge to itch her freckled nose as a hair danced across her cheek. Air slid between her lips, whispering to the surrounding wind.

She could sense the difference; the serenity she had seen in Quinn's eyes pulsing through her veins. But her mind raced, her emotions a reckless storm threatening to break from the clouds holding them back.

"Better. Gods, you are a fast learner." Quinn's voice broke her concentration. He frowned when she didn't smile. "What is it?"

"I felt the difference. I did." She sighed. "But I couldn't calm my thoughts."

The warmth in Quinn's smile was out of place from his usual scowl. Joseline's cheeks heated, surprised and embarrassed by her response. She folded her arms, glaring up though her lashes. "Is that funny?"

The warmth vanished. "No, not at all. I was a lot like you when Fallon started training me." He paused. "I was four, only a child. You

79

did well."

The heat in her cheeks increased and she looked away, wringing her hands. "So, how do I get better?"

"It's more like observing the thoughts as they pass. Did you ever cloud watch as a child?"

Joseline scoffed. "Don't be ridiculous, of course not. It would have ruined my gowns." Her head stung where it hit the firm ground as Quinn pulled her backwards. "Could you at least try and be gentle?"

He ignored her, pointing to a gap in the dense canopy, clouds nearly invisible in the dawn sky. "Tell me what you see."

With a sigh, she obeyed.

This is absurd, she thought. *I see nothing but the sunrise and some clumps of fluff.*

"Well?"

Joseline fought the urge to roll her eyes at his tone. "I can't see anything." She rubbed her temples, drawing a knee up to her chest. "It all looks like faint piles of white linen jumbled together."

"What else is on your mind?"

"Nothing," she huffed. "Only how pointless this is."

"Then you've learned the lesson."

"Which is what exactly?" Couldn't he give her a straight answer?

"Meditation isn't about clearing your thoughts. On the contrary, it's about allowing your thoughts to flow through you without consuming and absorbing all your focus. A cloudy sky has so many things to observe and notice with your eyes alone. However, if you simply allow the clouds to pass by in peace, it in turn brings peace to your mind. Make sense?"

She couldn't help but stare at him.

She'd always been a fast learner, but the palace scholars had never quite taught in a way she understood. Quinn connected with her intelligence, explained things as if he'd taught her countless times before. He pushed her knowledge, didn't submit when she wanted to give up. None of her former teachers had ever dared force her to do anything.

Joseline threw her arms around him, pushing her face into his neck before he could protest. "Perfect sense, thank you," she whispered.

He smelled of pine and frankincense, of Mikenna and the safety of the old healer's workroom.

Quinn tensed, but the grip on her elbows was gentle. "You're welcome, Your Highness." The blush on his cheeks was faint against his tanned skin.

Joseline blinked at his response. Was he embarrassed by her touch? He'd never blushed at her.

Quinn bit his lip, the color in his cheeks vanishing, though the strange look remained in his eyes.

"So, what next?" she asked.

"I think that's enough for today. We'll practice again tomorrow."

He didn't give her a chance to stand. She stumbled trying to keep up, his long legs carrying him twice as fast.

A soft yip echoed from the underbrush when she was two feet away from camp. Joseline spun, searching for the creature the sound belonged to, but she was alone. *I must be imagining things.* She continued walking with a shake of her head.

Maya greeted her as she approached the remnants of camp. Joseline took the handful of berries the younger girl offered, throwing them into her mouth, her stomach growling.

"Where did you two love birds run off to?"

Joseline coughed. "Excuse me?"

Maya laughed, handing her a water skin. "No need for pretense, he's handsome."

She drank. "He was teaching me to meditate."

"Only meditating? He does have an impressive reputation." Maya's gaze was kind, but touched with mockery and jealousy.

"There's nothing like that between us. Even if it was possible, I can't stand him." She fiddled with her curls, trying to settle the warmth forming in her cheeks. "The feeling is mutual for him, I assure you."

It isn't a lie, she thought, shifting uncomfortably under Maya's gaze.

Maya raised an eyebrow. "I don't know if it's possible for Quinn to resist a girl, especially not a red head."

Joseline's cheeks heated again.

"But don't worry about me, he's not interested. Besides, he's like an older brother."

"Yaya, would you leave her alone? I was meditating with her to better her mindset before physical training. Nothing more is going on." Quinn's voice was firm. He leaned against a tree, arms crossed, muscle bunching beneath his dark tunic.

Maya's confidence sank. She opened her mouth to reply and closed it.

There was a coldness in his tone as he added, "Even if there was, it wouldn't be your concern."

"Relax, will ya? I was just teasing her." Maya stalked off.

Joseline waited until she was out of earshot. "What was that about?"

Quinn frowned slightly but didn't meet her eyes. "Nothing."

Joseline frowned. "Quinn, if—"

"Don't worry about it, Your Highness." He walked away again.

Joseline sighed, following him. Bellona nickered as she approached, scratching behind the mare's ears before mounting. Her sore legs groaned in protest but she swung into the saddle nonetheless.

Day one of training hadn't been that bad, and it would only get better. It had to get better.

fifteen

They fell into a rhythm as they traveled. Quinn woke Joseline each morning before dawn to meditate in silence as the sunrise kissed the horizon.

The strange connection sparking between them was surreal, unnatural. It was terrifying. Quinn had never felt a tie like it with anyone. It made him uncomfortable.

Maya's feelings also made him uncomfortable. He loved her as if she were his own sister, but her feelings for him were getting in the way of her clarity.

The feelings had been there since Maya first joined Kynire years ago. After her return from the Assassin's Guild in The Redlands, he ignored them for fear of hurting her. In recent years she'd made snide comments about her dislike for his actions with other women. Quinn didn't blame her, not really. She was young, and her childhood had been nothing but hardships and abuse. But he couldn't help it if he didn't reciprocate her feelings, and her jealousy was impacting her opinion of the princess and their mission. It was becoming harder to ignore.

"Quinn, are you alright?"

The sound of Joseline's pretty voice sent a shiver down his spine. He kept his expression blank. "What do you mean?"

The look on her face was gentle. "You look troubled."

"I'm not. Even if I was, it isn't your concern." The response came out harsher than he wanted. "I'm sorry," he said, not quite sure why he was apologizing. "I haven't been sleeping well."

It wasn't a lie. The dreams haunted his thoughts every time he so much as closed his eyes, and he was no closer to figuring out what they meant.

Regardless, the apology was necessary. He needed to stop being so tense around her. He was her protector, not her captor.

Joseline touched his hand in understanding, and Quinn jumped, all too aware of the faint tingle where their skin met. She pulled her fingers away, but he reached for them again. "I didn't mean—"

Joseline shook her head. "Mikenna used to tell me it's often the unspoken things that soothe us the most; that we become aware of what we're searching for even when we don't know we need it."

Quinn blinked. "I don't know what frightens me more, your ability to learn so fast, or your ability to always know what I'm thinking."

Her laugh was like the sound of a Faerie's wings. "I thought you weren't scared of anything."

"I never claimed to fear nothing."

Jenson rode up beside them. "Didn't you know, Princess? Quinn has a real fear of spiders." Quinn flashed him a disapproving glare.

Joseline smirked, leaning toward his *sielapora*. "Is that so?"

Jenson ignored the glare, dark eyes dancing. "There was a spider in his workshop once and he squealed like a babe, running into the hallway until someone would kill it. Fallon was livid."

Heat coursed through him at the memory, but he refused to let it flush his cheeks. "For the Gods' sakes, Jenson, I was ten. Don't you have anything better to do than mock me?"

"Well it's true, isn't it? Everyone has a weakness."

"It could be worse." Joseline's voice was distant.

He tensed at the blank look as her eyes, forest-green flecked with that unnatural gold, darted toward the trees. His dagger was unsheathed in an instant. "Is everything alright?"

She blinked, the strange look vanishing. "I thought I heard something."

Quinn still scanned the underbrush cautiously, every muscle in his body on high alert.

"Quinn." Again, her touch was calming. He refused to jump this time. "I'm fine. Don't look so tense."

"I don't want anything to happen to you." He hadn't forgiven himself for the Pixie incident. It wouldn't happen again. It had been foolish and careless.

She smiled. "If I have you beside me, I'm safe."

The words made his chest flutter more than they should. "Something could still happen."

"Well, maybe you need to start teaching me combat skills."

He raised an eyebrow. "Alright, tomorrow."

She batted long eyelashes at him, her expression teasing. "I'm terrified."

Quinn leaned toward her in the saddle. "You should be. I'm not going easy on you because you're a princess."

Her eyes shimmered in the sunlight. For the first time, she didn't look frightened of him. It was soothing.

"I'd be offended if you did," she said, quickening Bellona's pace.

As promised, they began training at dawn. Quinn woke her from a restless slumber to lead her away from the group, motioning for her to remain silent. Only when they were several yards away did he explain what their training would involve.

Despite her grumbles, Quinn showed her the correct way to fall, insisting that it was a natural first step in perfecting combat. She'd been practicing for over an hour.

Joseline fell, trying to put her weight in all the right places, and creating new bruises whenever she forgot the technique Quinn taught her.

Everything ached.

Her right arm was numb from falling on it repeatedly, and her shoulder and ribs felt as though she had been kicked by a horse—though Quinn promised her form was flawless.

Wincing, she stood, meeting his eyes.

"Again." His face was an emotionless mask.

She didn't sigh, just obeyed, eyes squeezing shut as a jolt of pain lanced though her arm.

Gods, she was weak. It was pathetic and embarrassing. How was she supposed to fight off a demon king when she couldn't even fall without pain? She cursed her mother for never permitting her to undergo physical training and gnawed on the inside of her cheek until she tasted blood, relieved for a distraction from the ache in her side.

"Again." Quinn's voice had become nothing more than a metronome reminding her of her weakness.

Another lance of pain.

She gritted her teeth till they hurt, hitting the ground with a thud.

Pain, then another wince.

And another.

"Stop."

Joseline collapsed, fighting the urge to whine.

"Next, we need to work on core strength." She must have given him a disgusted look, because he shook his head. "This isn't negotiable. You need to do this."

Joseline's temper snapped. "Gods, you think I don't get how important this is? I'm trying. I'm not used to this. My body is exhausted, Quinn."

For the first time since they started training at dawn, he looked at her. Really looked at her. He swore, standing.

Confused, she accepted the hand he offered.

"Forgive me. I'm so used to training myself it didn't even occur to me that you've never trained before. This is a little different than dancing lessons."

Joseline glared at him. "Of course it's different from dancing lessons, you idiot." She bumped against a tree as they walked, cursing at the twinge of agony spreading through her shoulder.

Quinn put a hand on her elbow. "Would you like me to heal it?"

The question took her by surprise, as did the guilty look on his face. "What?" The words were quieter than she'd hoped.

He sighed. "Your shoulder, would you like me to heal it for you? I'm no healer, but I can at least try to dull the pain."

Yes, her mind screamed. *Please.* "No, I'm fine."

Quinn gave a half-laugh. "You aren't fine. I shouldn't have pushed you so hard." He paused before adding, "You need to be pushed. You need to find strength. But you can't if you're injured. I'm not trying to hurt you."

She took a breath. "Quinn, I'll manage. I have to."

"You don't have to be in agony to get stronger," he argued.

"No, but I need to feel the aches, the burns, all of it. I need to know it's working. That I'm doing something right. I won't get anywhere if you coddle me. I've been coddled my whole life."

When Joseline looked up, he was grinning at her. "What?" she asked.

"Nothing, it's nothing." He continued walking, not waiting for a response.

sixteen

The sun was just beginning to set by the time Jenson finally decided to approach Joseline that day. Quinn frowned when he rode up beside them, but Jenson smiled. "Why don't you go ride up with Maya for a bit? I'll watch out for her."

"If you think I'm going to willingly let you tell her more embarrassing stories about my childhood while I'm not here..."

"Quinn, just a minute?" Jenson lowered his voice, his eyes flicking toward Maya before he met Quinn's glare. "Please."

Quinn furrowed his brows, but nodded, and trotted Eclipse up beside Maya.

"Thanks, I owe ya one."

Joseline stared at him inquisitively. "Is everything alright?"

Jenson smiled, running a hand through his hair. "Everything's fine, I just wanted to talk to you about something."

"Oh?"

Jenson took a breath. He shouldn't be saying anything at all, it wasn't his business. But he'd become adept at reading his younger friends in the years they'd grown up together, and he sensed the tension looming no matter what they did to hide it.

"Maya doesn't mean any harm," he said at last.

Joseline narrowed her eyes. "I didn't think she did?"

"No, I...damn it." He wiped a hand over his face. "Look, I'm not here to play peacekeeper. But when Maya makes comments about Quinn...she isn't a bad person. She's just gone through a lot and it hurts her that Quinn doesn't feel the same way. She isn't intentionally taking it out on you."

Jenson was surprised to see her blush. "What are you talking about?"

He raised an eyebrow. "I saw what happened the other day. I feel the need to apologize, I guess? I told her to try and talk to you."

"Talk to me about Quinn?" Joseline asked hesitantly.

"No," he shook his head. "No, just in general. She's never had a close friend, and I thought if she talked to you, tried to connect, maybe..." he sighed. "I didn't mean to cause a problem."

"I don't think it was a problem, she just seemed a little hurt."

"She was, and it drives Quinn crazy. He cares about her, more than anything. But he hates that she does that, makes him feel bad about not reciprocating her affections." Jenson flashed a weak smile. "So, I'm sorry for dragging you into it."

"It's okay, Jenson," she said. "You didn't know."

He pursed his lips. "She did warn me she would probably say something stupid. I should have known what the stupidity would involve."

"Well, don't worry yourself over it, no offense taken on her part, alright?"

Jenson nodded. "Yeah, alright."

"Jens, are you done harassing the princess yet?" Maya called from ahead. "Quinn's getting restless."

Quinn rolled his eyes, turning away from her. "I'm not—"

"You are, don't even try to deny it," she teased. "It won't kill you to admit how you feel once in a while." Maya leaned over, patting Quinn's arm.

"Don't worry, I'm done." Jenson flashed a grin at Joseline, relieved when she returned it with a little nod and a smile. Leaning toward her he whispered, "Thanks, for understanding."

"Of course," Joseline replied.

Before moving forward, he added, "Oh, Your Highness, if you ever want more embarrassing stories of Quinn, you need only ask. I have plenty."

Joseline laughed. "I'll be sure to keep that in mind."

"One more thing," he said, turning in the saddle as Quinn passed him. "Don't be afraid to give Quinn more trouble. He needs a little challenge in his life, no one ever challenges him."

"If you find something discomforting in your bed, you'll know exactly who put it there, Jens," Quinn growled.

Joseline smiled. "I can do that."

"Good," Jenson replied, ignoring Quinn's threat.

After several minutes of silence, Maya asked, "What did you say to her?"

Jenson shrugged. "Don't worry, nothing bad."

"Jens, what did you say?" Maya whined.

He chuckled. "Nothing, would you calm down?"

"You're the worst," she grumbled.

"You're welcome," he replied, winking at her.

Maya stuck her tongue out at him. "Sometimes, I don't know what do to with you."

Jenson chuckled again, but said nothing, and Maya asked no more questions. The clouds rolled toward them as the sun met the horizon, lightning flashing against the scarlet-orange sky.

seventeen

Quinn cursed, blinded by the drenched hair sticking to his forehead. The storm had started over an hour ago and showed no signs of stopping. A campsite wasn't reassuring either; starting a fire in this deluge would be near impossible.

Thunder rattled the dark skies, Fallon's voice echoing, "Tell me what you see, boy," as Quinn rode up beside him.

His eyes darted between shadowy gaps in the surrounding trees, and he held his hands up, blinking away the rain obscuring his vision. His mind pulled at the deep well within him, blue-green glowing along his tattoo as tiny tendrils of magic danced on the violent winds and into the forest.

They raced, wild and determined, through the canopy and along the muddy, half-sodden ground. They searched, fighting to locate any dangers lurking through the storm. His ears twitched, trying to sense unwanted attention.

He heard it.

The soft hisses whispering in the trees. His eyes snapped into the growing darkness, but he was greeted by empty nothingness. "We're being followed."

"We are." Fallon nodded. "Be prepared for an attack when we stop. From what, I don't know."

"If Aeron's demons have been trailing us, I think it's safe to assume nothing good." Fallon nodded again but remained silent, jerking his head for Quinn to return to the back of the group.

Jenson sent him an inquisitive stare as he passed.

"Be alert tonight," was all Quinn said.

His eyes met Maya's in unspoken agreement. She gave a brisk nod and Quinn pulled Eclipse up beside Bellona.

His eyes scanned the trees for the remainder of the day, never picking up anything to worry over. But the uneasy feeling hovered. He kept the grip on his reins loose, holding them in his right hand so his left wrist was free to release the blade sheathed there.

They were more silent than usual when they stopped to make camp. The rain slowed to a light drizzle and trickled down through the canopy, echoing when it splashed off rocks and small puddles.

Quinn suggested they forgo a fire, but after hours of riding in the pouring rain, they needed the warmth. The trees above were thicker off the road, the ground drier. Joseline had been shivering since sunset, her long, thick curls plastered to her face and chest. They laid their cloaks over a fallen trunk, changed into dry tunics and hung the damp ones to dry as well.

Joseline seemed oblivious to the danger. Quinn thought about telling her, but said nothing, not wanting to raise her fears. But as they readied for bed, Quinn made sure to slip one of the daggers from his belt and place it under his pillow, his eyes still scanning the trees until exhaustion consumed him.

Shea had been trailing the group for almost a week now.

A week and still no reason for her to initiate another approach, not without a full awakening from the Goddess power dwelling within the fire-haired girl. The young girl knew Shea was following them. Sensing Shea's presence, her expression would change when she got too close, her eyes flecking with gold—with the Goddess's strength.

The pull she felt with the human girl was something very unusual, and Shea wanted to reveal herself. But her magic would shield her until the right moment, until the power slumbering within the girl awoke completely. The girl had nudged it, but the power remained asleep.

"You're thinking about her again, aren't you?" The whimsical voice said from over her shoulder.

Shea growled. *I am not,* she lied, her words echoing in her companion's mind as they always did when she communicated.

The tinkling and lack of pressure on her haunches alerted Shea of the Faerie's movement. Flying into view, the tiny creature hovered before her face, crossing his arms.

"Yes, you are." The clouds cleared and his iridescent wings shimmered in pale moonlight. He huffed a crop of silvery hair away from bright sapphire eyes.

Shea wrinkled her nose. *Fine, a little. Must you always be so obnoxious about sensing my thoughts?*

The Faerie flashed her a mischievous smile, settling on top of her head. "Don't worry, she'll prove herself soon enough."

eighteen

Joseline fought a terrified cry as she woke, a large, calloused hand clamped over her mouth. She met Quinn's eyes, swallowing the scream.

Without removing his hand, he flicked his gaze toward the forest. Her eyes darted to the darkness, though she saw nothing.

Joseline furrowed her thin brows. He jerked his head this time, releasing her mouth.

Then she heard it. A soft, hissing whisper. It was so natural it could have been the wind, but there was no breeze.

Quinn retrieved a dagger from beneath his pillow.

The shadows lurking in the dark stepped into the light, recoiling from the fire for only a moment. The same horrid stench from the hooded figures in Corae filled Joseline's nose, threatening to make her vomit.

Like a flash of lightning, all four of her companions stood in a defensive circle around her.

One of the creatures laughed, pulling back his hood with clawed hands. Joseline struggled to control the scream.

He was the largest of the four. His mouth, jagged and dripping with a dark liquid, looked as though it had been sewn together, ripped apart, and sewn together again in several places. Cracked lips were motionless as the laugh slithered through them.

Joseline covered her ears, desperate to block out the shrieking noise.

"Give us the girl and you will live."

The sound hissed through the trees, shrill and haunting.

Quinn flipped a dagger in his hand, his other fist clenching and unclenching at his side. Steel glinted at his wrist where he'd released the spring-locked blade. "She isn't for sale."

The shadowy creature stepped closer, followed by his companions, darkness churning beneath their slender torsos where legs should be. "I wasn't asking."

Maya cracked her knuckles, rolled her shoulders with a smirk, and gripped her staff as Fallon and Jenson unsheathed their swords.

"Leave," Quinn growled. "Now."

The creatures grinned—liquid oozing around the stitches holding their lips together, soulless black eyes glittering in the moonlight—and lunged.

Fast, too fast.

But Quinn rushed forward, the tip of his dagger just missing the creature's side.

It spun, whirling on Quinn's unprotected back, but he was there, steel flashing to meet razor-sharp claws.

"You have no chance of attaining victory. Aeron will emerge, and you will die," it hissed, black liquid spraying Joseline's cheek.

She blinked, confused as she reached up to wipe the blood away, her eyes finding the spot where Quinn sliced open the creature's chest.

It roared.

Joseline shouted for Quinn to watch himself, but he was three steps ahead. Deflecting, spinning to the side, daggers reaching again.

He misjudged the distance.

Seizing the window, the creature slashed at Quinn's shoulder. Blood dripped down his arm, but he didn't falter.

Maya was a whirlwind of fists and kicks, twisting about the monster before her like a lethal blur with a staff twice her size. Her piercing eyes blazed with determination.

Jenson stumbled to her left, his short sword slashing at his opponent, dark blood splattering into his tunic.

Joseline watched, helpless, barely able to follow the actions with her untrained eyes.

The shadowy creatures dodged and weaved every attack, their speed impossible, but her companions showed no signs of tiring.

The strange feeling inside Joseline stirred, ancient and hungry. It seeped into her soul, adjusting to her body, tasting the air caressing her senses and urging her to fight as well.

Awakened, she could hear the same dark wind as before.

She scanned the trees, her chest tightening, but saw nothing.

Quinn stumbled toward her, flashing a wild grin and launched himself at the shadow being.

The look on his blood-splattered face was inhuman.

His eyes blazed like blue wildfire.

He was bleeding heavily, oblivious to the pain but he lagging from a deep wound running from collarbone to stomach. Joseline frowned at the color of his blood, the normal crimson a darker shade than normal.

Like poison.

She had helped Mikenna treat the injured enough to recognize its effects. The world spun at the panic, the only sound echoing in her ears that awful, shrieking laugh.

The creature before Jenson fell to one knee, his arm hanging limply as Jenson yanked his blade free of the shoulder, dark blood dripping from his sword.

Maya, swift and lethal, blocked a blow aimed at her ankles.

Fallon sliced up his creature's torso, its chest and neck soaked with dark, stinking blood.

With each strike, her heart fluttered.

A fool's hope.

Fallon cried out, stumbling to the ground.

He wasn't bleeding, but he hugged a wrist to his chest, his grip tightening on the hilt of his longsword to remain balanced, the blade buried in the dirt.

"I can handle it." His jaw clenched as he fought another cry, holding up a hand when Quinn started toward him. The shadow being before Fallon sagged to his knees in the damp earth, dark teeth visible as he snarled.

"I can't let you—" Quinn deflected a slash of the shadow being's claws with his attention turned to Fallon.

They almost found their mark in his already wounded chest.

"You can, and you will," Fallon commanded. "Protect Joseline, not me. That's an order, boy."

As they argued, Joseline saw it—the fifth creature she'd sensed lurking in the shadows.

It stepped into the light, shrinking from the flames as it staggered toward Quinn's turned back. This one was even larger than his companions.

The feeling inside her shook, fear shifting, vanishing, willing her body to stand.

Her blood pounded in her veins, her mind blanking as the ancient power consumed her, vibrating through her core.

She couldn't stop it, didn't want to stop it from protecting him.

Maya screamed his name, but Joseline was faster, her movements not quite her own as the light guided her.

She didn't cry out. She didn't think. She merely ripped the bloody dagger from Quinn's hand, and lunged.

nineteen

Quinn's face paled.

Joseline, small fingers clutching his dagger, launched herself at the Shadow Beast.

That sticky black liquid spurted from the deep gash in its neck, spraying over her thin face. The creature didn't even have time to scream as he collapsed to the ground.

The entire forest froze.

The second shadow being stared, shocked, at its fallen companion, up at the frail girl standing before it, and back at its companion. Black eyes burned, a demonic cry escaping its lips as it surged toward Joseline.

Quinn moved, but not quick enough.

Joseline, still clutching the dagger, tried to step away from the nails reaching for her. She stumbled, her shriek piercing as nails dug into her arm.

Frantic, she swung the dagger forward, drawing blood even as it flung her to the ground. She didn't rise again.

Quinn tackled the creature, his well of magic surged too fast, overflowing with a lack of control. The fire raged, engulfing him, fueling the sense of panic and terror.

He would not be too late to protect her.

Quinn unsheathed two more daggers. His cry echoed through the forest, his crossed blades decapitating the demon in one swift blow.

The Shadow Beast was still laughing as its head rolled along the ground.

Dark blood sprayed everywhere, the blood covering Quinn's face hot and stinging as his mind flooded with an untamed calm.

Standing, he turned to face the remaining creatures. They stared at their fallen companions, frozen and unsure.

Good, Quinn's magic purred. *They should be afraid.*

Turquoise shimmered, intertwining with the dark swirling ink on his skin, blue-green flames glowing, growling for more power. Wildfire erupted from his fingertips in a thin, lethal shard, slitting the shadow creatures' throats in one sweeping motion.

They fell, dark blood pooling, soaking into the earth. Flames enveloped their bodies, incinerating them to nothing more than ash.

He stumbled to Joseline's small, motionless form, shuddering. The familiar sting of poison pulsed through his veins, stabbing into the wound along his chest. The glow faded from his skin.

Quinn sagged to the ground, his eyes heavy. He'd lost too much blood. His chest tightened, his body convulsing from the poison that must have coated those black talons.

Maya was beside him. "Quinn, calm down, they're gone."

Gone.

His mind swirled, forcing the magic threatening to explode again to retreat and stay inside the well. He'd overdone it.

They're gone, he repeated. *Gods above, the world is spinning.*

"Joseline," he murmured. "Her arm...I think there was poison..."

The darkness consumed him. Everything went black.

twenty

The effort to breathe was unbearable as he fought to swim toward the surface. The water engulfed him, almost blinding. The energy slowly ebbed away as the movements became more difficult. He shook, his legs beating against the vicious current struggling to pull him back, to suck him down into her frigid blackness. One more second, and he would be free. If he could just break through the darkness...

"He's losing too much blood. He can't afford to lose anymore."

Her voice shattered everything even as the dark, empty void surrounded him, maintaining its hold on his consciousness.

Light exploded through the darkness.

He screamed.

His body thrashed, convulsing uncontrollably, the pain threatening to swallow him whole.

"Help me hold him, child, I can't do this if he keeps thrashing like that." A different, unfamiliar woman's voice. Aged and firm.

"I'm trying! He's too strong."

"If you want him to live, you must. I need to close that wound."

Her voice whispered in his ear, warm and reassuring. Soft, phantom touches stroked his cheek and through his hair with her voice. "Hold on, Quinn, please. This is going to sting, but we must stitch it. Please try and hold on."

He wanted to listen, even as the light and the darkness swirled together in his mind.

The agony was burning him alive, taunting him. His throat was so raw from screaming that no sound emerged. His chest tensed, the shock sending a chill through him until he couldn't control the shaking.

"I'm almost done, keep him still."

"Hold on, Quinn. Hold on."

Her voice relaxed him, soothing the fire threatening to engulf his soul. The flames within him dulled, sputtering several times before dying.

Air rushed into his lungs and Quinn gulped it down greedily. He took several shuddered breaths, then lay still.

The darkness vanished, consumed by the light.

He faded into oblivion once more.

twenty-one

Quinn woke in a dim room.

The soothing scent of sage and lilac clung to the air. Ivory lace curtains draped the four-poster bed he lay in, the bedside table covered in an assortment of ointment bottles, salves, and clean cloths. Steam curled from the spout of a tea pot painted with pastel-colored peonies beside an empty ceramic cup and saucer, all the same design.

He tried to sit up, his body immediately burning in protest. His chest and left arm were layered with thick bandages, and from the throb in his ribs, he guessed one of them was broken. The rest of his body was covered in various bruises and cuts. He'd survived much worse, but the pain was still vicious. At least the poison was gone.

His mind swirled in vague recollection of slipping in and out of consciousness while someone stitched the wound running from collarbone to abdomen.

A light breeze danced through the open window, sage and lilac blinding his senses once more.

Lilac. Her sweet, floral scent.

She slept in an oversized armchair near the small hearth across the room. She seemed even smaller somehow, with her knees drawn up to her chest, freckled nose and cheeks flushed with sleep, and those scarlet curls spilling over the chair.

So small, yet so wild. So alluring.

So forbidden and off-limits.

She could have died for him. The thought sent a chill down his spine. He was here to serve *her*, not the other way around.

But aside from sheer exhaustion coating her face even in sleep, she looked unharmed. Quinn released a breath.

She stirred, yawning. "Quinn, are you awake?" She tucked untamed curls behind her ears. "How do you feel?"

"I've been through worse." He ignored his body's protests, forcing his back to straighten against the pillows.

Moving to the bed, she poured steaming liquid into the teacup and passed it to him. He sipped slowly, the bitter taste soothing his throat.

"You've been asleep for two days."

He nodded. "I'm not surprised. I don't practice magic often enough to maintain control without using too much energy. My magic hasn't slipped since I was a child. It's more draining than I remember."

Quinn was unsure what to make of the strange look in her eyes. When she spoke, her voice was so soft he almost asked her to repeat herself. "I worried about you."

Quinn laughed, regretting it as pain shot through his ribs. "It's going to take more than that to kill me."

"I don't remember what happened, during the fight." Joseline's voice was a whisper. She fiddled with her curls, something he noticed she did when she was nervous or uncomfortable. "Maya said I killed one of those...those things...I don't remember any of it. It's like I gave my actions over to the...my mind went blank." She was silent for a moment. "What were those creatures?"

Quinn bit his lip, sipping the tea again. "I don't know. I've never seen anything like them. If I had to guess, some of Aeron's demons."

"They weren't human."

"No, they weren't. That alone is reason why you shouldn't have done it."

The look she gave him was ice. "I saved your life."

"I don't need you to protect me. You have no experience and no training. What you did was reckless and stupid." It was an effort to keep the growl from his voice. "You got lucky. Not to mention I was poisoned, and you had no way of knowing if the poison might infect you too."

Joseline opened and closed her mouth several times, gaping at him. "I—"

A plump, elderly woman swept into the room. "So, you've decided to return to the world of the living." A smile touched thin lips. "How miserable do you feel? No need for pretense with me, I've seen enough wounded in my life to know the truth."

Quinn turned his attention from Joseline, the woman's gentle demeanor easing the tension between them. "Nothing I can't handle."

Wrinkles sprouted around watery eyes as she laughed. "I have no doubts. You're covered in too many scars for someone your age."

"Quinn, this is Anita. She helped clean your wounds." Joseline studied the floor.

Anita held out a hand in greeting. Her leathery skin was covered in wrinkles and freckles, her hands calloused—healer's hands. "I don't know what you were attacked by, but the Gods must be watching over you. You should be dead from the blood loss, not to mention the poison."

Quinn shook her hand, taking another sip of hot liquid as his eyes began to droop.

"Not much of a talker, are we? Well, we should let you rest anyway, and I have pot-pies to finish." Anita wiped flour-covered hands on her apron. "I'll be back after the evening meal is prepared to change those bandages. If you need anything, send word for me or Joen, my husband."

The door clicked shut behind her.

They were silent for another moment before Quinn spoke. "How's your arm? You weren't poisoned too, were you?"

"I'm alright. Anita said it must have only affected you or all been gone by the time I was attacked. There was no trace of it in my blood."

Quinn barely had the strength to nod. "The others?"

"Minor scratches. Fallon twisted his wrist wrong. It's bruised, but he's fine."

"Good." He eased down in the bed, wincing. "I meant what I said. You aren't ready for combat."

Her fingers brushed his as she took the mug from his hands. He snarled at the flash of sensitivity flickering in her eyes, the action sent a ripple of pain through his chest.

"Maya said you were stubborn when you felt helpless."

The remark caught him off-guard. "I'm not—"

"You are, but it's alright. I would be, too." She paused, fingers limp on the doorknob. "I've been meditating without you, just thought you might want to know."

Quinn closed his eyes as her footsteps grew faint, allowing his mind to fade into darkness once more.

twenty-two

Fallon sat at the bar long after the other guests retired.

He ran a hand over the scar accenting his chin, waiting for Anita to return with an update on Quinn's condition.

The outburst had been unexpected. Quinn hadn't lost control since he was a child. He'd burned down an entire building.

He possessed more magic than he knew, his lack of training a potential threat to his safety and the safety of anyone around him. But Fallon had taught Quinn as much as he could without exposing the truth he'd worked so hard to keep hidden from lingering demons. It had taken years of rigorous training and meditation for the vast amount of power coursing through Quinn's body to dwindle to normalcy.

He'd been fine for years, until the princess's life was in danger.

Interesting indeed.

Fallon heard the woman's footsteps in the hallway upstairs. He drained the mug, inspecting the faint bruising along his wrist.

"Will you be wantin' any more, Sir?" Joen, the innkeeper, spoke in the common tongue, but his voice as thick with the Dorwynn accent as his wife's.

Fallon shoved the mug along the wooden counter with a brisk nod. The man filled it then limped toward the swinging doors connecting the bar to the kitchen.

"My wife's seen worse and healed worse." He called over his shoulder. "She was a young healer when she saved my life, and no stranger to the wounded then. Your son is in good hands."

Fallon didn't correct him as Anita slipped into the room. She sent her husband a smile, eyes twinkling. Joen returned the gesture before leaving them to their privacy.

Anita eased onto one of the tall bar stools. "So, would you care to explain what's going on here, or should I make assumptions?"

Fallon wiped a hand over his face. "I'm not obligated to explain anything to you."

Anita laughed. "No, you are not. But when you've seen what I've seen, you learn to pick up on the unspoken things."

Fallon eyed her over the rim of the mug. Her once-brown hair was peppered with gray and pulled back into a tight bun at the nape of her neck. Her round face was littered with wrinkles, yet there was still a youthfulness to her expression.

"You know nothing about age," Fallon said at last, his voice soft.

Her voice was softer. "When you've survived terrors and lived amongst immortals, it isn't difficult to recognize a full-blooded Fae when you see one, let alone two."

Fallon went stiff. "I beg your pardon?"

Anita's smile was warm. "I was a healer on the Dorwynn border. I helped victims of Aeron's demon uprisings for almost forty-five years before I met Joen. I nursed him back from death and we settled here, away from the fighting. It's been thirty years since we removed ourselves from that part of the world, but we aren't blinded in the presence of your glamours."

Fallon swore, running a hand over his scar. "He doesn't know that he's Fae."

"I would assume that's why he wears the charm around his neck...that it hides his true identity. Did you enchant it so he won't take it off as well?" Anita's voice was calm.

Fallon nodded, no longer seeing the point in lying, and turned to her. "Is that why you let us in, because you knew he was Fae?"

Anita shook her head. "In all my years of healing demon wounds, I've never seen poison like that. Fae or not, he wouldn't have survived much longer even with that raging wildfire fighting to burn it out. With his Fae abilities weaker than normal, I'll need a few days to monitor him before you continue traveling, to make sure none lingered. The Gods are with you. The girl would not have survived in his place. What attacked you? Don't expect me to believe it was an animal."

"Since you already seem to know it wasn't I have no intentions of lying to you." Fallon eyed her, sighing. "I've never seen anything like them, either."

"Was it Aeron?" Her voice was laced with fear.

"I don't know who else it could be."

"That young girl, she's the fire-haired princess from the prophecy." He nodded. "Will the royal houses come together, seal him within the demon realm as they did before?"

A question, and a plea.

Fallon wiped a hand over the scar along his jaw again, sighing. "The legends don't do the reality justice. The seal came at a great cost. The Dwarfs and Witches haven't been heard from in three centuries, and the naïve humans don't believe Aeron is anything more than a nightmare made to scare children into their beds. The Fae are so busy fighting lesser demons along the Dorwynn border, the disbelief of mortals is our last concern. Our forces don't have the strength to make them believe what they refuse to."

"I know the perils faced at the border," she said, folding her arms on the bar. "I faced them myself."

"Even with the might of Dorwynn's armies and naval forces, King Reul could not defeat Aeron alone. Without the other royal houses' support and an heir to keep King Reul's bloodline on the throne..."

"Navarre will be at Aeron's mercy," Anita whispered, finishing what Fallon didn't dare say.

"The world can't afford to be at his mercy, not again. It wouldn't survive this time."

"But Reul has no heir, Aeron saw to that when his demons

slaughtered them all."

The comment sent a ripple of pain through Fallon's chest.

Anita wiped a hand over her mouth. "During my time healing on the border, I heard whispers of a protective order of warriors. They called it Kynire, meant to be an alliance to defend Navarre should the seal ever break, to help keep the Promised Princess safe and fight in her defense." She was staring at him. "Do you know of such a thing?"

It was the wiser choice to stay quiet. Their safety and the safety of the realm could depend on secrecy and silence. But the woman and her husband deserved to know something. He owed her that much for Quinn's life.

"Kynire is no myth." Anita's eyes widened. "However, their business is kept secret. The less common knowledge, the better."

"Well if that young girl is the Rathal princess..." Fallon put a hand on her arm and her voice trailed off.

"The less you both know, the safer you are. We don't know who or what might be following us, and I would feel responsible if any knowledge you learned was used against you."

Anita nodded in understanding. "I shall ask no more, but I will alert the lord in Rivedas of a friend's arrival." She stood from the bar, holding his stare a moment longer. "Just know you are not the only survivors. Even after he was sealed, Aeron's chaos shattered many lives. Should the need arise, help will follow."

A reminder, a promise.

Without another word, she left. Fallon stared after.

twenty-three

Shea was tired of wet fur. Yet the red-haired girl, Joseline, stayed within the inn, so there was nothing to do but wait.

The barn kept her dry at night, and during the day she refused to stray from the back door of the rundown, homey inn. She pressed her body against the stone, shielding from the rain and ignoring Azuri's teasing.

"You can still see from the hay loft..."

Shea growled at the Faerie. *If you don't want to get wet, go in there yourself. The smell of contained horses makes me nauseous.*

Azuri shrugged. "If you say so."

Their vigil pressed on in silence, Shea curled against the weathered stone while Azuri sprawled on her haunches. She was just nodding off when the back door creaked. Her ears shot up, pale blue eyes darting toward the noise.

"I still don't think this is a good idea."

It was Joseline.

She walked with Quinn, the scowling brown-haired warrior. Her arm clung to his heavily bandaged torso despite the deep growl rippling through his chest.

Taking advantage of the break in the rain, they headed for the barn. Shea padded behind them.

"The lack of fresh air was starting to suffocate me," Quinn said, wiping a hand over his face. He approached the jet black stallion whose stall warmth Shea had shared the past three nights.

"We don't know how safe it is out here. You're still healing."

Any moment now. Shea kept her eyes on Joseline.

"With you and Anita fussing over me, I'm fine." He turned to face her, and Shea froze. Quinn sucked in a breath.

"Still, I...what?" Joseline turned.

Their eyes synced, flashing in unspoken connection.

"You..." she whispered. "You *were* following us."

A hesitant step forward, and another. Their gazes never faltered.

You had to prove your strength before I could show myself. Shea's knew her words echoed in Joseline's head.

"Prove myself, what do you mean?" Joseline knelt.

Worthy of my companionship. You are chosen, but you weren't ready for my help, not until you awoke the power within you. Control will come with practice. Her eyes flickered toward Quinn. *Trust him.*

The air rippled with raw power, shimmering like golden flecks of starlight. "I don't understand..."

"What is she saying?"

The shimmer surrounding them dropped.

"You can't hear her?" Joseline asked, brows furrowing.

"No."

Shea allowed her thoughts to flow into Quinn's mind. *My name is Shea. I was sent as a guide to travel with the princess.*

When she spoke, Joseline held out a hand for her to sniff. Shea rubbed her cheek against it, a soft purr rising in her throat.

"It's been two weeks since the Pixies lured her to that pond," Quinn said. "Why wait?"

Shea wasn't surprised he knew.

"Pixies? Friends of yours?" Joseline's voice shook.

More like cousins of my companion. Shea's ear twitched as she said it, but Azuri buried his face in her haunches. She huffed. *Stubborn creatures, all the Faerie Folk. But the Pixies are dangerous*

111

where their Faerie cousins are merely tenacious, though harmless.

Joseline laughed, scratching the fur of her chin. "Well, they should get along with Quinn here just fine."

Anger flashed in Quinn's eyes. "I'm going back inside." He didn't wait for Joseline to follow him, refusing to let the pain Shea could smell on him show.

Joseline jogged after him. "Well, come on Shea. I'm sure you'd like something to eat."

Shea trotted behind her, pale blue eyes never leaving those scarlet curls.

The smoky dining hall, filled to the brim with inn guests, echoed with laughter and music. Travelers huddled around worn tables covered in cards, coins, burnt out cigars, and empty mugs. Women dressed in low-cut shifts sat in men's laps, their smiles sultry.

Anita and her servant girls shuffled amongst the crowded tables, balancing trays of fresh food and pitchers of overflowing ale. A band of traveling minstrels played in the dim light of a secluded corner, beautiful melodies floating through the thick, hazy air.

Healed enough to be out of bed for more than ten minutes, Quinn joined the others downstairs. He hadn't expected the lighthearted atmosphere in the hall.

Anita was the chef she claimed to be. One of the regulars drunkenly boasted of travelers who ventured out of their way just for the chance to taste some of her famous pot pies. When he said they were the best in the Rathal, Quinn believed him.

He and Fallon sat in a private booth near the bar. Fallon refused to leave him alone despite his protests. Maya and Joseline lounged near the large fire warming the stone hearth, laughing with a group of young maidens. Shea, having eaten three pot pies, dozed on the rug beneath Joseline's feet. Jenson leaned in the archway on the opposite side of the room leading upstairs, flirting with a young scullery maid. Anita rushed by, sending them a wrinkled grin, a tray of dirty plates balanced on her shoulder.

Fallon's voice pulled his attention away from the room. "Feeling alright?"

"Yes." Quinn tugged at the cloth holding his hair back from his face, tightening it. "I told you the wound already started scabbing."

Fallon said nothing. He'd been distant since the previous evening, but Quinn knew better than to ask. Whatever weighed on his mind, Fallon would tell him in his own time. He always did.

"You're surrounded by pretty women and you haven't even batted an eye, how unusual." Jenson's body swayed with too much ale as he approached them.

Quinn flashed a dark smirk. "I like women and I like bedding women. Doesn't mean I have to bed every single one I lay eyes on like some people."

Jenson's own grin was lazy as he leaned against the table. "More for me."

"Be my guest."

Jenson's dark eyes glowed in the firelight as he walked toward the group of ladies near Maya and Joseline. "While you're not competition for their attention?" he called over his shoulder. "I plan to."

Quinn shook his head as Jenson threw a casual arm around a pretty blonde and whispered something in her ear. She laughed, eyes sparkling.

"He's more of a handful than you sometimes." Fallon didn't try to hide the amusement from his voice.

Quinn raised an eyebrow. "I simply enjoy the company of women as much as they enjoy mine." He paused. "How much farther until we reach Rivedas?"

Fallon's expression hardened. "Should only be a day's ride, two at most. I plan to spend quite some time there to train and regather our strength and supplies." More silence. "Quinn, I—"

"I wondered where you two were hiding."

Whatever Fallon had been about to say before Maya approached, the moment passed.

"We haven't moved." There was no amusement in Quinn's tone.

His eyes flickered to Joseline, still sitting near the hearth. "I hope you aren't getting the princess drunk. I suppose I should be grateful there's no spiced wine, you and Jenson have a terrible habit."

Maya slid into the booth beside him, giving a little pout. "I may like liquor, but I don't corrupt innocents." She grinned up at him.

Quinn snorted, raising an eyebrow at her. "If you expect me to believe that, Yaya, you're more of a child than I thought."

Maya narrowed her eyes. "You're just jealous I'm a better staff fighter than you."

"Oh, is that it?"

"But of course." She took the untouched mug of ale from before him and sipped.

Quinn rolled his eyes. "You beat me one time."

"Yep." She nodded, setting the mug back down and wiping her mouth with her forearm. "And you're never going to forget it." She patted his arm, sliding out of the booth once more, then frowned, folding her arms as she studied him. "Joseline is right though, you still need to rest. Your stubborn habit of pushing yourself too hard is showing." She gave his cheek a swift kiss and walked back to Joseline before he could argue.

Quinn shrugged, turning to Fallon. "I suppose she's right. If I don't go to bed now, you aren't going to like what time I wake up."

The older man couldn't quite hide the laugh. "Goodnight, boy."

Quinn barely made it into the hallway before he heard footsteps behind him. "Yaya, for the Goddess's sake I can put myself to bed."

"Having issues with females, are we?"

Quinn swore, turning to face Anita. "I apologize. I thought..."

Anita held up a hand. "It's alright. I've seen enough young ones walk in and out my doors to know when to mind my own business. I wanted to make sure there was nothing you needed before you retire."

"There isn't anything to mind your own business about. She's interested and I'm not. It's been that way for years." He gripped the railing with a steady hand.

Anita paused, as if pondering whether to say more, then added, "And the other?"

Quinn hesitated. "The other is under my protection and that is all."

"Her fear of leaving your side and worry for your health the past five days say otherwise."

His jaw clenched. "There is nothing else. I'm not interested in such things, especially not with her."

Anita held up her hands again. "Suit yourself." She smiled. "If there's nothing else I can do for you, I'll be going." She disappeared into the smoke-filled hall.

Quinn returned to his rooms, pushing her words from his mind.

twenty-four

The darkness was blinding. But his companions preferred the darkness. It did nothing to ease his growing temper.

They didn't trust him.

He knew they didn't, not after his first failure, but their taunting glares still infuriated him.

Kellen had been ready to leave for almost two weeks, but their commander insisted they remain in the capital to gather strength. Kellen convinced him to station their party outside the crumbled city walls, but he refused to move out for at least another week, despite Kellen's urges.

"You seem distraught, *Captain*."

After six years, those hissing voices still made him shudder.

"What does it matter to you if I am?" He pushed sandy hair back from his forehead, his own deep voice raspy from lack of sleep and food.

They didn't need to eat often either. The Shadow Beasts preferred the pain and suffering of their victims.

"It doesn't, but your anger is useless and doesn't change my leader's plans."

My leader, not our leader.

Kellen wiped a hand over his face, the new scar still tender. "I *am* your leader." He knelt, patting the dirt to make a fire circle. Darkness or no, he needed food before he killed them all.

"What do you think you're doing, *mortal*?"

"I'm making a damned fire. Stop making idiotic comments."

Before the being could formulate a reply, Kellen slashed into the darkness with his long sword. The headless body slithered to the ground, followed by silence.

Kellen let out a half laugh, shocked he'd been fast enough to end the miserable life. "For creatures from the Shadowplains, you have no sense of danger. Any other challenges to my authority?" No response. "Good."

The commanding shadow creature watched him with soulless black eyes.

Kellen ignored the stare, pointing to the nearest creature. "Get me some firewood." The order was obeyed. "For the next week, I don't want to hear any arguing with my commands. I council with your commander only, I don't give a damn what your opinion is. *I* am in charge here."

He stalked off towards the woods to hunt the first thing he could find, the commander's eyes burning into his dark cloak. "Anyone who feels like arguing or challenging me," Kellen said over his shoulder, "can end their own life before I return."

twenty-five

Evalyn's fear of displeasing the foreman never faded. His well-known temper was enough to make anyone cower in panic, and each day she fought to maintain her sense of sanity. A feeling her fellow slaves no longer had any control over within themselves.

The interior of the dimly lit mountains were spacious enough to fit a dozen slaves per cavern. Each day, they paired off into groups as they entered the stale air, the foreman barking orders at the men and Shadow Beasts to keep them in line and on task.

And each day, he followed her group into whatever cavern they entered. Watching her, waiting for her to falter.

Evalyn held back a cry of pain as the ax slipped from her grasp, the blunt end of the shaft landing with a hard smack against her ankle. She bit her lip, blood swelling in her mouth as she trembled, fighting the urge to collapse to the ground.

The foreman's whip cracked in the dirt beside her. "Back to work, girl."

Evalyn gulped down the air, swinging the ax into the stone before her. To her left, Elyon sent her an inquisitive look and she gave a small nod in answer to the unspoken question.

The foreman saw it as well. Pain sliced along her spine as the whip split her flesh, blood stinging as it dripped down her back. "No socializing, insolent girl, you know the rules."

She braced a hand against the wall, clenching her fists against the dark stone, refusing to show him her fear. *I will not let the darkness consume me.* She repeated the words. *I will not let the darkness consume me.*

The whip cracked a third time, stone crumbling inches from her cheek. She clenched her teeth as agony rippled through her scalp, the foreman's grip on her hair painful as he pulled her to the ground.

"You aren't special," he spat. "Just because the captain looks at you more than the others doesn't mean shit. You are no one."

"He doesn't...he doesn't look at me," she whimpered.

The whip cracked in the dirt beside her face, the fresh cut stinging her cheek. "Shut up. No one asked you, bitch." He raised the whip again.

Evalyn closed her eyes, ready for the fresh sting. But it never came.

"I thought I ordered you not to whip slaves to uselessness, Toren. We have deadlines to maintain and we have enough slaves dying of exhaustion or sickness without you injuring the healthy ones."

Evalyn opened her eyes at the sound of Dax's voice. He stood beside the foreman, dressed in a deep green coat embroidered with golden swirls, his cutlass hanging from his hip.

"She was conversing with the others again. She deserves this punishment." The foreman spat on his boots. "Why is it you always seem to favor her, *Captain*?"

Dax raised an eyebrow. "I'm not favoring her. But you've whipped her, and now she's going to go back to work." He turned to her, his expression daring her to argue. "Isn't that right?"

Evalyn nodded but struggled to stand on her throbbing ankle. She bit her lip, trying again.

Dax swore, hefting her to her feet. "So pathetic," he grumbled, shoving her toward the line of slaves spaced against the cavern wall.

She let out another involuntary whimper, bracing herself against the stone so she wouldn't collide with it.

Before moving away from her, Dax paused, whispering in her

ear, "Are you alright?"

Evalyn debated shoving him away, but thought better of it, turning to face him. "Don't worry about me, your foreman will just whip me again when you're gone," she purred, smiling. "I'm a big girl, I think I can handle it."

Dax took a step back, blinking at her in surprise. After a minute, he smirked. "I suppose you are." He shrugged, the dangerous, lazy look he wore around the foreman returning. On his way out he called, "You will leave her alone, Toren."

The foreman looked as though he might argue but sent her a final glare and walked down the line, deeper into the cavern.

Dax watched her for a moment longer, then walked away.

I can only try to keep you safe in so many ways.

Evalyn gritted her teeth, picturing the foreman's head in the rock before she buried the blade of her ax into it. The stone cracked, chipping off and crumbling at her feet. She swung again, ignoring the agony spreading along her spine as her ax stuck.

I will not let the darkness consume me.

She couldn't escape yet, she knew. They would kill her as soon as she tried. But she refused give up, refused to stop fighting in any way she could.

I will not let the darkness consume me.

The words echoed in her head, strong and unyielding, even as she knelt to fill her satchel of obsidian and followed the other slaves out of the caverns.

I will not let the darkness consume me.

twenty-six

It had taken Quinn hours to fall asleep, Anita's comments pulsing through his mind. He shouldn't be thinking about it at all, but he couldn't stop the racing thoughts.

Joseline rode up beside him, smiling despite his scowl. "Don't worry, I wasn't going to ask if you were alright. I'll leave the mothering to Fallon and Maya."

He forced a smile. "I don't notice it. I'm just grateful you weren't poisoned as well."

Excitement flickered in forest green eyes. "Does that mean we start training again tomorrow?"

"If you'd like."

She let out a half laugh. "I wouldn't *like* to. But I need to."

He glanced up at the dark imminent rainclouds. "Goddess willing it doesn't rain. I personally don't like training in mud *all* the time."

Her grimace answered for itself.

Shea, already bored of walking beside the horses, jumped up, settling onto Bellona's rear. *How much longer until our next stop?* she asked lazily.

"At most, Rivedas is a three days ride from here."

Perfect, wake me when the day is over. Shea rested her chin on folded paws and closed her eyes.

As usual, they traveled in silence until the setting sun bathed the dirt road in hues of deep red, honey orange, and gold. As Maya and Jenson prepped the evening meal, Quinn gave Fallon a curt nod, and motioned for Joseline to follow, a suspicious glare in his narrowed almond eyes.

"I'm changing our training for the next few days while we travel. Mornings for meditation, evenings for physical." Before she could complain, he added, "I need to train as well. You'll train with me. Stop when you need to, I don't want you exhausting yourself, but I'm not going to decrease my own training to a lower level for you."

He pressed his chest to the ground, elbows tucked into his waist, and waited for her to follow. He pushed himself up, steadying his arms. She copied him, almost gasping at the uncontrollable shake in her wrists.

"No, like this." He shifted, kneeling beside her and gripped her elbows until they were angled against her waist. "It's harder, but you don't have to go all the way down if you can't."

She nodded, but said nothing, forcing herself to repeat the movement halfway five times before she collapsed to the ground in defeat.

Quinn continued, his biceps and chest burning as he pumped up and down. "For someone who's never trained a day in their life, five is impressive, Your Highness."

"How do you manage this every day?" she panted, rubbing at her left arm.

Quinn swung his legs around to sit cross legged. Despite the scabs now formed over his wounds, his chest still burned. Once it healed, he'd need to ask Jenson to fix his tattoo. The thought of sitting still for hours while his friend etched the black ink back into the scars of his skin was comforting.

"When I was a boy, Fallon would test all Kynire's trainees on who could do a certain skill the longest or most efficiently. Whoever won got freedom for the next hour. Whoever lost...Fallon would decide what our punishments were based on the degree of our weaknesses."

"He punished you for losing?"

Quinn cracked the knuckles of scar-littered hands. "You don't want to know." He lowered himself again, not waiting for a reply. This time, he braced his forearms on the dirt, lifting his hips off the ground. She lasted all of twenty seconds. "Giving up already?"

Joseline glared at him, pushing herself up for another ten seconds before she fell, defeated.

After several minutes he relaxed, his biceps and abdomen screaming once more, and stood, drawing two daggers from the belt strapped around his hips. She eyed him warily as he flipped one in the air, caught it by the flat of the blade, and held it out to her, steel kissing his wrist.

"This is a horrible idea," she murmured.

With a shrug, Quinn picked up a fallen branch from the ground and tossed it to her. She almost missed it.

"I don't want you to hit anything," he said, steadying his voice. "Watch what I do, swing your arms through the same movements, and I'll help where you struggle."

She did fairly well. Her form was sloppy, but she tried her best to swing the stick about her tiny body with the same movements he did. The meditation had paid off splendidly. Her movements were steady. He only stopped her mid-swing several times to adjust her grip or the angle of her elbow.

By the time he'd finished his exercise routine they were both sweating.

"How...how do you move so well?" she panted. "You're so graceful."

Quinn took a step toward her and sheathed one dagger, flipping the other in his hand. "That's what fighting is, Your Highness. A graceful, lethal dance."

He spun around her, prodding and poking his dagger toward different parts of her body with deadly accuracy.

He never touched her, the steel in his hand always an inch away. The breeze surrounding them rustled, tugging at her curls, cooling the sweat visible on their faces as she followed his movements with her eyes.

She watched a long while before daring to bring up her stick, blocking or jabbing the steel on her own accord.

Turquoise eyes met forest-green, shimmering with raw power. Light and fire.

Faster and faster they circled, their bodies humming to one another, whispering some ancient melody only they could hear as if they'd done it countless times before.

Closer and closer they spun, the fire blazing through their veins, the whirling light threatening to lift them into the air.

The wind stopped, the dance slowed.

Joseline's eyes never left his.

Her back pressed against a large tree, one hand at her side gripping the bark, keeping her steady. Steady and grounded.

Her breath shuddered from her body, warm as it brushed against his chest.

He braced his own hand against the tree above her head. The world spun yet didn't move at all, her lilac scent sweet and intoxicating, clouding his senses. "You...that was good. Clumsy and inexperienced, but good."

"Thank you, Quinn." Her pretty voice was barely audible.

His eyes left hers, fluttering to her mouth for a split second, then back to her eyes. Joseline held her breath.

"Are you two going to stand there all day staring at each other, or are we going to eat?" Jenson's voice broke the spell.

Joseline released the breath, her grip on the bark loosening.

Quinn blinked several times, hardening his expression before he turned from her and walked toward the others.

Whatever just happened, he would not think about it. He wouldn't allow himself to think about it.

He didn't even look to see if she followed him.

twenty-seven

The last day of Ryneas, Julia's eleventh birthday, was usually a day of merriment and love. The celebration was the most extravagant the palace had seen since Ostaras, the spring equinox celebration in Rinoa. Filled with grandeur at every turn, the ball was meant to honor her, to *distract* her.

But as Julia watched the ladies whirling in their fancy gowns with charming lords at their sides, she could see right through her mother's attempted façade. King Nathaniel, who'd finally begun to speak after several weeks of mournful silence, wasn't impressed either. But mother insisted the festivities continue, insisted their people see they were strong amidst the tragedy hovering over the capital.

Julia huffed at an onyx curl framing her face, letting her chin fall into her hands against the armrest of her throne. Balls were no fun without Josie. They would giggle and laugh, guessing which courtier would ask them to dance next, or merely dance with one another while sipping on bubbling cider. Alone it was, well, boring.

"Your Highness, try not to look so miserable, people will notice eventually." Niven didn't turn to her as he spoke, his thickly accented voice almost inaudible amidst the music.

Julia pouted, crossing her arms. "Just because Kellen left you in charge doesn't mean you have to notice everything."

Niven laughed, the sound warming the hollow feeling in her chest slightly. "I'm also your personal guard, don't forget. It's my job to be observant of you." He peered down at her, raising an eyebrow. "You do look miserable though." He paused, scanning the ballroom before he asked, "Would you like me to escort you back to your rooms?"

Julia glanced to her mother, knowing the queen would be furious if she left her own party, and smiled. "I'd like that very much."

"As you wish, Your Highness."

She hopped from the throne, skirts billowing around her. Queen Talia turned at the motion, pine green eyes narrowing. "What are you doing, dear?"

Julia swallowed. "I'm returning to my rooms. I don't feel like socializing."

"I think not. This ball is for you, and you'll stay until it's over." Queen Talia's voice was laced with authoritative demand.

Julia opened her mouth to argue, but Nathaniel put a hand on his wife's. "Talia, if the girl wishes to retire for The Twelve's sake let her retire. It isn't hurting anyone."

Talia sighed, then nodded. "Niven, you'll see her back to her rooms?"

The knight stepped up beside her, bowing slightly. His dark hair fell across bronzed russet skin. "On my life, Majesty."

Julia rushed toward the back entrance of the ballroom before her mother could change her mind. The music faded into a distant hum as Niven shut the doors behind them. The halls were empty, aglow with candlelight from the chandeliers hanging overhead.

And still, the haunting feeling that shadows lurked around every turn, always a step behind, followed with unseen eyes.

"You're still worried about your sister." Julia frowned as Niven spoke, but the guard continued, "Kellen won't return without her."

Julia fiddled with the laces of her corset. "How can you be so sure?"

A gentle hand on her shoulder stopped her, and Niven knelt. Silver armor gleamed, the Waeshorn crest decorating his chest as it did all the Jade Cloaks of the royal guard, gauntlets covering his forearms like scales. She felt safe, protected, with him at her side.

"A knight's duty, above all, is to their kingdom, to serve and protect their people no matter how weak. But the duty of a personal guard is a sacred honor few knights are given. When I vowed to protect you, I promised to never cause you harm, to end my own life if it meant keeping you safe. What good are those vows if I can't uphold them?"

"And Sir Kellen, he made the same vows to Josie?" Julia bit her lip.

"He did. Granted, he was significantly younger when he made them, but he still knew what he was doing."

She blinked. "You aren't that old..."

The corners of Niven's mouth twitched up into a smile. "Perhaps not, but age doesn't matter. I swore the oath same as Kellen. A personal guard who betrays that vow deserves a fate worse than death, the worst fate The Twelve can bestow."

He stood, his forest green cloak fanning out around him as he walked. Julia remained beside him. "I miss her," she whispered.

"I know," Niven replied. "We all do, Your Highness. She brought light to everything she touched. But so do you."

Julia gave a small nod but said nothing else as they continued the walk to her rooms. Once outside the door, Niven cleared his throat. She turned to him, confused, her hand falling away from the door.

The large knight knelt again, pulling a small box from a pocket. It was no bigger than the palm of her hand. The ribbon, tied into an elegant knot, was the same forest green as his cloak. He held it out to her, blushing.

"What's this?" she asked.

Niven shrugged, running a hand through his hair. "You know my mother. She refused not to give you something."

Julia laughed weakly. "Mikenna is a wonderful woman, a wonderful healer. Thank you, for thinking of me."

"Of course, it is your birthday after all, Princess," Niven mumbled, looking down at the eagle pommel of his longsword.

Smiling, Julia pulled on the bow, gently removing the lid. She lifted the necklace, the black stone pendant fashioned into a single teardrop on a silver chain, radiated in the candlelight. She gasped, clutching her free hand to her chest. "On, Niven, it's beautiful!"

"She got it from a merchant in Orira, said it came all the way from a woman claiming to be a Silvermist witch in Rekiv. She thought it might suit you. It matches that hair of yours." He tapped her nose.

Julia grinned, fastening the clasp at her throat. It hung between her collarbones. "Did the merchant say what type of crystal it was?"

"Jet stone. It's mainly for protection. Mikenna infused some of her own protective spells into it as well. Nadie mentioned something to her about you seeing shadows outside your windows."

Julia's pulse quickened, her eyes involuntarily shifting to the windows behind him. But there was nothing, only the shimmer of candlelight illuminating her reflection.

Noting her gaze, he added, "We thought it might help you feel..." His voice trailed off.

"Safe?" she asked meekly.

Niven nodded. "I will do everything in my power to protect you, Julia, always. Mikenna and Nadie too. I know you miss Anya. And I know you miss your sister. But you have people who want to keep you from harm no matter what."

"I know that."

"Good, don't forget it." He stood just as her evening guards approached to take up their post outside her rooms. "Sweet dreams, Princess."

"Goodnight, Niven." Julia replied, slipping into her room.

As the door clicked shut, she gripped the jet pendant at her chest, the stone warm. She smiled, soothed by the security. For the first time since Joseline's disappearance she felt completely safe. Glancing down at the necklace, she wondered how long it would last.

twenty-eight

Evalyn woke before dawn.

She bit into stale bread, almost choking as a piece threatened to fall into her lungs, then turned to the pile of dry meat tucked into the corner. Part of her debated not eating it just to spite Dax, but not a very big part. Besides, with the still healing wounds on her back, she could use the extra strength. Eyeing the hallway to be sure no one else saw her reach for the food, she scarfed it down.

The door at the end of the hall opened, chains rattling as the other prisoners moved to glimpse the unusual visitor.

A hooded man stopped before her cell.

She glared up at him, holding her chin high, refusing to let her body shake and betray her fear.

"Are you Evalyn?"

Her grin was wicked. "Who's asking?"

He opened the door, jerking her up by her wrist. Her chained ankles rattled, and she lurched forward clumsily, biting back a cry of pain. "You'd do better to watch your mouth, girl."

Evalyn was silent as he led her through torch-lit fortress halls. It all looked the same. The darkness lingered everywhere in pockets of shadow where the torch light couldn't reach. The stench of blood was so strong in some places, she wouldn't be surprised if it coated the walls.

Even the blood red moon, visible through high, barred windows, had an uneasy darkness to it. The smell of death and fear was overpowering.

She had no idea how large the fortress was. But she calculated every turn, every sound, every window.

At last they reached a set of heavy iron doors. They towered upward, vanishing into the dark stone so well, it was difficult to say where the doors ended and the ceiling began. The corroded metal was carved with swirling shadows and faceless men, demons, and monsters. Horrors only nightmares could make reality.

It creaked as it opened, grinding against the stone floor.

The hooded man yanked her into the center of the room, shoving her to her knees. She snarled, pale flesh scraping where she fell.

Three men stood in the middle of the large, barren room. Dax, the foreman, and another hooded being trailed by shadows. She lifted her head as the third lowered his hood.

He was inhuman.

The fire surging through her blood screamed in protest, warning her to get away, far away from the black shadows swirling around him.

He looked as though he had been human once but was no longer, the stench rolling off him like rotting flesh. He hovered above the ground, thick black shadows swirling below his torso where legs should be. Soulless dark eyes gleamed down at her, the space between them branded with two crossed scythes. His mouth, ripped and torn, oozed black liquid where it was sewn together in a jagged line, sharp teeth visible behind dark lips.

Her entire body wanted to recoil from him.

But she stood her ground, ignoring the goosebumps rising on her arms, and tilted her head toward Dax and the foreman with a feral smile. "To what do I owe this pleasure?"

The foreman's fat hand contacted her cheek, her face twisting away from the impact.

Her skin stung where it would bruise in the morning. "How

many times must I tell you to watch your mouth, insolent girl?"

"At least once more, *Sir*."

He made to slap her again, but the shadowy man held up a gloved hand. "That's enough." Evalyn wanted to cover her ears to block out the sound of his hissing voice. "We do not have time for useless bickering. Stay your hand."

The foreman obeyed.

Dax, dressed in all black save for the large indigo feather tucked behind his ear, was a mirror image to the shadow creature, his silky voice cold and bored. "As you know, it has been brought to our attention that you are still helping your fellow prisoners. You know by now this isn't permitted and what types of punishments this behavior results in."

Her eyes blazed with hatred. "I haven't the slightest idea what you're talking about."

Dax smirked. "Don't be coy."

The shadow creature hissed. "This island's sole purpose is to isolate the realm's magic wielders and mine every volcano dry of the obsidian it contains. We have a deadline to maintain. A deadline pushed closer, and we need strong slaves, not weaklings. The orders your master received were specific. You will not get in the way."

Dax knelt before her. His dark eyes met hers daring her to argue, his grip on her chin painful. "You are not permitted to aid those who fall. If they are incompetent, they are to be tossed aside."

Evalyn could have sworn she saw pain flicker in his eyes as he spoke, as if his words were a plea for her to be careful rather than a statement. But the feeling passed quickly.

"Anything you say," she purred.

His grip loosened, his expression softening for only a moment before he slid calloused fingers along her cheek, stroking his thumb against dirtied skin. He tucked a knot of silvery hair behind the subtle point of her ear. She forced her body not to cringe from the touch.

"Pity," he said, louder for the others to hear. "Pity such a pretty thing had to be enslaved."

The foreman chuckled and Evalyn swallowed her disgust, not

breaking their stare.

He really would have been handsome if he weren't such a pig.

Her nostrils flared as she chewed her bottom lip. "Pity indeed."

Dax's grin was too hungry as he slid his eyes down her neck, lingering at the dip of breasts visible beneath her rags. "I always did like your sass, even as a child." He looked at her face again, her chin aching. "Are we clear?"

"Crystal clear." Evalyn's voice dripped venom.

He yanked her up, chains rattling, eyes still lingering. The throb spread through her shoulder and arm, the beginning of another bruise.

Sometimes it surprised her the man hadn't dragged her into his bed yet. He had a horrible reputation.

I can only try to keep you safe in so many ways.

Evalyn shook the confusing thought from her mind. It didn't matter.

Her escort detached himself from the doorway, yanking once more on her chains. She stumbled slightly, trailing after him into the hallway.

"Foreman," Dax said. "If she gives you any more trouble, expose her and chain her to one of the fortress towers for a few days." She could hear the smile in his voice without seeing his expression. The goosebumps coated her flesh once more at the thought of the punishment he referred to. "The men seemed to enjoy that last time."

"As you wish, Captain."

The iron door closed. She ignored the burn in her cheek and arm as her mind churned, planning.

The pirate captain might very well be her key to freedom. She hoped she could tolerate him enough if she planted the seed, sparked the full force of his desires. Rare kindness or no, he was a lustful, heartless man, the pirate captain who found her—a nearly drowned six-year-old child—and subjected her to this fate.

Dax had never hurt her, not the way the foreman had, but she detested the way he watched her with those hungry, indigo eyes. Hated the way he did nothing to stop the foreman's abuse her as if she couldn't feel it, then tried to comfort her with secretive words and glances. Perhaps he thought she forgot all he and the foreman had put her through.

But she never could.

The familiar chains rattled in the distance as they approached the other prisoners on their way to the mines. She fell into line, not speaking a word to anyone. She needed to figure out whatever it was Dax wanted. What he *truly* wanted.

She still needed to become stronger, to learn any weakness she could use to her advantage.

Strong, so when she was ready, her freedom would let her walk away a new woman, the fearful child cowering within her no more than a pile of ash scattered across the mountain floor. The foreman's skull the first one she'd crack against the wall as she burned them into oblivion.

twenty-nine

Malous was upon them.

With Ryneas and the Midsummer festival over, the days grew short, making for less daylight. Already they'd traveled a day longer than Quinn anticipated, and Joseline longed for the warmth of a real bed once more.

She fiddled with her hair, letting out a wistful sigh. *I missed Julia's birthday. I've never missed her birthday. I hope she won't hate me too badly.*

Bellona nickered, and Shea opened an eye from her usual spot on the mare's rear. *We're almost there don't look so down on yourself.*

Joseline still wasn't used to the echo of Shea's voice in her head. "How do you know?"

Shea let out a lazy huff as Eclipse pulled up beside them, Quinn motioning for her to follow him ahead of the others. "Your Highness, come."

After the attack and the days she'd spent helping him heal, Joseline's slumbering power had begun opening to him, trusting him despite his continual coldness. They were cordial, more civil than usual, but they hadn't spoken of the evening several days past. The connection between them from their sparring match in the forest vanished as if it had never been.

They trotted their mounts up the crest of a slight hill, the golden orange sunset blinding. Joseline squinted to see the expanse of Rivedas, painted in evening hues at their feet.

Rivedas, governed by Lord Gavin Clemonte, was home to the main farming guild in Rathal. Half the size of Corae, it was surrounded by Farowa Forest on all sides, the northern road cutting through its center like an arrow. Lord Clemonte's estate stood in the northwestern corner, a shadow to the tall, sturdy towers of the temple. The empty grounds were covered in fields, the harvest just beginning for the approaching winter months.

It had no protective wall, its border a wide dirt road big enough for two large carts to travel comfortably. Having never left the capital, it was strange to see a city unprotected by ancient black stone.

The buildings reflected every shade of the glowing horizon against their sand colored bricks and ashen wood. A fountain decorated the center of town, a large statue depicting Ryneas, the God of Trade and Agriculture, at its center. Two large streets branched off from its structure, intersecting the northern road. To their left, a cluster of small houses stood near large fields, the faint shapes of grazing animals dotted amongst their pastures.

The serenity was beautiful until Quinn stiffened.

A squad of armed guards gathered at the base of the hill, bows drawn. Quinn moved Eclipse closer to Bellona. Fallon, Maya, and Jenson flanked them, weapons ready.

With a wave of their leader's hand, the guard halted a step behind him. Light armor gleamed in the evening sun, their cloaks decorated with a golden sword thrust downward, a black thorn branch twisted around the blade. The sigil of the Clemonte family.

Fallon's stallion moved down the hill to meet their leader, a tall, burly man who seemed to be about her father's age, with steady, golden-brown eyes.

The other man met his gaze. "Are you and your comrades friend or foe?" His voice was rugged, but kind.

"Who's asking?" Fallon replied, his expression unwavering.

"We received word from a tavern along the main road several days behind you, alerting us of friends traveling north from King Reul's ancient Order." The other man's horse pranced as he stroked a hand over his full, dark brown beard. "So, I repeat, are you friend or foe?"

Joseline leaned toward Quinn. "Reul the Fae King?" He gave a sharp nod, his attention still on the guards below. "But I thought he died in the Second Demon Wars centuries ago?"

This time he glared at her.

She said nothing else, twisting a scarlet curl around her finger.

"It would seem our new friend decided against the secrecy I advised. My comrades and I just came from an inn south of here."

"Anita sent word of your arrival. It seems the legends of Kynire are remembered after all." Both groups were silent for a moment. Then the other man smiled warmly. "Welcome, my friends, to Rivedas."

Lord Gavin Clemonte hadn't stopped staring at Quinn since Fallon introduced them. Quinn could feel the older man's golden-brown eyes following his every move—not with caution, but awe. Gavin's eyes darted to him whenever he spoke, moved, or so much as shifted.

Quinn shivered, taking another sip of ale as he fiddled absently with the pendant at his throat.

The tavern Gavin and his men escorted them to was near empty. A few groups laughed or talked amongst themselves, paying no mind to the newcomers accompanied by their liege lord and city guard. At least being with familiar faces hadn't attracted much attention from the town's people.

"So, friends, where did you say you traveled from?" Gavin said at last.

Quinn took another bite of beef stew, eyes wary. "We didn't."

Fallon, seated beside him, clapped him on the back. "No need to be rude to our hosts." The older man grinned, an unfamiliar gesture even Maya raised her eyebrows at. Fallon ignored them. "Please forgive Quinn, he's not the friendliest to unacquainted faces."

"He's not the friendliest anyway," Jenson muttered.

Quinn scowled at him.

"Nothing to forgive, I assure you. I would be hesitant too if I were traveling these days." Gavin leaned toward him, his rough voice softening. "There are tales of strange creatures wandering these woods. After the incident in Corae, I don't blame you folks for being cautious."

"What happened in the Capital?" Quinn questioned. Joseline shifted beside him, and he brushed his knee against hers under the table, a silent request to say nothing.

Mercifully, she obeyed.

Gavin frowned. "You don't know?"

Quinn raised an eyebrow.

"The entire city was attacked by shadows or rather, thick clouds of smoke. Everyone tells a different story it seems. But the city outskirts are occupied by shadowy beings. Some think them men, others say they're demons in Aeron's host. After the princess's disappearance, nobody knows for sure."

"These creatures, they just walk around, they don't terrorize the citizens?" Joseline asked. Quinn refrained from smiling at the calmness in her voice.

Gavin nodded. "Yes, it's peculiar."

"Interesting indeed," Fallon said.

"As I said, some people say Aeron is responsible, but I have a hard time believing in children's stories."

They continued eating in silence for several minutes. "I'm so sorry for asking again, I know it's not my business, but where is it you come from?" Sensing Quinn's growl, Gavin rushed on. "I only ask because of your eyes."

Quinn blinked. "My eyes?"

"Turquoise eyes are rare, unheard of in most races. They are said to be seen only in the Elirona bloodline. If you believe in such myths.

I've never come across another with eyes like yours."

Quinn laughed outright. "The Elirona bloodline, as in the royal Fae? I've lived in Rathal my entire life." He glanced at Fallon, who laughed as well. "I'm definitely not Fae."

Fallon's shoulders seemed to tense slightly at his response, but his mentor added, "My *son* and I have lived in Rathal's capital since his mother died. I regulate Kynire's headquarters there, taught him everything I know. He's my second in command."

The strange look was still on Gavin's face, but it faded as he tugged on his beard. "I must be recalling the stories wrong. My apologies." He didn't mention it again.

They finished eating when an excited shriek sounded from the other end of the room.

Quinn turned toward the young child running unsteadily across the hall, golden brown curls bouncing about her round face. A lean woman chased after her, always a step behind.

The child launched herself at Gavin, squealing. "Papa, Papa!"

Gavin took the toddler into his arms, cradling her against his chest. "Ari, my little troublemaker. Giving your mother a hard time, I see?" He tickled her, shrill giggles echoing through the room.

Gavin looked up at Ari's mother. She sent him an exasperated look, but it softened as he stood, taking her into his arms as well. Ari giggled again.

"Your sweet daughter learned how to climb out of her bed and thought she could sneak out of the manor."

"It would seem she succeeded, Mereen, my love." He leaned down to kiss her, his smile kind. Ari's small nose wrinkled, and she stuck her tongue out at the gesture.

Gavin held them both tight, sending his daughter a sly look. "Now, Arrietty. I need you to be a good girl for your mother and go to sleep. Do you think you can do that, princess?"

Ari nodded, wide chocolatey eyes covered by her curls as she reached small hands out for her mother. Mereen hoisted her daughter against a hip, kissed her husband fiercely, and left.

Gavin sighed. "Arrietty, my little princess. She's going to be a feisty one. I pity the lord who marries her." Several of the men sitting with them laughed or shook their heads.

"Sounds a lot like someone I know," Quinn said, his eyes lingering on Joseline.

Her cheeks heated. "Speak for yourself, idiot."

Gavin let out a loud, booming laugh at the retort, the sound so pure Quinn couldn't help but chuckle. Maya winked at Jenson, snickering. Even Fallon smiled.

The rest of the evening was filled with much needed serenity. Gavin and his men told countless stories about Rivedas and its history, the normal routines they went through daily, the best merchants to purchase supplies from at the morning market. Joseline soaked it all in, spellbound by the opportunity to learn about her country from the people who inhabited it.

"Quinn." He blinked, shaking himself from a daydream at the sound of Maya's voice in his ear.

He furrowed his brows at her face inches from his on the table. He lifted his head.

Maya did the same, smiling, and jerked her head toward the door. "Go on, clear your head. You look...confused."

"I'm never confused." He glanced over at Joseline, who was deep in conversation with Jenson, Fallon, and Gavin. Fallon had relaxed again, but Quinn still couldn't ignore the tight feeling rooted in his gut that his mentor was keeping something from him.

Sensing the direction of his attention, Maya's smile deepened. She reached over, giving his hand a little squeeze. "Jenson and I are perfectly capable of keeping her safe without you. We're all in this together, remember?"

The corner of Quinn's lip twitched. "I know. I guess I just need to be reminded sometimes." He sighed. "I don't know what I'd do without you both."

Maya shrugged, releasing his hand. "No idea, probably die of boredom with only Fallon for company."

"Oh, Gods, I can only imagine."

Maya grinned, showing the gap in her front teeth, and Quinn

chuckled. Feelings aside, she did have a sweet smile, and despite her age, she was quite often the most sensible of them all. She deserved better than him. She deserved someone who could care for her the way he never would.

"What are you still staring at me for? Go." Maya gave him a little shove.

"Right," he nodded. "Thanks, Yaya."

"Don't mention it," she replied, turning back to the conversation as he slipped outside.

In all his travels with Fallon, Quinn had only passed through Rivedas. The town was so peaceful.

Few citizens occupied the streets in the growing evening. Some lugged home wobbling carts from the market, while others, arm in arm, simply admired the cool evening breeze as he did. Quinn climbed onto one of the many rooftops, resting his head against arms crossed behind it.

After several minutes a voice said, "How'd I know you would find a rooftop somewhere to be alone?"

Quinn spun.

Jenson, tall and slender, was almost invisible in the shadows. He pulled his hood back, dark eyes shining in the moonlight as he approached, sitting beside Quinn. "Maya said she sent you away to *think*. Do you want to talk about what's bothering you?"

"Sometimes, I hate you both for pointing out my feelings."

Jenson chuckled. "Someone has to. What else are kindred souls good for?"

"I just hate that it means you can always read my thoughts somehow," Quinn mumbled.

Jenson raised an eyebrow. "I'm your *sielapora*," he mused. "I'm always here to listen. But you don't have to talk about it if you don't want to."

Quinn sighed, looking up at the stars. "I can't stop thinking about what Lord Gavin said. If that's true, it could be connected to why I don't remember the first four years of my life. It could explain the questions about my past, the flickers I dream about. Maybe they're memories..."

"Do you believe that?" Jenson's voice was almost a whisper.

Quinn chewed his lip, bracing himself on an elbow as he faced his friend. "I don't know. If they were, I can't understand why Fallon would lie about them."

"Does not telling you mean he lied?"

"Well, no." Quinn dragged a hand through his hair, laying back once more. "But why wouldn't he tell me who I was, return me to my family? You know the stories of the Demon Wars as well as I do. Another living royal child could change everything, not just for me or Joseline, but Navarre. Even if I wasn't a royal, just a pure-blooded Fae, that would still explain so much, change so much, especially if I really learned to control my magic."

The moonlight illuminated the thoughtful look on Jenson's face. "Fallon thinks of you as his own son. If he knew and neglected to tell you something about your past, he must have a good reason for it."

"I suppose...it just doesn't make sense." Quinn sighed again.

"Well, you can ask him or do nothing. Fallon will tell you if it's important, you know he will. He made you his second for a reason."

The dull ache gripping his chest lessened. "You're right."

Jenson flashed a playful smile, crossing long legs. "Sauda's ass, when did you turn into a worrying old crone?"

Quinn gave him a shove and pointed down to the heap of stinking manure along the side of the building. "You'll be sleeping in that dung pile if you don't watch it. I'm still a better wrestler than you."

Jenson crinkled his nose. "You've always had a nasty sense of humor." They both laughed, the sound echoing into the forest.

thirty

Evalyn knew exactly why several of Dax's guardsmen pulled her out of line as blood-red light rippled along the horizon. They escorted her through the same unfamiliar halls, a step away, golden hilted swords ready.

She'd seen the pirate captain watching them work twice since the incident with the foreman. Each time, she'd flashed him an indiscreet, flirty smile, fluttering long eyelashes.

They spiraled higher into the fortress, cracking stone under foot leading to Goddess knew where. She kept her chin high, forcing her breathing to remain even.

She would not let the darkness consume her.

At last they stopped before an open door, smoke billowing from within. A middle-aged woman with narrowed, deep-set eyes met them at the door. She grabbed Evalyn's chin, clucking at her dirt-caked hair and skin, and pulled her by an elbow. The door clicked shut.

The woman dragged her toward one of the wide tubs lining the room, steam rising from the water, thick enough to blind even Evalyn's precise vision. Several wenches chattered in hushed voices near a long window. The woman snapped her fingers and they dispersed.

Rags ripped from her body with no effort. The woman undid her long braid and tossed her into a tub, water sloshing onto the stone floor. Neither Evalyn nor the woman spoke even when the wenches returned, their arms filled with various vials, oils, brushes, and cleaning cloths. The woman muttered something in a language Evalyn didn't understand and dunked her head into the scalding water.

It took an hour of scrubbing with salts and lathers to remove the dirt and grime from her skin.

The water, so dirty from years of poor hygiene and grime, had to be drained and refilled twice. Evalyn refused to cry out, even as they pried off her iron shackles to scrub the already raw skin beneath. The woman gave her a narrowed look, but Evalyn only flashed an innocent grin and shrugged.

Her hair was a nightmare.

A slave of eighteen years, the silvery locks knew nothing but neglect. She kept it braided, but even that couldn't stop the dirt from consuming the natural color. It took another hour of brushing, soaking, and unknotting to tackle her hair alone. They had to cut out several unsalvageable knots.

Then, for good measure, they layered out the spots where the knots were cut away and scrubbed her skin raw again.

Evalyn relished in it.

The fire surging through her breathed in the pain with open arms. It called to her, coaxed her, begging for the sweet relief of power she'd experienced only once before they shackled her. The magic hummed through her veins, her soul, threatening to escape, to burn her alive.

The iron prison clamped around one ankle, then the other. The flickering embers simmered and died. Cold rushed through her, but the well of power still slumbered, waiting.

They dragged her from the tub and toweled her dry, then guided her to a connecting room. There, the woman and several wenches twisted and pulled at her hair. Pins held back the long damp strands framing a too-narrow face, falling over her bare breasts.

They shoved her into a gown of light teal, tightening the laces of a black leather corset over top. She pushed the loose fabric up to her elbows. The cotton gown grazed stone as she approached a mirror on the opposite side of the room.

Evalyn had never seen a reflection of the woman she'd become. She wasn't sure what to make of herself.

Her hair, straight, thick, and shimmering like moonlight, brushed the small of her back. The turquoise of her dress accented the vibrant blue-green of her eyes. She touched her neck, pale flesh lovely before her hands fell to her narrow waist constricted beneath leather and trailed a finger up her side to brush along her breasts which, popped somewhat noticeably despite years of malnourishment. She frowned, patting the extra fabric along her chest, but refrained from rolling her eyes. She wasn't surprised.

And the ears. She touched the delicately pointed tips, the unignorable indication of her heritage.

Evalyn smiled in admiration. She was quite beautiful.

The woman huffed. "Shame you were enslaved so young. You have the elegance of a fine court lady."

Evalyn frowned, gnawing her lip.

"Not when you scowl like that! Smile, you have such lovely lips."

She batted long eyelashes, her melodic voice silk. "Something like this?"

The woman rolled her eyes. "He always liked women with character. Go on, then."

Evalyn tried not to let panic rise in her chest as the hooded man appeared and escorted her from the room.

They'd removed the chains from her wrists and unhooked the rings of heavy iron connecting her feet. But the soft clank as her iron-clamped ankles rubbed together reminded her of her imprisonment, and her wrists were red and bruised where the chains left the skin raw.

Evalyn knew the guard was examining the feminine body that had been revealed. She held her chin high, refusing to cover her chest as his eyes lingered.

The stairs leading to Dax's chambers made her iron-clamped ankles throb. She gritted her teeth, clenching her fists at her sides.

The guard knocked once, twice, before the door swung open.

The captain. Every inch of him was covered in masculine elegance.

Shoulder-length dark hair was half pulled back, a burgundy plume tucked behind his ear, and his beard was dark and trimmed. Black pants blended with the leather boots covering his calves. A belt, decorated with a dagger and cutlass, slung across his hips. His chest, tan and sculpted, was visible through the half-buttoned collar of his white tunic. The burgundy coat swung around his knees as he walked, clinging to muscled arms. His long fingers were covered with various gemstone rings.

Lustful eyes trailed down her body, warranting a chuckle from the guard.

She chewed her lip, filling her own eyes with innocence.

He could never know how terrified she was.

Evalyn stepped past him into the room, refusing to flinch as the door clicked shut. "Curious already? I've heard stories of your...appetite. It makes a woman a little nervous." She flashed a wicked smile.

He motioned to the candlelit table beside the glowing hearth.

Evalyn struggled not to drool at the feast amidst the gold plates. There was enough food for twenty slaves. She blinked at the dishes covered in various cheeses and exotic fruits, mixed vegetables, an assortment of buttered breads, roast pig, and chicken.

She wondered how much she could stomach before she was sick.

He guided her, a gentle hand at her waist to the seat beside the hearth. His touch sent a sudden jolt rippling through her, but she ignored it, blinking away the confusion of the strange comfort his touch warranted. Coals crackled under the bed of flames. She didn't argue as he pushed in her chair, poured her wine goblet halfway, and seated himself opposite her.

He was still staring at her as he lifted his goblet, but his dark blue eyes seemed softer somehow, less ravenous.

I can only try to keep you safe in so many ways.

Again, she pushed the words from her mind. She couldn't see

him as anything but a monster.

"No need for formalities with my title, you may call me Dax." He sipped, then wiped his mustached upper lip. "What may I call you? Knowledge of names is rare among the slaves, and if I remember correctly, you refused to give me your name when first we met."

She sipped as well, focusing on keeping her hands steady. "Evalyn."

His dark eyes glinted in the firelight. "Evalyn, a lovely name." He sliced off a pig thigh, tossing it and a clump of grapes onto his plate.

"Why thank you, Sir." She chose cheese and berries, not wanting to overdo it. Sweet juice tickled her tongue. She stifled a moan at the delectable flavor. She'd forgotten what berries tasted like.

"Dax, please."

"Dax," she repeated.

"So, it seems you've been eating the extra food despite your incessant nagging on the subject. Honestly, Evalyn, I didn't mean to startle you or anger you with my actions." His collected expression faltered. "It's just...you are the youngest I've ever brought here, I would have felt personally responsible if something happened to you."

Evalyn kept her own expression calm despite the rapid flutter in her chest. "I still don't understand why you feel the need to do it in the first place."

Dax's crooked smile was kind. "Regardless of that you think, I'm not heartless. I saved your life only to give you to the wolves, the least I could do was try to keep a better eye on you."

"But—"

He waved her off with a jeweled hand. "No need for thanks. We needn't discuss it if it's going to fluster you, little dove."

They finished eating in silence, Evalyn doing her best not to stare at him.

Dax stood, unsheathing a blade from his hip to pick a piece of pork from his tooth. Sheathing it once more, he walked to her and extended a hand. She allowed him to pull her to her feet and grip her waist.

Again, the jolt of energy sparked, igniting her core when they couched. If Dax noticed it as well, he didn't show it.

"Such a pretty young woman you've become." He stroked her cheek with his other hand. "I knew I wouldn't regret bringing you here all those years ago. You just need to keep that sweet mouth shut around certain people. It's a dangerous game we play here, little dove."

Her throat bobbed, her pulse quickening. "That sounds rather perverse, even for someone with your reputation."

Dax laughed, the sound warm and comforting. "Oh, don't be ridiculous, I didn't mean it like that. I simply meant...well, I couldn't just let you die, you were only a child."

"You had all this planned from the day you—"

He stopped her with a finger over her lips. "I've had a lot of things planned since the day I found you, but we needn't get into all that now. I know how to spot beauty when I see it. Yours was easy to see, even in a half-drowned child. I had to do something to protect it, didn't I?" He took a step toward the bedroom, still bracing her thin body against his chest.

Evalyn managed a laugh, releasing some nerves as she trailed a finger along Dax's jaw. His beard was surprisingly soft. "Here you had me thinking I was just another slave to fuel your unhealthy obsession with obsidian."

His chest rumbled as he chuckled. "Unhealthy?" He set her on the edge of a large four-poster bed, moving toward the dresser lining the wall by the door. "Obsidian is a powerful stone."

Make him want you, the voice in her head whispered.

She fiddled with the laces of her corset, looking at him through long lashes. "Anything can be powerful in the right hands."

Dax's hand froze on the dresser. He turned. "You really think that?" She didn't answer, only batted her eyelashes flirtatiously. He grinned, his smile crooked. "Something, like you?"

Evalyn bit her lip, returning the gesture as he walked toward her. "But of course."

Dax tossed a nightgown to her. "You'll wear this to bed." It was smooth, silken in her fingers.

"If I refuse?" Ever hard to get, ever innocent.

Again, that lazy smile. "You won't refuse."

"Won't I?"

"No, you won't." Those dark eyes flickered, daring her to challenge him.

Then, gently, he tucked a silvery strand behind her ear, leaning so close his breath heated her neck. "I don't have to be a gentleman. If you aren't careful, little dove, that sweet mouth of yours is going to get you into a lot of trouble. If not from me, then something much worse."

A finger trailed down her spine and goosebumps covered her skin, unsure if they were from the fierce challenge in his eyes or the subtle gentleness of his touch.

But she refused to let any hint of fear show. "Anything you say, Dax."

He chuckled, pulling away. "I was always curious what Fae women were like. Quite the little she-demon, aren't you?"

She responded by tugging at the laces binding her chest. Dax turned away and she blinked. "You don't want to watch?"

Dax peered over his shoulder, raising an eyebrow. "I'm not a savage you know. My interests lie more in keeping those enslaved here from harm." He reached forward, caressing the curve of her neck. "Besides, I have no interest in forcing you to do something you don't want to. If you ever have those feelings for me, they'll be mutual, for both of us."

He turned away again and Evalyn unlaced the corset and gown, replacing them with the satin nightgown. The fabric brushed her thighs, clinging to thin curves.

Her pulse quickened. His strange comments meant nothing. The sensation of energy shimmering between them meant nothing.

She could do this.

She *would* do this.

Get close, let him trust her, let him think he was in control. Evalyn nodded, all too aware of the garment's shortness.

She watched as Dax removed his coat, boots, and pants. For a man in his early forties, his body was still in near perfect condition.

He let out a low whistle, and Evalyn blushed despite her mental protests. "You know you're a lovely young woman, don't you?"

Evalyn flashed that wicked smile. "I know."

His laugh was heavy as he pulled her close to him again. This time, she braced a hand on his chest. They were about the same height, but he was so much stronger. One pull on her waist and they were laying in the middle of the bed, Dax leaning over her.

His eyes trailed to her mouth, her breasts, then back again. "So many things I could do to you. But I won't, not yet. Not until we both want to. You're safe, and we have all the time in the world." He kissed her cheek, his lips surprisingly gentle. Goosebumps rose on her arms and neck.

"Is that what you want?" she breathed. "With me, I mean."

Dax pursed his lips. "I suppose I never thought about it. I want you to be safe, little dove, I won't deny that, but it's never been because I see you in that way." He tugged on the sheets, then again on her waist to pull her up. Her head sank into soft pillows. "Maybe someday. But as I said, only if it's mutual." Dax rolled away, and she adjusted the sheets crumpled beneath her.

Rather than look at him, Evalyn stared at the ceiling as she asked, "Not to be ungrateful for such generosity, but if you weren't planning to seduce me, why am I here?"

She gasped at the sharp tug as he pulled her toward him. "I meant it when I said I want to keep as many people safe as I can. What better way to protect a precious gem from thieves than to conceal it in plain sight, little dove?" His voice was a low whisper against her neck.

Evalyn said nothing, her breath ragged as it shuddered from her throat. Dax drifted off to sleep, his arm draped across her waist.

But Evalyn couldn't sleep.

The fire slumbering within her grew stronger with her hatred. The strange kindness and soft touches didn't justify years of cruelty. She couldn't let it. She needed her hatred. Without her hatred she had nothing left.

So her mind whirled with plans of how she might escape, and

how Dax would pay for all he'd done in the process.

Evalyn woke to the sound of Dax grumbling.

She yawned, hands stretching over her head, back arching. She'd long forgotten what a warm bed felt like.

He was already dressed and fiddling with his boots when she turned to him. "Is everything alright?" she murmured sleepily, eyelids heavy.

"No, everything is not alright," he muttered. "The Shadow Beasts are demanding more meetings to discuss the failure of the princess's name day several weeks ago. It's ridiculous if you ask me." She had no idea what he meant but didn't stop him from rambling.

Realizing it as well, Dax shook his head. "Wear what you were brought up in. I can arrange to have something more suitable sent up today, and a servant will be along to begin your lessons."

She blinked, clutching the silky ivory sheets to her chest. "Lessons?"

"You're under my protection now, Evalyn. My little dove is going to know how to read, which I'm assuming you don't, since you spent the past eighteen years in a cell."

The response took her by surprise.

"You won't be returning there. So, behave yourself. I have enough problems without you causing more."

Before she could think up a sassy reply, he was gone.

Evalyn wasted no time.

She slipped from the bed and tugged off the nightgown. Her eyes glanced down at the clean, gleaming skin. She ran a hand along her stomach, over her navel, wrapping her arms around her waist with a pleased smirk. Reaching for the cotton gown she hesitated, tossing it to the side.

The nakedness didn't bother her, and it didn't interfere, only prevented the gown from getting sweaty. With a satisfied huff, she pushed herself through more exercises than she ever had in the stone cell.

Strength and patience, her mind whispered the words over and over. They were her motto, her will.

Strength and patience.

I will not let the darkness consume me.

By the time a servant girl entered with breakfast, she was in dire need of a long, hot bath.

thirty-one

Three uneventful weeks all but blurred together, the dreams continuing in undistinguished distortions.

Rushing water churning, violent, almost blinding all his senses. A woodland cottage. A silver-haired Fae girl. A dark, tragic mistake. But it was all hazy, uncertain.

Quinn tried to ignore them by filling his time with distractions. He trained with Joseline in the mornings and explored local stores and markets with Jenson or Maya in the afternoon. Most days, Lord Clemonte would invite them to train with his men in the barracks of his estates, but Quinn preferred to venture off into the woods to train away from prying eyes.

The part of Farowa Forest surrounding Rivedas was thick with hidden groves—most likely ancient Faerie homes from the days when the Faerie Folk still inhabited Navarre. Sometimes, Quinn could even pull Fallon away for a few hours to train.

Despite the secrets he might keep, Fallon was the only one who could truly match Quinn's speed, and he'd missed training with his mentor before Joseline's name day.

Each evening, he and Jenson found a different rooftop, either to talk or just watch the stars shimmering down from the heavens. As *sielaporas*, his relationship with Jenson had always been different, calm and trusting. There was no pretense between them, and Jenson always knew just what to say to put him at ease.

This particular evening they'd both managed to doze off, tucked into one of the many flat spaces between the high stone turrets of the temple. A loud gong jolted them awake as the city warning bell trilled from the tower above.

The first gong still echoed against the coppery metal by the time Quinn's feet touched the ground, swift and wary, Jenson a step behind with that same feline grace. They followed Gavin's men to the barracks near the front of his estate. Gavin swept past, giving a curt nod, then signaled for the soldiers to remain vigilant, cautious, as they moved south.

Fallon and Maya approached a moment later, checking various weapons.

Quinn flashed Maya a questioning look as he tightened the belt slung over his hips, checking each dagger along with the self-sheathing blade at his wrist.

Reading his expression, she said, "Joseline is on her way to the catacombs with the other women and children."

He nodded. "Any idea what it is?"

"No, but whatever it is...I hope it wasn't following us." Maya's voice was quiet, nervous.

Five dozen men gathered toward the southern tree line. The sound of shifting steel and chainmail echoed on the breeze, their light plated armor all engraved with the Clemonte crest on cloaks or breastplates.

Not even a chirp echoed from the spreading darkness. Quinn shivered.

The air was too black. The breeze blew into the forest as if drawing them toward whatever waited beyond.

Gavin called out, his archers kneeling in front with drawn bowstrings, awaiting the command to fire. Another dozen crouched on rooftops, all arrows aimed into the woods. Jenson knelt with them, drawing his longbow.

The minutes ticked by. Still there was nothing. Maya sucked on her gapped teeth, fidgeting beside him. But just as Quinn opened his mouth to question the alarm, the wind shifted, blowing that horrible rotting scent toward them.

His chest tightened.

A group of twenty shadow beings emerging from the forest, those eerie black clouds churning against the dirt. Aeron's symbol, etched into the dark leather of their vests, was a stark contrast to their pale gray skin.

Leading them forward, eyes gleaming with bloodlust and hatred in the moonlight, was Kellen.

thirty-two

The warning gong sent the tavern into a frenzy of disarray and panic. Food plates clattered to the floor, shattering, as villagers pushed away from clustered tables. Women huddled against one another, clutching young children to their breast. Lord Clemonte's men shouted orders and reassuring words before rushing out into the night.

Maya and Fallon exchanged a silent look.

Maya gripped Joseline's shoulders with steady hands, easing her to her feet. She shook, her vision blinded by images of those horrid shadow creatures. She wasn't sure when Shea was placed in her arms, but the rapid, thumping pulse at her throat dulled from the fox's warmth.

"What's going on?" Joseline asked.

Shea, sensing her fear, nuzzled against Joseline's chest. She stroked the fox absently.

Maya put a hand on her arm. "Your Highness, I need you to follow the other women and children. You'll all be safe, I promise, but I need to ensure that you're unharmed."

"What about you?" Her pulse quickened again.

Maya smiled. "We'll be alright. You're strong, you can do this. But you aren't ready to fight beside us yet." She scratched Shea's chin.

"We're counting on you to protect her, little one."

Shea nodded.

Another look passed between Maya and Fallon before they sprinted off with the other men.

Joseline forced a shuddered breath through dry lips. She tried not to think about her companions as she followed the large group.

The temple was enormous compared to the crypt-like stone caverns beneath. The temple priestesses ushered them down a steep flight of stairs, patches of moisture dripping from the ceiling. The walls were lined with crevices, each containing small urns or ceramic jars of what Joseline assumed were ashes of those long dead.

The floor flattened before descending into another staircase, which opened into a circular room made of that same gray-black and pewter ledgestone. The high ceiling was almost invisible, save for the massive candelabra dangling from its center. More crevices lined the walls, empty and waiting for urns to fill them.

The Goddess statue, standing beneath the candelabra and just as enormous, faced the stairway as if it could ward off any evil threatening to enter this sacred place of death and prayer. The circular base came up to Joseline's thighs; the lip of stone, littered with flower petals and candles both half-burned and untouched, was wide enough for someone to sit on.

"Goddess protect us, there are so many," she murmured into Shea's fur as she moved past the statue.

Those who entered the cavern first pushed toward the back wall, making room for others. Several women clutched infants to their breast, whispering comforting words to dull their cries. The clank of canes and boots alike echoed off the high ceiling.

Joseline could almost smell the fear. Shea continued to nuzzle against her chest, one vigilant eye on the stairway.

"Mama?" Arrietty huddled in Mereen's arms, curls falling across her face as she gripped her mother's skirts, her eyes filled with terror.

Mereen stroked a hand over her cheek, bringing her daughter closer. "Hush, sweetheart, we're going to be fine."

"Papa too?"

156

Joseline's heart tightened.

Held back tears shimmered in Mereen's eyes. "Your Papa is very strong, very brave. This is the type of thing he trains so much for. He and his men are going to take care of everything, you'll see."

Joseline listened to similar conversations echoing in the space around her. The fear was suffocating. She sat in a corner, knees drawn up, Shea curled against her chest. Her hands still shook, but she balled them into fists, gazing up at the Goddess statue.

She watched from her vigil in the room's center, slender arms raised above her head, reaching for the ceiling. Aged moss covered the elegantly carved gray stone in several spots, her body etched with an elaborate tree, the symbol of the Goddess's connection to the earth and its life. Moss consumed the deep grooved spiral beneath her breasts, and the triple moon between her conjoined hands loomed above her, signifying the abundance of power within.

The statue's energy pulled her toward it, and Joseline ignored the soft whine as Shea tumbled to the ground. The ancient feeling slumbering inside her stirred as she took another step, then another, placing an ivory hand on the spiral. She closed her eyes, the feeling drifting through her mind, her body, awakening once again like a whispering breeze.

This time, she fought to keep control.

Joseline, are you alright? Shea's tail curled around her ankle.

She glanced around the room. The group of priestesses huddled against the base of the Goddess's spine watched her. The shudder drifted through her once more.

She wanted to help them.

These people, *her people*, they were in danger and she was defenseless, unable to give them anything but her voice and the false hope of her council.

She exhaled.

Shea nuzzled her. *Your aura's changing, I can see it in your eyes—they're gold.* Joseline picked her up and the fox licked her chin.

She loosened another breath.

The inner power swelled, the drift warming her blood, reassuring and sturdy. The warmth grew as she removed her hand from the statue, as if the Goddess herself had given her strength.

Joseline cleared her throat, facing the room as best she could from the base of the statue. "Everyone, please, remain calm. We will be protected, all of us. The Goddess grants us strength and courage in times of suffering, and her children watch as well, unable to turn a blind eye."

The whimpering and crying ebbed away as fearful eyes turned to her.

She met them all evenly, calmly.

One of the elder priestesses stood, her cane clanking against the stone as she steadied her thin body. Dark hair peppered with white brushed her shoulders, beady hazel eyes shifting to Joseline suspiciously as she approached. "You and your companions arrived several weeks ago. No sooner than you arrive, our peace is disrupted by an attack from an unknown enemy. What do you know about this?"

"Nora, please, the girl is trying to comfort us," Mereen said. Ari still clung to her skirts as Mereen turned to Joseline, eyes bright. "Do you know what's out there, what they face?"

Joseline shook her head, returning Nora's accusing stare. "I do not know what they face, and I cannot say we are blameless. But I can promise you my companions will do everything within their power to protect you, all of you, even if it costs them their lives. As I would give mine."

Nora's eyes narrowed. She laid her cane down on the lip of the statue and crossed her arms. "Just who are you?"

"We are not your enemies. The comrades I travel with, they are part of the Fae King's Order. They are tasked with the protection of Navarre and all who inhabit it." Several gasps followed her remark and Joseline repeated, "We are not your enemies, Nora."

She sounded stronger, firmer this time, and she spoke with that voice not her own—the Goddess's voice.

"No, no you aren't." Acceptance flashed in Nora's eyes as she looked first at Joseline and the white fox in her arms, then the Goddess statue. She turned back to Joseline. "One blessed by the

Goddess, capable of using her light as you are, couldn't be."

More gasps. "Blessed by the Goddess?" Again, Mereen. She gripped Joseline's arm. "Please, can you help us, do you know something we can do for them?" Fear, hope, desperation filled her voice.

"I don't," Joseline replied.

Nora gestured to the others, palms facing upward as she motioned to them. "We will pray. The Goddess, The Twelve, they listen to our plea."

A tranquility eased in, replacing the fear. Joseline watched, awed, as those around her sat. They clasped hands, some holding one another, some smiling and others crying, the Goddess statue attentive from her almighty perch. Children, women, elders twined their fingers together and closed their eyes, chanting ancient prayers in unison.

A cool, small hand squeezed her fingertips. Arrietty stared up at her, eyes shimmering. They eased to the ground together, Nora and Mereen on either side of them.

Joseline glanced around at all assembled, most praying aloud with Nora, though others bowed their heads and prayed in silence. Joseline whispered her own prayer into the damp, stiff air. Shea, purring softly, paced the room, nudging and soothing those who would accept her comfort. At last she stopped before Ari, curling into her lap.

The presence remained within Joseline, emitting a peaceful calm amongst the room as the fear ebbed away.

It resonated, bouncing between her body and the statue. It submerged itself in the energy of the room, fueling the change in emotion and air. Joseline and Shea exchanged a look, sensing the ever-shifting aura. The Goddess's essence filled her, seeping into her body—guiding, calming, and protecting.

It remained even as the sound of clashing steel rattled from above.

thirty-three

Kellen.

Quinn gritted his teeth, his blood boiling in silent rage as Fallon put a hand on his shoulder.

Kellen.

The captain who had been at Joseline's side for years, protecting her, until he decided to sell her soul to Aeron.

Kellen's betrayal to the royal family, to Joseline, infuriated him.

Loyalty wasn't something to be taken lightly.

Gavin's men trembled. From fear, the smell, or both, Quinn wasn't sure. He prayed, for all their sakes, these men had combat experience. If not, this could end tragically for many innocent people. Last time, they'd struggled against only five, now they faced off against three times that many.

Quinn nodded to Fallon, then stepped forward, but it was Gavin's voice that boomed across the dirt path. "Who are you, and what business do you have in Rivedas?"

Kellen held up a gloved hand, motioning for the shadow beings to halt. The larger one standing just behind him flashed a disapproving snarl, but remained.

Ignoring Gavin, Kellen fixed his eyes on Quinn. "You and your companions have something that belongs to me. Give her back, and we'll be on our way."

A savage smile tugged at the corner of Quinn's mouth. "You're even worse than I remember, Captain." He unsheathed the double-handed long sword at his hip. "She isn't going anywhere with you."

Kellen took another step. Quinn's grip tightened on his hilt. "Princess Joseline is under my protection. Give her to me, and no innocents will be hurt."

Several men gasped at the mention of Joseline's title. Others shifted uneasily.

"Tell me one good reason why I should believe a traitorous rat like you."

"You don't have to believe me, only obey." The shadow beings snickered. The larger one gave what seemed to be an approving nod.

"Sauda's breath, I will," Quinn gritted his teeth. "If you want the princess, you'll have to kill me."

"That can be arranged," Kellen challenged.

It was all the invitation Quinn needed.

He shot forward, no more than a flash of lightning and steel, gripping the hilt with both hands.

Shadow creatures blurred past him as he lunged for Kellen, running toward the others. Heat pulsed through his veins, magic surging, fueling his energy.

Kellen was slower but didn't lack strength or skills. He moved like a snake, twisting his sword in flawless movements around his body, his eyes following Quinn's actions as if he could predict what he would do next. Clever, controlled, and unpredictable.

Quinn shook the unease away, tightening his grip on his sword and swung his blade in a crescent moon toward Kellen's chest.

Kellen stumbled back, barely avoiding contact, blood dripping down his cheek where Quinn's blade sliced open a fresh scar.

Quinn didn't allow the window to open as he lunged forward again, wind whistling around his blade.

Kellen twisted sideways, their steel slashing. Quinn mimicked the movement, bringing the sword up over his head to deflect the blow aimed at his back.

Quinn's breath was deep and even, the steel an extension of his arm as his body fell into the motions of the lethal dance. He knew every moment, every step, as if it were a part of him.

Attack, block, repeat.

Faster and faster they twirled around, oblivious to their surroundings. He wasn't sure how long it had been. He didn't care.

Steel clashed together, screeching.

They broke apart.

The flames clawed at Quinn's skin, begging for release. But he kept the magic at bay, flesh and black ink alike glowing a vibrant blue-green in defiance. His breathing remained even, the swelling flames calm.

He would not lose control. Not this time.

Chilled raindrops ran down his face as the storm erupted in the sky. Shrieking, pained cries echoed from Gavin's men, the smell of blood and the demons' repulsive stench overpowering. Quinn glanced back, relieved to see more shadow beings motionless in the mud than men.

But he paused too long.

Kellen's sword gripped his attention as it tore through cloth, slicing down his bicep in a bloody streak.

Quinn gritted his teeth, choking back a groan. He switched his sword to his equally-adept right hand, hot, sticky blood running down his fingers.

Water dripped down his forehead, and he wiped it away, focusing on Kellen as another shriek sounded from Gavin's men.

"They don't stand a chance, you know that, don't you?" Kellen taunted. Quinn growled in response, hurdling toward him; the Captain blocked, but his growing exhaustion slowed his movements. "Mortals are so pathetic."

"If mortals are so pathetic, what does that say about you?" Quinn challenged.

Kellen drove his blade forward and Quinn stepped back, losing his footing. He slammed into the mud, cursing. His head cracked against the ground, blurring his vision, his sword splashing in the mud just out of reach.

Dark spots flickered across his eyes, his pulse racing as he tried frantically to clear his vision. The world was tilted, hazy, his blood pounding against his temple.

Kellen loomed over him, grinning. He brought his sword up over his head, ready to deliver the final blow.

Quinn rolled, steel diving into his right shoulder instead of his heart.

The scream erupted from his lips before he could stop it, blood flowering his tunic as Kellen ripped the blade free. The burning sensation pierced clean to the bone. Quinn gasped, tears of pain stinging his eyes. Kellen's footsteps splattered mud against his cheek.

His pulse thundered through his veins as he released the dagger hidden along his wrist, springing the blade free of the guard leather and concealing it against his chest. Fire flared, threatening to unleash, but Quinn swallowed it, rallying the reserves of his strength, twisting onto his back with lighting fast reflexes.

The confident gleam in Kellen's eyes vanished when Quinn's dagger plunged into his gut.

Kellen coughed, blood coating his teeth and splattering Quinn's face. The sword clattered to the ground behind him.

"You bastard," he hissed. "I'll kill you."

Quinn scrambled to stand as Kellen fell to his knees, gripping his stomach where blood oozed through his fingers. Quinn swayed, but mercifully stayed upright.

Kellen tried to reach for his sword, but Quinn stomped a boot on the steel, sinking it further into the mud. "You never deserved her," he growled, the bloodied dagger sharp against his fingers.

Kellen spat onto Quinn's boots. "Aeron will have her. Maybe not today, or tomorrow, but he will have her. There is nothing you can do to stop that."

Quinn knelt, swinging his fist low and hard, driving his knuckles into the fresh wound in Kellen's gut. Kellen roared, coughing up more blood as he toppled backward.

He stayed down.

Quinn winced, clutching his shoulder as he joined the others. Only five shadow beings remained. Several of Gavin's men moaned on the ground, but few seemed unconscious. Gavin himself was still standing. Swaying, but standing, as were Maya, Fallon, and Jenson.

The metallic smell of blood coated the air.

Fallon sent him a weary look. "Kellen—"

"Is no longer an issue." Quinn rasped.

"You survived an attack from these beasts before?" Gavin sliced toward the shadow creature before him, panting. He was bleeding from a wound at his temple and claw marks scraped down his thigh.

Goosebumps covered Quinn's arms. He sent a prayer to Noria, Goddess of Healing, that the nails responsible hadn't been poisoned.

"Behead them, just to be sure." Jenson wiped a forearm across his cheek, smearing the mud and dark blood splattered on his skin.

Quinn would never forget the shiver those hissing voices sent down his spine.

"You mortals are so pathetic. So oblivious."

"You have no idea what we're capable of." Flames prickled his skin in defiance, his tattoo glowing with blue-green wildfire.

The shadow being laughed. "I know quite well what you and your Order are capable of, Son of Dorwynn." He glanced to where Kellen lay unconscious. "Even so, you still sound like that boy Aeron has do his dirty work. The Master should have killed him for the first failure, insolent fool."

Quinn sheathed the dagger at his wrist and spat. "I am nothing like that traitor."

Challenge gleamed in the emotionless eyes, that dark liquid oozing from gnarled lips. Quinn prepared to lunge, to wipe that hideous smirk from the creature's face.

"Aren't you? If I'm not mistaken, you are the one who left that pretty, naïve princess alone and defenseless beneath the temple."

Quinn froze.

The smirk widened as the remaining four creatures began to slither forward. "I sent one of my men to find her the moment you two engaged in combat. The mortal fool thought he knew best because

Aeron entrusted him to guard the girl. Thought he was our leader, thought just because he was under Aeron's command, we were required to obey him without question. But he's almost as foolish as you."

The words escaped him, panic rising once more as all thoughts faded from his mind but Joseline, facing one of those monsters alone, surrounded by innocent people.

He forced his mind to clear as he jerked his arm free of Jenson's grasp and ran, ignoring Maya's shouts from behind him. His body was exhausted, his shoulder burning. The flames pulsed, reaching into his eyes and encircling him as if to protect his dying energy.

Faster, they seemed to shout, *run faster*.

The wind nipped his face, the rain blinding as he willed himself to keep going.

Damn it. He should never have left her side.

The temple loomed overhead, lightning flashing through the sky, illuminating the stone turrets. He staggered up the steps and into the building, searching for a shadow being lurking in dark pews. The temple was empty.

His breath rippled from him, the wind chilling his bones, but his thin shield remained intact. He willed his breathing to calm.

She's fine, the magic hummed. *She's fine.*

Quinn believed it, until the temple echoed with terrified screams.

thirty-four

Joseline smelled the creature seconds before its shadowy form appeared atop the second set of steps.

She was on her feet instantly. Shea snarled, hackles rising. Every instinct told her to run, to run far away. But they were trapped, that monstrous thing between them and the only exit.

The shadow being sauntered down the bottom steps. Women and children alike shrieked in terror, the fear rising once more as they retreated against the back wall, as if that would save them from the living nightmare. Mereen fainted, Arrietty clutching her blouse.

The only fearless one amongst them, was Nora.

Fearless or foolish.

She stood before the creature, her expression calm. But the shadow being, much to Joseline's horror, was grinning at her.

Nora spoke first. "What are you doing here, demon? This is a sacred place, a place for our dead and worship of the Great Mother Goddess and The Twelve. Your kind are not welcome here."

The creature turned, staring at the elder. "You are in no position to ask me anything, human half-breed."

He loomed more than two feet over her, but Nora stood tall. "You aren't welcome here," she repeated. "As a priestess of this temple, it is my duty to keep demons like you from setting foot on this sacred ground."

Joseline, freed from whatever spell held her captive, stepped forward. "They're innocent people, leave them alone."

"Ah, Princess."

Joseline wished she could block out that wretched hissing. Shea hadn't stopped growling, and the ancient presence fought to keep her calm. "Yes, here I am."

"You will leave her be, demon. You aren't welcome here," Nora said again.

The demon shot forward with a feral hiss, long fingers contacting Nora's throat and shoving her to the ground, shadows swirling around him. The elder lay unconscious at the base of the Goddess statue, blood trickling down her forehead. The shadow being leaned against the wide-lipped stone, still grinning at Joseline, sharp teeth dripping with dark liquid.

She'd forgotten how fast they were.

Screams clouded the room. Several priestesses knelt beside Nora. The others paled, shrinking further back against the wall.

Joseline couldn't take her eyes from the creature. "That's so much better." His hiss chilled the air. "She was becoming obnoxious, wasn't she?"

"Leave," she said again, her voice weaker. "Or...or I'm going to make you."

That laugh. She *hated* that laugh.

"Aw, the little princess is going to put up a fight, is she?" His lips parted, that vile liquid oozing down his chin. "I don't think so. Where are those mighty protectors of yours? You're helpless without them." Another laugh. The children whimpered behind her as he took a step. "Now come with me, little girl, I'll be gentle."

The ancient power shuddered, shrinking away from him, but Joseline held her ground. "No, I'm not going anywhere with you."

"The hard way, then." The creature gripped her wrists and she cried out, blood swelling where his nails dug into her flesh.

She ground her heels into the stone, swallowing the surging panic.

167

No, her mind roared. *No, fight back, do not let him take you.*

"One more step, and I'll kill you before you can make a sound."

The air evaporated from the room. No one spoke, no one moved.

Quinn, bloody and shaking, stood at the foot of the stairs. He shimmered with raw fire, the flames encompassing him the same blue-green as the fire in those feral eyes.

He clutched two daggers in his hands, blood dripping from a wound along his left bicep. His right shoulder, soaked with blood, drooped to the side, though his grip on the dagger remained strong. The storm outside left his hair and tunic soaked, the thin fabric clinging to every inch of muscle, the dark ink of his tattoo swirling along his skin, shimmering with blue-green fire, stark and vivid beneath his tunic.

He was inhuman, a wild animal ready to kill.

The shadow being dropped her wrist and she stumbled back. "Make me, Son of Dorwynn."

Quinn snarled, shooting forward.

It was like the first time. That first attack in the forest.

Watching him fight was fascinating.

Joseline held her arms out, a shield between her and the innocents, as if she could protect them from the nightmare. Even Quinn looked small next to the monster.

Flames danced with him, swirling around his body gracefully despite the sweat dripping down his brow. Exhaustion coated his expression, but he didn't succumb to its control. "I'll tell you the same thing I told Kellen before I dealt with him."

Joseline's heart fluttered and tightened at the Captain's name.

"Oh? And what's that, Son of Dorwynn?"

Steel clashed against nails, the impact echoing. One little girl covered her ears, crouching on the ground.

"Stop calling me that. I'm not Fae."

The creature's eyes gleamed. "If you say so, Son of Dorwynn. What did you tell Sir Kellen? It was time someone dealt with him. He's such a weak, obnoxious mortal. Determined, but weak. Aeron should never have asked for his help. He was so much weaker than his father."

The flames surrounding Quinn flickered, threating to die as his energy faded. But he gritted his teeth, knuckles white. "I told him he didn't deserve the princess. He didn't, and neither do you."

Quinn moved like lightning, the only sound his daggers slicing together as the shadow being's head thudded to the ground, dark blood pooling where his body fell.

Quinn collapsed to his knees, bracing himself with his good arm.

Joseline rushed to him, screams echoing from behind her. Tears burned her eyes, but she ignored them, falling to the ground beside him. "Quinn?" She gripped his face in small hands, forcing him to look at her.

He smiled thinly. "Are...are you..." He swayed, unable to form the words on dry lips.

Joseline caught him, his weight forcing her to lean back against the ledgestone. But he looked so small, so young and frail as the color continued to drain from his flesh. "I'm alright," she whispered. "But you..." she glanced at his shoulder again. Blood stained her hands where she held him. "You need help."

"I'll be fine."

She laughed, the tears stinging her cheeks. She wiped the wet, dark strands from his forehead. "You stubborn idiot."

"I'm...I'm not..."

You are a stubborn idiot, Shea murmured, approaching them.

Quinn turned to growl at the fox, but pain contorted his face. Shea rolled her eyes with a flick of her tail.

He sighed. "It's not deep, I need a bath and sleep is all." Their faces were so close his breath tickled Joseline's skin. He pushed her away. "I don't want your help." He gritted his teeth and tried to stand.

He nearly toppled over again, but Joseline resisted the urge to reach for him. "Quinn—"

"Your Highness, I can manage."

She didn't argue with his tone as a groan from Nora diverted their attention. The elder woman leaned against the base of the statue. The blood trickling down her temple was dry and several women fussed over her, but she shooed them away.

"What happened?" she asked. "What happened, where is the girl?"

Mereen, conscious once more, answered, "She's alright. She..." But the elder paid her no mind as she caught sight of Quinn.

Nora's eyes widened, her face paling as though she'd seen a ghost.

Quinn met her stare, shifting uncomfortably.

Joseline wondered if he might finally faint from blood loss. He was so pale.

"Where are you from, boy?"

The awe in Nora's voice took Joseline by surprise.

Quinn frowned, but made his way toward her, extending a hand. Nora took it, bracing the other hand against the statue as he eased her to her feet.

"Corae." He paused only to steady his breath. "I'm a member of Kynire." Their hands remained clasped, the strange look still on Nora's face. "The name's Quinn."

"Quinn," she repeated, her voice no more than a whisper.

Everyone was still staring at them. Nora, realizing it, released Quinn's hand and cleared her throat. "Well, Quinn of Kynire, on behalf of the Great Mother and our village, I thank you for saving us."

He chuckled, the wince following. "That's what I'm here for."

Shea yipped at Joseline's feet and she picked her up, stroking soft ears. Nora's attention flashed to her. "This man is your companion?"

Joseline nodded, her nostrils flaring. "He is. Though it would appear he has a terrible habit of showing up when you need him most, in no condition to fight, and then pushing himself to exhaustion."

Quinn raised an eyebrow at her, the humor a strange sight in his eyes. "A thank you would do." Under his breath he added, "Insufferable princess."

"Idiot," she replied.

Quinn swayed again, and Nora caught his uninjured shoulder. "She's right you know. You need a healer."

The humor vanished, replaced by that familiar stone mask. Quinn waved her off. "I'm fine." Those watchful turquoise eyes darted around the catacombs. "No others were injured?"

Nora shook her head. "Just me." She gave him a long look, old eyes trailing over every wound with a healer's gaze. "Well, me and you that is."

"We should make our way back out to the village," Quinn said. "The monsters should be taken care of by now, and there are wounded that need healers."

Accepting he wasn't going to budge until they'd seen to their own wounded, Nora began the climb toward the temple. The others followed, avoiding the headless corpse still crumpled before the stairs.

Joseline motioned for Quinn to go as well, but another soft yip from Shea stopped her. She turned back toward the statue. Mereen stared at them, clutching Arrietty's hand. The child's eyes shimmered with held-back tears.

Joseline wasn't expecting the bow that followed. "Thank you, Princess." The child's whisper was barely audible beneath her unbound dark curls.

Joseline blinked. "I...I didn't do anything deserving your thanks."

Mereen stood, taking Ari into her arms. As they walked past, she touched Joseline's arm, her smile warm. "It is thanks to you that we are alive and well." She cast a quick glance toward Quinn. "You and your brave warrior. Gavin..."

Quinn gave a small nod of acknowledgement. Without another word, she hurried up the stairs, leaving Joseline and Quinn alone.

She motioned to the stairway. "Well, *my brave warrior*, shall we?"

Quinn chuckled, releasing a sigh. The corner of his mouth twitched upward in a smile. "As you wish, Your Highness."

She almost shoved him, but his wounded shoulder stopped her. "You're really the insufferable one, you know that, right?"

He sent her a sidelong glare as they began the climb into the temple.

thirty-five

Moonlight shimmered from the cloudy sky by the time Rivedas relaxed.

The wounded rested in the temple infirmary under the watchful eyes of Nora's novice healers. Mercifully, the injuries were minimum. Several men would have larger scars and bruises requiring several days of bedrest, but most remained unharmed aside from sheer exhaustion. Even the stab wound in Quinn's shoulder wasn't as deep as he feared once he had allowed Nora to clean the blood away.

Fallon approached Nora's cottage at the edge of town, running a hand through sweaty hair.

Lord Clemonte, disheveled and weary, answered his knock with a sharp nod and locked the door behind them.

The cottage interior smelled of lemon verbena. Plants and flowers draped in vines over every surface in sight. Ivy climbed the walls, and soft yellow curtains swooped across small, tinted windows. The furniture was cedarwood, save for the couch and matching armchair near the hearth.

Nora hobbled in from the kitchen, motioning to the circular table near the window. Gavin took the tray teetering in her shaking hands, setting it on the lace-covered surface, and helped her ease into a chair.

Fallon contemplated yet again how this conversation would go. He'd known for a few weeks the healer was Demi-Fae, but she remained isolated in the temple most of the time, and they'd exchanged sparse words during the recent hectic hours about what to say now.

Gavin spoke first. The Lord sounded as exhausted as he looked. "I'm going to get this out of the way, then." He took a long sip of steaming liquid.

"A special herbal concoction of mine, to help settle those nerves." Nora's wrinkled smile was thin.

"It sure does the trick." Gavin sipped once more. "I'd like to know what exactly is going on. As Lord of Rivedas I have a right to know."

Fallon and Nora exchanged a look. "Yes, you do," Fallon agreed.

"Sauda's ass, of course I do." Distress coated his voice. "What in the Gods' names were those creatures? What are they doing here? They were not human, not anything from this world."

Fallon took a ragged breath. "They are Shadow Beasts. Creatures in Aeron's army from The Shadowplains."

"And the human?"

"Kellen, the Waeshorn family's Captain of the Guard and Princess Joseline's personal man-at-arms."

Gavin frowned. "I was a member of the palace guard. The King and I are close friends, and he gave me the honor of serving with the Jade Cloaks for many years until he insisted I retire. That boy...he isn't Emery's boy, is he? He was a babe when I retired twenty years ago to raise my first daughter. But Gods, the boy looks just like him."

Fallon sent him a wry smile. "He's been Aeron's spy for years. Exactly how long, we don't know."

Gavin bit at his thumb nail, scratching the dark brown beard along his jaw as he let out a low whistle. "You're sure?"

"He has Aeron's mark of power tattooed on his wrist, Quinn saw it the day we..." Fallon trailed off, glancing to Nora.

"The red-haired girl traveling with you is Princess Joseline."

An acknowledgement, not a question.

"She's the spitting image of her father. Even if those monsters

173

hadn't said something, it wasn't hard to guess," Lord Clemonte said.

"The plan was always to return her to the castle, but Kellen tried to take her." *To Aeron*. The words were unspoken in Fallon's tone. "Once we learned her safety would be compromised in his presence, we took her into protective custody."

"Where are you headed, then?" Nora asked.

Fallon turned to her. "The Order of Kynire was created to keep any demonic threats from the royal houses and ensure the safety of those with royal blood. We take the princess to Raenya in the north."

"Her life is in considerably more danger now that Aeron has attempted to retrieve her," Nora muttered.

Gavin cleared his throat. "I'm sorry, I'm confused."

"You know the legends of Kynire, and you know the history of Aeron, but you don't know why the princess's safety is vital?" Nora demanded.

Gavin met their stares. "I don't. Some legends I'm aware of, but the mortal storytellers stopped repeating those myths with our history a long time ago."

Fallon's anger flared despite his exhaustion. "They are *not* myths." He drained his mug, Nora pouring another.

"Aren't they?" Gavin's voice was softer.

Fallon closed his eyes. "The four royal houses of Navarre—Waeshorn, Elirona, Stormwood, Ashguard. Through the royal bloodlines, the ancient rulers sealed Aeron within The Shadowplains during the Second Demon Wars. The seal, bound by both magic and blood, would remain intact provided an heir of the four bloodlines remained on the thrones. The Waeshorn bloodline, and the Goddess's purity within it, are the keys to his complete return. The Promised Princess's possession of her power must be protected at all costs."

When Fallon opened his eyes, Gavin stared at him, but still he continued. "After the seal was secure, the Fae King, Reul Elirona, created The Order of Kynire to keep any potential threats at bay and secure the promised one's safety. There are branches throughout Navarre, some unknown to the country's inhabitants. We communicated for years until Aeron's underlings began to rise up, executing children of royal blood. The communications stopped, to protect both Kynire's secrecy and the King."

"You are its leader?" Gavin asked. "So, you're..."

Fallon gave a thin smile, the truth almost hard to speak aloud after so many years in secrecy. "I am Fae."

"Pure Fae warriors are also myths, you know."

"There are ways to conceal my heritage. I keep my appearance hidden through glamours. But lifting the glamour slightly to use my Fae abilities in battle increases defense. I've always scouted for Demi-Fae when looking for new warriors."

Gavin's eyes flickered to Nora at the mention of Demi-Fae. "Your warriors, the princess, do they know?"

Fallon shook his head. "The dark-skinned archer does, he's one of my strongest Demi-Fae. The others, no."

"And the boy with turquoise eyes, does he know—"

"We do not speak of that." Fallon cut Nora off sharply.

"It's because of you and your companions that my family, my men, and my home are unharmed," Gavin said. "I have a life debt to pay you, Fallon."

"You owe us nothing."

"I cannot accept that. My wife, my youngest daughter, they are alive because of your help." Gavin drained his mug. "Just know, should you ever require my help, the Clemonte family guards will come to your aid. I may not be a Fae warrior with centuries of training, but I am still a lord of Navarre and a knight of this realm. I'll gladly lend you my sword should you need it." Fallon nodded. "In addition, I will retell those ancient stories. I am no storyteller, but I'll share what I can remember."

"You would do me a great honor."

"The world deserves hope in times of chaos and the memory of your people's stories. The knowledge of those tales may save Navarre." There was a spark in Gavin's eyes, a promise. "Go get some rest, old man. Looks like you need it."

Fallon chuckled, the release of energy comforting. He ran long fingers against the scar on his chin. "Old man? You do realize what it means to be a pure Fae blessed with the Gods' eternal light?"

Nora, still as silent as she had been for most of the conversation, smiled.

"Being blessed with immortality doesn't mean you aren't old."

A pressure deep within Fallon's chest loosened. A pressure that hadn't been released for over two hundred long years.

"You are correct. Sometimes I feel even older than I am. But having friends to ease the loneliness makes the centuries I've spent alone more than worth it in the end."

Gavin tilted his head. "Are we friends?"

"You remind me of someone I grew up with. Someone I was, and am, quite fond of." He paused before adding, "I think we'd make good friends, you and I." They clasped hands.

"Friends then, Fallon." Gavin left without another word.

Only then did Fallon face Nora, knowing the elderly woman was watching him.

"You know the truth, I'm assuming?"

"I do."

"He has no idea."

Nora picked up on the unspoken demand in his words. "I figured as much. What is he capable of?"

Fallon ran a hand through his hair, pulling a ribbon from his pocket to tie it back against the nape of his neck, the cool breeze refreshing against his hot skin. "He knows how to use the minimal amount of his magic for defense and healing."

"But?"

"At only twenty-four, he's almost a better fighter than I am, his skill in combat equal to any Fae I've fought beside in all my centuries, even his immediate kin. But he has no real experience with his magic. He possesses a great amount, yet using it for a long time threatens mental exhaustion he doesn't know how to prevent. But I couldn't risk anything else. His life is too valuable. He's only alive because I was in the wrong place at the right time. I knew the princess would need him one day, so that lack of knowledge seemed a necessary sacrifice to keep him alive."

Nora collected the cups from the table. "You blocked his memories then?" Fallon nodded. "You'll need to tell him. It will be easier coming from you than anyone else."

"I'm aware." Another sigh escaped his lips as he stood. "You knew upon seeing him?"

Nora's eyes were old and tired, but alert. She didn't break his stare. "I did." Sensing his question, her gaze hardened. "How is of no importance. We're all entitled to our secrets."

Fallon shrugged, turning to the door. "Indeed we are. Now isn't the time to discuss that knowledge."

"No." With a huff, she lifted the tray onto her shoulder, gripping her cane in the other hand. "I hope she lives up to what is expected of her."

"Trust me, so do I. Quinn's been training her."

"Good." He tugged on the front door, a light breeze kissing his skin. But before he took a step, she added, "I hope *he* lives up to what is expected of *him* as well." She vanished into the kitchen.

Exhaustion took its toll as he walked back to the Clemonte estate. For once, Fallon ignored the thoughts racing through his mind.

thirty-six

From the expression on Quinn's face, Joseline was surprised he hadn't burst into flames.

When she walked into his room that morning, she hadn't expected he'd still be asleep. He usually woke before dawn. But before she could let herself out, he groaned, lifting his head from the bed.

The glare that followed prickled goosebumps along her spine.

He dressed in silence, his anger rolling off him in waves as they walked toward the large fountain of Ryneas at the center of town, Quinn grumbling something about the open space for training.

Her body craved it. Her dreams had been haunted by a million ways the previous night could have played out. Each time she woke in a cold sweat, determined to prevent the scenarios from becoming reality.

From the groggy look in his eyes, Quinn hadn't slept well either.

"Well, Your Highness?"

She blinked, cursing the daydream.

Piercing turquoise eyes flashed in annoyance. "If you aren't going to pay attention when—"

"No, I'm sorry," she said quickly.

He knelt with a grunt.

Her eyes flitted over his back and broad shoulders to the rippling muscle under his tunic. Despite the thick bandage beneath, the fabric bunched as he moved, clinging and accenting. The pendant matching his eyes shimmered in the morning sun as it slipped from his shirt.

Then there was that tattoo.

She could never stop staring at the black swirls of ink running across his skin, twisting and turning like a river over golden-tan flesh. It was massive, wrapping around the left half of his body in beautiful tribal patterns.

Dark and dangerous, strong and masculine.

"Are you going to train, or are you going to stare at me all morning?"

She blushed, joining him on the ground. "So, what are we—"

"Do what you want. I need to wake up before I strangle you," he interrupted, the growl still in his voice.

She shouldn't have bothered waking him up at all. But she said nothing else, only followed him through a series of exercises, mimicking him as best as she could. Despite his wounded shoulder, she could barely keep up.

Sweat dripped into her eyes and down her chest. Joseline managed ten push-ups before she collapsed, gasping.

Quinn did significantly less than usual before he sat up, cursing as he rubbed at his shoulder. "Ten is better than last time, right?" She nodded. "Well done." Despite the praise, his tone was cold.

Shoving her feet at him with a forward thrust of her chin, she rolled onto her back. He raised an eyebrow, bracing her ankles with a firm hand. Joseline hoisted herself up, her stomach clenching in defiance. Quinn was so close she could feel his breath tickle her cheeks as she panted, nose flaring.

"Again," he whispered.

She repeated the action, her weak body already shaking. She hated herself for that weakness.

Enough already, just grit your teeth and do it.

Joseline hadn't heard Shea approach. The Aonani fox sat beside her, an annoyed look in her eyes.

You could do this if you stop fighting and let him push you.

Either that or push yourself and stop being pathetic.

Joseline's nose flared again as she gritted her teeth and forced her body through the discomfort.

Push yourself and stop being pathetic. You can do this. The words echoed in her head even as her stomach screamed in protest.

Several moments passed before Quinn eased her to her feet. She watched him, repeating every movement as he showed her how to punch, holding up his palms for her to strike.

She paused once to wipe sweat from her eyes.

Faster and faster she fought her doubt, even as her core numbed. Quinn never left her side, Shea an ever-present shadow at her feet. She blocked out everything but the training, honing her focus on perfecting the movements. Punch after punch, her waist twisting.

Better, her mind screamed. *Stronger.*

"Joseline, I said that's enough."

She stopped, her hand frozen in mid-air at the sound of her name on Quinn's lips.

"What?" Her tunic and leather vest stuck to her body, drenched in sweat.

He jerked his head toward the small crowd watching them. "Enough." He gave her a long look before adding, "How about a run?"

She snorted. "I've never run a day in my life."

That rare mischievous look flickered in his eyes. "Exactly. It will build endurance. One step closer to being strong enough to try learning some magic." He started toward the outskirts of town. "Come on, Your Highness. I won't tell the others if you're sick afterwards."

Joseline sent him a narrowed look, though her chest fluttered in excitement at the promise she'd all but forgotten. "I won't be sick."

Quinn waved a hand at her, not bothering to turn back as he said, "No? Prove it."

Without another word, she jogged to catch up.

To her credit, Joseline only threw up once.

Quinn expected worse.

He made an effort to keep his usually quick pace slow as they ran one lap around Rivedas, every few feet reminding Joseline to focus on her breathing. Shea jogged beside them, an additional support.

When they rounded the final corner, she put a hand on his arm. Panting triumphantly, she took one look at him, turned to brace herself on the brick wall, and vomited.

Then, as if nothing happened, she wiped her mouth with a sleeve and continued walking toward the Clemonte estate, Shea trotting at her heels.

It was all Quinn could do to keep the grin from his face as he stared after her.

Despite the horrors of last night, merchants and farmers lined the streets of the northern road, pushing heavy carts or holding baskets of fresh fruit. Shopkeepers opened their doors with warm smiles, nodding to anyone who passed. With Malous halfway over, harvest season was growing closer—Corae, Orira, Rivedas, and Adoa crowded with traders eager to sell various goods. The main roads were congested with traveling caravans between Rathal's largest cities, trading goods a necessity before the harshness of the frigid winter months.

The sun was blinding, though a light breeze dimmed the humid heat. It danced through the streets, brushing over his sweat-soaked tunic and sending a shiver down his body.

Quinn's shoulder throbbed, but he ignored it. The loss of blood made the stab wound look worse. It wasn't as deep as it felt, no more than a phantom pain, and the cut down his arm was barely a scratch. Thanks to the milk of the poppy Nora forced him to drink, the ache was already dull. Even so, the healing would take longer if he pushed himself too hard. He rubbed his shoulder, swallowing a wince.

"Quinn!" Jenson's smile contagious as he joined him, running a hand through onyx hair. "You've already exercised." There was a hint of disappointment in his voice.

"With the princess." Quinn raised an eyebrow. "Why does that matter?"

Jenson tilted his head to the side, fixing him with a long,

calculating look. "It doesn't." A pause. "You...you look happy."

Quinn's brow furrowed. "Happy? What do you mean?"

Jenson let out an exasperated sigh and rolled his eyes. "Gods above, Quinn, happy. Haven't you ever felt happiness before?"

Quinn took a step back, crossing his arms. He'd never allowed himself to think about it. His past was never more than striving to reach Fallon's standards, and trying to recall memories from the first four years of his life resulted in pounding headaches.

"I guess I never thought about it," he admitted, twisting the pendant between his thumb and forefinger.

Jenson whistled. "Our Fallon. Quite the father, wasn't he?"

Quinn gave him a close-lipped smile. "It was always about perfection."

"I'd believe that." There was a moment of silence. "Well, you do. Look happy, I mean." Quinn followed Jenson's gaze as he stared toward Joseline and Shea disappearing behind the estate doors. "It's like she brings something out in you. Something I've never seen. Something you don't quite see either."

Quinn kept his expression neutral, not wanting to think about the statement and the truth it might hold. Last night...the princess hadn't brought up the way she'd held him or the tears she'd shed. He planned to keep it that way.

He had always, *always* been careless with women.

A young, foolish boy, he'd revelled in it, once he'd grown into his man's body and discovered how to please a woman beyond end. Gods, he and Jenson had used it as another form of competition. His reputation was awful, yet he'd been so proud of it.

But with Joseline, just thinking about that reputation made him ashamed, as if he didn't deserve to look at her let alone touch her. It bothered him, yet he wasn't sure why, didn't quite understand.

"Quinn?" Jenson waved a hand in front of his face.

Quinn blinked. "What?"

His friend chuckled, making his way toward the barracks on the east side of the estate. "Your little audience this morning has been buzzing everywhere about the handsome warrior who saved the town." Jenson flashed that mischievous grin. "So, are you going to show them how much you don't live up to those expectations?"

Quinn glared at him. "If you wanted a challenge, you need only ask."

Jenson laughed, shoving Quinn with a shoulder as they walked. "Eager to show everyone who's better at throwing daggers?"

Quinn bit his lip, sending his friend a menacing smirk. "You have no idea what you're getting into."

Jenson returned the expression. "After all the years we've trained together? I know what I'm getting into."

"Are you two fighting again?" Maya teased, jogging up beside them.

Quinn turned to her. "There's nothing to fight about. Jenson seems to think I'm going to let him beat me."

"Doesn't he always?" she asked, sending Jenson a wink.

"I never think he's—"

"She does have a point, Jens," Quinn chuckled.

Jenson scowled. "I hate when you guys gang up on me."

"While we're on the subject, does that mean I get to beat you at staff fighting again?" Maya's eyes danced.

"You aren't going to."

"Oh? I thought you weren't being a sore loser?" Maya jabbed at him with her fists playfully.

Quinn laughed, slinging an arm around her shoulders and ruffling her hair. Maya squealed, shoving him away and jogging toward the barracks now in plain view. Gavin, standing outside one of several fenced arenas, waved.

If it weren't for the bandage Quinn knew wrapped his thigh, the lord looked unharmed, the cut along his forehead no more than a faint red line. Ari clung to the wooden gates circling the arena, her wide eyes shining with young curiosity.

Gavin smiled as they approached. "Glad to see you're doing well."

Quinn glanced at the half-empty arenas, slinging his arm around Maya's shoulders again. "How are the injured?"

Gavin followed his gaze. "Healing, thanks to Nora. Honestly that woman is a goddess. How Rivedas ever survived the winter sicknesses before she arrived, I will never understand."

"Glad to hear that," Maya said.

Quinn turned to Jenson, who leaned against the fence beside Ari, laughing at something she said. She was pointing to the sparing men with fascination.

"She's going to be a little fighter one day," Gavin said, beaming. "Watching the practice yards captivates her for hours."

"I'm gonna be like Papa." she boasted, turning back to Jenson.

Quinn cleared his throat. "It would appear my training with the princess this morning warrants a duel with my friends." When Jenson flashed a smile, he added, "He thinks he can best me at dagger throwing, but we both know that isn't the case."

Maya snorted.

"Are you sure that's wise with your shoulder healing?" Gavin asked. "I don't want you injured further on my watch."

Quinn swallowed a growl. "It's fine. Besides, I need to keep it moving."

Maya put a hand up to her mouth, whispering, "Quinn, captain of pushing himself too hard. You get used to it after a while."

Quinn rolled his eyes.

"Can I help, Papa? Can I?" Ari hopped down from the fence and raced over to her father, pulling on his pant leg with excitement.

Gavin scooped her into his arms, the action releasing a shrill giggle from her lips. "Of course you can, princess."

He motioned for Quinn, Jenson, and Maya to follow as he entered the yard.

thirty-seven

The mouthless, shadowy horrors attacked in the eerie gloom just past midnight. The mortal who led them targeted the man with brown hair and eyes that matched hers. The man's inner fire raged, flickering around him, glowing along his flesh. But he lacked the control to unleash it without burning out. She watched, numb, unable to stop it as the two warriors clouded in light and dark slashed and weaved through pouring rain.

The light fell, crashing down into waiting, reaching darkness. His shriek erupted into the night as steel plunged into his shoulder.

Evalyn was still screaming when Dax shook her awake.

It was the third time in four days the dream haunted her. Each time she awoke, her head ached, her body drenched in a heavy sheen of sweat as she shook, paralyzed.

"What in Sauda's name is the matter?"

She shivered, clearing her throat as she met Dax's eyes. "I'm sorry, I..."

He shoved the covers away. "It's fine," he grumbled, though his voice said otherwise.

The hand she reached toward him dropped to the bed. "I'm sorry, Dax." She took a breath to settle her nerves.

For almost two and a half weeks she managed to keep up the

facade, until the nightmares began plaguing her at random. She wasn't sure who the male was, and she didn't care. The visions were driving her insane.

Dax found the pants he'd discarded the previous evening and pulled them on, fastening the leather belts to his waist with practiced efficiency. The bed creaked as he sat, gripping her chin with calloused fingers. "Try not to let it happen again."

He said the same thing each time before. Evalyn hoped he wouldn't have to repeat it a fourth time. She nodded.

"Good." His hand dropped to his side. "I'll be gone most of the day." That was nothing unusual.

In the past few weeks, they'd fallen into a peaceful rhythm. They barely acknowledged one another, save for the small talk at dinner. But despite years of tension and hatred she thrust at him, he continued to show her kindness, continued to claim he had her best interests in mind.

It surprised her, the strange feeling that he might not abandon her again, might not leave her like the others, like he had before. The adjustment still made her cautious, wary. But she rather liked it, the growing warmth and comfort of having someone else around.

It didn't alter her opinion that much, but the feeling was nice.

Nevertheless, they kept playing the game, and didn't speak of the unspoken.

He yanked the bedroom door open, a long, emerald coat embroidered with swirling gold draped over his shoulder. "I'm told you're doing well with lessons, even though you hate them. You're progressing. Try not to be too much of a pain, alright, little dove?" She nodded again.

He left without another word.

Her feet hit the hardwood floor with a soft thud, and Evalyn began her exercises. Her mind blocked out all images of the male she felt strangely connected to. For now, anyway. She even added several variations to her movements as well as attempting a few new exercises. She liked having more room to work.

Strength and patience, her mind whispered. *Strength and*

patience.

I will not let the darkness consume me.

When the servant girl, Naomi, entered, she was sitting at the long oak wood table, bathed and dressed, the brown-haired man nothing more than a faint memory in the back of her mind.

After more than an hour of leaning over the cluttered table, Evalyn wanted nothing more than to bash Naomi's head into the wall.

Books, blank parchment, ink wells, and feathers littered the wooden surface. Evalyn stared, expressionless, at the confusing words, fighting the urge to send everything clattering to the floor.

Naomi pointed to the damned word, the same word she'd been pointing to for fifteen minutes. The paragraph blurred together, the letters mocking her with cool, beautiful swirls.

She growled, braiding her hair into an efficient twist. "I already told you, I don't know." Evalyn glanced toward the window, bracing an elbow on the table and resting her chin in her palm.

"We can start from the beginning again if you prefer? Go over what you already know? You're reading beautifully so far."

The servant girl was young and frail. Black hair framed her narrow face, moving limply as she reached for the large leather-bound book across the table.

Evalyn put a hand on her arm. "No, enough."

"But Captain Dax insisted we continue—" A viscous glare from Evalyn silenced her.

"I need a break." She walked to the window consuming the wall near the hearth, folding her legs beneath her as she sat on the wide ledge.

Though the sea was visible in the distance, the steep mountain was littered with that ugly black ash. It cloaked the air in thin clouds making it near impossible to see anything but the entrances to the mines. Even from within the fortress, obsidian glistened in the sunlight through the clouds, the volcanic stench enough to make her gag. The clank of swinging pickaxes echoed from the caverns beneath the dead volcano where the slaves exhausted their energy mining the black stone.

Guards stood vigil outside. Some were Dax's pirates, but most of his men had been replaced by the Shadow Beasts, expressions stone while screams resonated in the air around them. She flinched, imagining the snapping leather whip's sting against her skin.

Mercifully, she'd learned at a young age to keep her magic in check and not provoke the foreman. One extreme incident had been excused by her youth, her punishment the iron shackles to prevent it from happening again. Her fingers trailed over them now.

A second incident found her bound, naked and freezing, to the turrets of the fortress. For a moment, her mind involuntarily flickered to the memory. To the way Dax had almost begged Toren not to kill her for the insolence. There had not been a third incident.

Others weren't so lucky.

She thought of Elyon, wondering how he was managing without her to keep an eye on him. As if sensing her thoughts, the young Dwarf stumbled from one of the lower cavern entrances.

He fell to his knees, blood dripping down his back. The pain on his face was visible even from so far away. His shredded rags exposed ruined skin along his spine. The foreman, whip raised, loomed over him like a menacing shadow.

Evalyn's nails cut into her palms as she returned to the table. Naomi gasped and hurried to the bathing room, fetching some damp cloth to wrap her hand.

The lessons continued until a second servant entered with the noon meal. Evalyn wasn't hungry. But she forced herself to eat, to focus, refusing to allow the image of Elyon, shaking and bloody on the ground to disrupt her concentration.

She would find a way through this, to help him and find the male in her dreams. Useless worrying would get her nowhere.

"That was correct." Evalyn blinked at Naomi, staring down at the Sauda-cursed word—*comfortable*—and released a shuddered sigh.

More progress. Slow and steady, but progress, nonetheless. She must be patient to succeed.

So, she gave the girl a sweet smile. "Looks like I'm getting it after all."

"You're just stubborn. You're learning faster than you give yourself credit for." She tapped the next page with a finger. "Shall we?"

They continued, sounding out words she struggled with. Before long she read several pages aloud entirely by herself.

But still she craved more.

She wanted to read books, every book she could get her hands on. Even as a child she adored the late nights her mother spent reading to her.

Make yourself useful. You can't be expendable to him if you want to survive.

They worked till the sun dipped below the horizon, Naomi's other duties beckoning her elsewhere. Evalyn returned to the window, watching the slaves march back into the fortress. Exhausted, they struggled to put one foot in front of the other, menacing whips waiting.

Elyon wasn't with them.

She shook her head. His life meant nothing to her. She was leaving without him as soon as she was strong enough to escape.

Even so, her well of slumbering magic surged. Pain twanged around her ankles at the anger she couldn't deny. She wished she could snap the iron prison away. The thought sent a spark of agony along her skin.

She was so tired of fighting the shackles. Tired of seeing her fellow slaves never return from this fortress. Maybe she would never return, slinking into the encompassing darkness and vanishing like the others before her.

No.

She would get revenge.

Redemption for those who had given their lives for her, a nobody, an orphan with no claims.

They'd helped her, even if it forfeited their own lives.

The old, dark-skinned woman who dried her foolish tears and

helped her find strength the first year of her imprisonment.

The leathery-skinned man who gave her his food rations when she was sick, and died a week later from his own starvation and sickness.

The young, innocent Dwarf boy.

The countless others who had died or vanished. Their rare smiles, the kindness they showed despite their inevitable end. She would not let their deaths be in vain, would not let their sacrifices go unnoticed.

Kindness or not, Dax was to blame. He had to be. She couldn't forget that.

Dax, the foreman, the guards, the mouthless horrors. The list of monsters was endless.

Evalyn would survive.

She'd survive and unleash her magic to burn them all. She would not let the darkness consume her. The words echoed through her mind like a beacon of light.

I will not let the darkness consume me.

Over and over Evalyn repeated the words and the list of names. She opened one of the leather tomes, sounding out the words and gritting her teeth when she struggled.

By the time Dax entered the room, muttering about the incompetent failure of a boy, her teeth ached.

thirty-eight

You know he'll see you eventually. You can't hide forever.

Azuri folded his arms over his chest and stuck his tongue out at Shae when she spoke.

They'd watched the practice yards every afternoon for the past four days from Joseline's window. Azuri's eyes never left Quinn.

He had extraordinary skill, Fallon's dedication to his training exceptional. Each day, someone challenged him to one contest or another. Each day, he bested them flawlessly.

His aim with those daggers, well...Shae snorted, her tail swishing behind her. She pitied any unlucky idiot be on the lethal receiving end in a real fight.

Her eyes flickered up to Azuri, perched between her ears. Despite her efforts to make conversation, her Faerie companion remained silent. *You can't ignore me forever either,* she grumbled.

Azuri huffed out a breath, flicking Shea on the back of the head. Her ears twitched in response. "Stop telling me what to do."

So, he does speak.

The Faerie narrowed his eyes. "Yes, I speak. Birdbrain."

You're the one being a birdbrain, Shae growled. *Just talk to him.*

Outside, Quinn swigged from a water jug. Azuri's folded arms fell onto Shea's head, and he sighed. "I can't."

You can, you're being stubborn.

"No, I can't. He...he can't see me."

Why not?

Another sigh. His iridescent wings shimmered in the sunshine. "He doesn't know his own strength yet, let alone his heritage. So, until he does, until he learns the truth, I'll remain invisible to him. That's how it must be. That's how it's always been between Faeries and humans."

He isn't human.

"No, but he thinks he is. And right now...that's basically the same thing."

But why—

"It's not like I don't want to see him," Azuri grumbled. "It doesn't matter anyway."

With one last look at Quinn, Azuri flew out the window and toward the woods, not bothering to wait for Shea's reply.

thirty-nine

He was so cold.

The blackness coated his body in an impenetrable cloud of shadow.

He couldn't move, couldn't see.

His back screamed in agony. The whips, the crack of leather ripping through his flesh, tormented his mind.

Then, utter darkness.

Voices swirled, seeping into his skin from the shackles binding him.

Laughing. Mocking.

I promised myself I'd be brave. I wouldn't let the fear control me.

But he was not brave.

He'd been foolish, and he'd failed.

The whispers hissed along his skin, tingling like venomous snakes ready to strike. He longed to block out the horrid noise, but it filled every crevice of the dark, slithering into the blackest corners of his mind.

He couldn't fight it. The pain would kill him, swallow him whole. He opened his mouth to scream, but no sound emerged. His lips cracked and bled.

Don't let them see they get to you.

He bit down on the shriek as darkness continued to consume him.

forty

Snarling accusations echoed from the stairway outside Dax's chambers. Evalyn wasn't sure what to do other than sit in silence.

It was the third time the foreman and Shadow Beasts had joined them that week. Dax claimed it was to make sure he stayed in line and discuss plans. Regardless, Evalyn hated it.

Her arm ached where Dax's fingers gripped it for talking back, and her cheek still stung from a slap. Dax never physically hurt her unless one of them was around. The need to show control was absurd, and she told him as much, but it didn't make the growing bruise throb any less. It didn't help that the spy Dax spoke of had failed again. It set him, the foreman, and the Shadow Beasts all on edge.

Dax had begun opening up to her since she'd left the mines, small details about his past, his childhood, but for the most part he still concealed his emotions fairly well. He watched her only when he thought she wouldn't notice the gleam of pride in his eyes.

But she noticed everything, even the scrolls sprawled on the table, laden with ancient Dorwynnian runes and images of four horrifyingly beautiful figures. Dark hair fell past their shoulders, white teeth flashing behind black lips. The two in the center appeared younger, teardrop scars etched into pale skin below their eyes, the flesh beneath shimmering molten gold.

She fought to hide her shiver, focusing on the large book before her. After only one day, she sounded out some simple words, and wrote each letter twice. Today, she read five pages aloud without any trouble and wrote her name.

The door creaked open and Dax stumbled inside, his elegant coat crumpled and hanging off his shoulder slightly. Glaring at the door, he slammed it shut, then clenched his fists. Blood dripped down his jaw where she assumed one of the Shadow Commanders split his lip.

"Dax, is everything alright?" Her throat bobbed slightly as she watched him, a miriad of emotions flickering across his face.

"Shut up, I don't need your pity," he snarled.

Evalyn blinked in surprise at the hatred in his voice.

"No, of course not," she muttered, tucking a strand of hair behind her ear. "I...I'm sorry."

His expression softened almost instantly as he turned to face her. "Evalyn..." the emotions faded until only the pain remained. "I didn't mean—"

"Don't bother." She held up a hand. "I don't need excuses or apologies. You don't owe me any kindness anyway, I know that." She shoved up from the table, wrapping her arms around her waist. "I shouldn't have expected any."

He crossed the room in seconds, gripping her shoulders. "Little dove, I'm sorry. That anger wasn't directed at you."

"No?" She snorted. "Shocking."

"I—" he stopped. "I thought you knew by now that I don't hate you."

The softness in his voice caught her attention. She raised an eyebrow, her gaze drawn to his lip and the blood still running through his beard. Biting her lip, she picked up a napkin from the table and dipped the tip into a half-filled water glass before reaching toward him. Her chest fluttered, anticipating his hesitation, but he didn't pull away, only winced slightly when she touched his lip.

Gently, she wiped the blood away, focusing on his lip rather than meeting his eyes. "What do you hate so much then?" she whispered.

Dax stiffened, moving toward the window and opening it with a swift push. "Them," he murmured. "I can't stand them."

"That's an understatement," she grumbled, following him. They said nothing else as the sunset unfolded before them.

The setting sun illuminated the mountains in beautiful shades of burnt orange and fiery red. Light glistened, more visible in some spots than others. The sky was stunning and soothing, vibrant peach and ruby hues swirling and twining together among the clouds.

Then, she heard it. Her head tilted, a soft gasp escaping her lips.

"Beautiful, isn't it?"

She nodded, her eyes finding the shimmering water between massive mountain peaks. The waves crashed into crumbling foothills, misting over dead volcanoes as if they could somehow cool the ancient flames that no longer existed. The water was calm, aquamarine depths radiating from the distance. "I always assumed it was further away."

Dax's chuckle was soft as he placed a hand on the small of her back. "Narcio isn't that large, the mountains just close in around the fortress, but the ocean's been there all along." He paused. "I miss it, being out at sea."

The sadness in his eyes unsettled her. "How long has it been?"

Another soft chuckle. He pulled his hand away from her, but she reached for it, willing him to face her. There was no sadness in his eyes as he said, "Since I found you, Evalyn."

She wasn't sure how to respond.

The hatred ever-boiling within her simmered lower. "What?"

"I haven't been out at sea in eighteen years. It kills me a little more each day."

"Why?" she whispered.

He ran a hand over his beard, closing his eyes. She waited for him to speak, her Fae hearing all too aware of the waves crashing against the mountains. "It was their way of punishing me." His hand, still holding hers, tightened. "Their way of letting me know I have no power over them." He scoffed. "I hate it, seeing good people, *innocent people* suffer and die around me. I've always tried to defy them, to keep as many slaves as I could from real harm, but I defied direct orders when I brought you here rather than letting you die."

Evalyn bit her lip, unsure how to feel about the pain in his voice. Something flickered in her chest, doubting the wall she'd built more than ever.

"Twenty-five years ago." Dax's eyes remained closed, but he stroked her palm with his thumb. She didn't dare move. "Twenty-five years ago, those demons barged onto this island and started mining obsidian for their banished king."

She waited.

"They destroyed everything with their cursed shadows, blocking out the sun. It was suffocating. They brought boatloads of slaves from the southern continent they conquered, most magic-wielders, and began mining. Then, just for sport, they destroyed the inhabited parts of the island and took its people into slavery as well."

At last, she dared to speak. "Did they ever...I mean, were you ever a—"

"No," Dax interrupted. Laughing, he added, "They needed my support to command the island and the seas. I was a young, established pirate captain. The sea and every pirate armada on the continent were mine to command. They needed me, needed my men and my ships to regulate their work here, keep tabs on the slaves, and do their dirty work. Without my help, they never could have gained control of the island and its trading routes on the northern continent. But once they got it, I became nothing more than a pawn."

The doubt flickered again. "*Were* an established pirate captain?" He was silent. "Did you ever try to stop them?"

Maybe she'd been wrong.

Dax released her hand and straightened, walking back to the scrolls littering the table. "Once. Many of my men died in the process." The pain vanished from his voice. "They got exactly what they wanted. I no longer have a say in their actions. Sometimes, I doubt I ever did. It doesn't matter anymore. They can bring all the slaves they want if it means they'll mine their obsidian, leave my people alone, and get off my island."

Evalyn gritted her teeth, nails digging into her palm again. She hadn't been wrong at all.

With a curt nod, she took a step toward the bedroom. How could she think he might be unselfish? Kindness or not, he was a horrid, greedy man who didn't care for anyone but himself.

"My biggest regret, after all these years, is that I couldn't think of a better excuse to keep them from enslaving you."

Evalyn's hand froze on the bedroom door.

She turned back to him. Pain flashed in dark indigo eyes. She opened her mouth and closed it, unable to hide her shock.

Dax smiled. Genuinely smiled, then turned away from her.

He really had wanted to save her. To stay with her, not abandon her. And he had, in the only way he knew how without risking her life.

Evalyn covered her mouth with a shaking hand. Her knees buckled as she tried to remain upright, a hand braced against the doorframe.

"Evalyn."

She couldn't look at him.

"Evalyn." His arm slid around her waist and she closed her eyes. If she looked at him, she would be unable to maintain the facade.

She wouldn't cry. Not in front of him.

Those cool, callused fingers gripped her chin gently. "Evalyn, you're trembling."

"I...I'm not." It was hard to keep her voice strong.

"Look at me."

She couldn't.

"Look at me." His voice was stronger that time.

Slowly, she willed her eyes to open. They burned with held back tears, but she didn't flinch, didn't blink. Dax took one look at her and swore.

"What?" Her voice cracked.

He shook his head, sweeping her into his arms. "That's the look." He set her on the bed, sitting beside her. "The look of a starving, drowning six-year-old who refused my help. The look that still haunts me because I couldn't do anything to save the innocent child it belonged to."

Evalyn sniffed, a tear sliding down her cheek. "I don't like it when you talk about your past." Another tear fell. He brushed it away. "It reminds me that I'm not as strong as you think I am."

Dax smiled. "You're right. You're stronger than you think you are."

Evalyn blushed. "You're a fool, Dax."

They readied for bed, Dax turning away from her as he spoke. "I may be a fool, but I'm tired of pretending to be someone I'm not." Slipping between the sheets, Evalyn fell back against the pillows, Dax propping up on an elbow. "Every time I look at you, it's harder to keep up the lie."

"What lie is that?"

He brushed a hand over her silvery hair, stroking the soft skin of her cheek. "Of pretending I'm cruel, that I mean you or anyone enslaved here harm. That's the last thing I want. It's what *they* want."

She wasn't sure what to feel without the sense of revenge or hate. "Then what do *you* want?"

"To protect those incapable of protecting themselves." He leaned over to the bedside table, blowing out a candle. "But I can't do that without pretending to the outside world, to the shadow creatures. I need them to believe I'm a cold-hearted pirate captain they can trust. But I can't pretend with you. Not anymore."

Dax draped an arm over her, his touch warm and, for the first time, comforting. "Good," she murmured. "I've never been one for lies. The truth is always more important."

Dax laughed again, the sound somehow soothing. "I'm glad there's someone else in this world that thinks so."

forty-one

"That dopey grin is freaking me out."

Quinn frowned at her. "You really don't think I smile that often?"

"It's just a fact." Joseline wiped at the sweat dripping down her forehead. The summer air was humid, the Malous heat alone vicious, and they'd run twice their usual distance.

He chuckled. "You didn't vomit up your stomach today. I was admiring you for it."

He was right.

For the first time since they'd started the morning jogs, Joseline hadn't been sick afterward.

"Are you starting to see the difference?"

Maya's voice cut off her response as she came up behind them, looping her arm through Joseline's. "Of course she is, she can hold her own against you in a fist fight. That's enough to be proud of."

Joseline blushed, her stomach grumbling in approval as they headed for the tavern. "For no more than a minute, if I'm lucky. He let me win once, it hasn't happened again." Maya burst into laughter.

The tavern was empty, as it always was this time of day. Shea greeted them, twirling her tail around Joseline's ankles. Fallon and Gavin sat at the bar sipping on mugs of ale.

"How was training?" Fallon asked, his back still turned.

He had a way of knowing when Quinn was near. The internal connection was strange, even after seeing it so often.

"We ran two laps today," Quinn said.

"Your stamina is increasing I see."

The young bar maid approached them. Her long chestnut hair, swept back from her forehead, tumbled freely over one shoulder, her matching eyes trailing over Quinn's body and the sweaty grey tunic clinging to it.

Joseline, all too aware of the sultry look she gave Quinn, tried to ignore the twang of annoyance.

Maya however, bristled.

The young woman batted long lashes, pressing her busty chest against the counter. "Same as always?"

Quinn gave her that dark smile. "You know us so well." She walked away, brushing thin fingers against his. "Thanks, darling," he called after her as she vanished into the kitchen.

"A week of healing has you back to your usual self I see," Fallon said. "Jenson will be so disappointed."

"Jenson will what?" their russet-skinned comrade asked, pushing through the doors.

Quinn laughed as Jenson crossed lean arms against the counter. "Nothing. I was just being polite."

"Oh, is that what you call it?"

Joseline cringed at Maya's tone, the jealousy rolling off her in waves. Her shoulder brushed against Quinn as she inched away.

Jenson, sensing her unease, leaned against the bar between them and engaged Maya in conversation. Joseline sighed in relief.

"Everything alright?" Quinn's breath tickled her ear.

Not trusting her voice, Joseline nodded. Her eyes met his, then shifted toward Maya. She flashed a weak smile.

Quinn growled softly. "I've got to do something about that."

Before she could reply, the bar maid returned, balancing several mugs of ale and a water jug on a wooden tray. Joseline reached for the jug, taking a grateful swig.

"You seem to gather quite the audience, does that always

happen?"

Joseline's eyes followed the woman's raised finger.

The tavern had gained at least a dozen new occupants since they entered, most of them giggling and blushing when Quinn turned. He flashed a smile, running a hand through damp, tangled hair, before pulling it back into a half-bun.

Joseline laughed. "What do you expect when you act like that?"

He glanced sidelong at her, fiddling with his pendant. "Like what?"

The giggling continued as the smell of warm oats and honey filled her nose. Joseline's stomach growled again, overpowering the twang of jealousy. She shoveled a spoonful of sweetness into her mouth before reaching for the small pitcher of milk.

"Like that, like...I don't know how to explain it." She wiped a hand across her mouth, milk dripping down her chin.

"So lady-like." She gave Quinn a shove.

"It could be worse," Jenson said. "It used to be we couldn't make it halfway down the street without being stopped by at least one girl he'd flirted with or bedded. Quite the gentleman, Quinn."

"Oh yes, so gentlemanly." Sarcasm drenched Maya's voice. "If I were you, which I never would be, I'd be ashamed for my inability to keep it in my pants."

Without waiting for a reply, she shoved away from the bar, the stool clattering to the ground in her wake, and stomped outside.

The room went silent.

"Is she really always like that about you and girls?" Joseline breathed.

Quinn drank from his bowl. "Usually." He didn't look at her.

"She doesn't seem to have a problem with me...I haven't seen her get so..."

"Quinn, you know why she is," Jenson interrupted, his reply almost inaudible.

Quinn's eyes flashed to his friend. "Kyaos be damned, I don't care why she is."

"Yes, you do."

Quinn sighed, his head falling into the crook of his elbow. "I get it, I do. But it's infuriating, and she knows it. She acts like it's my fault she had a crappy childhood because I don't reciprocate her feelings. I care about her, she knows I do, knows I would die for her, yet I'm still horrible for not feeling the same way she does. Tell me how that's fair to either of us, Jenson."

"Quinn," Fallon said, "you can't blame her."

"I don't, but it still doesn't give her a right to act like that."

"Maybe not. But despite what you know, you do nothing to prove her wrong when she gets like that."

"I shouldn't have to prove her wrong," Quinn grumbled, swigging from the mug of ale.

Joseline found herself standing. "I'll go talk to her."

All three men stared.

"That's not a good idea," Quinn growled.

"Perhaps not, but I'm still going to." Quinn reached for her as she walked away, but she shook her arm free. "Quinn, it's alright."

She followed Maya out, Shea on her heels.

It took some asking around, but at last she found Maya in the catacombs beneath the temple. She clutched her knees in the middle of the floor, staring up at the Goddess statue. She wiped a hand along her nose, the sniff echoing off stone walls.

Shea bounded down the stairs and Maya turned. "What do you want?"

Joseline released a breath. "I just wanted to talk to you." She sat near the bottom step, leaning against the stone. Images of that headless corpse and Quinn's too pale face flashed in her mind, but she shoved them away.

Another sniff. "What could you possibly want to talk to me about?"

"Why do you get so upset when Quinn...I mean..." She fumbled for the words.

Maya's laugh was sarcastic. "I am not having this conversation with you."

"I just want to know."

The younger girl glared at her. "Why, because you want to know if it's safe for you to be flirty with him too? I don't care what you do."

Joseline ignored the light blush that heated her cheeks. "Maya, if it didn't bother you, you wouldn't be down here crying."

"I'm not—" A tear fell down her cheek even as she tried to deny it. She swore. "What does it matter to you anyway?"

Joseline chose her words with care. "You're right. It doesn't matter to me. But it matters to you, and that makes me want to understand."

Maya stared at her, red eyed and quivering, but didn't glare this time. Sadness coated her expression. For a long time, Shea's tail swishing against stone was the only sound.

At last Maya spoke, tucking a short strand of blonde behind her ear. "You don't get it." She wiped at her nose again. "You have everything. You've always had everything. You don't get what it's like to have nothing, truly have nothing, and then have nothing stolen from you."

Joseline waited for her to continue. "When I was a girl, I wanted nothing more than a family. A real family, a father." Maya crossed her legs, fiddling with the laces of her boots. "But I never got to meet my father. My mother used to say he was some ass who lodged at her inn for the night, seduced her, and left the next day. He didn't know I existed. I wanted to believe her."

"But you didn't?"

Sensitivity flashed in her eyes. "I refused to believe he would just leave us. I refused to believe he would let my mother treat me the way she did, that he could be worse than the jerks my mother brought around who would..." Maya's bottom lip quivered.

Joseline wanted to comfort her but couldn't bring herself to move. Shea approached instead. She yipped, her tail swishing over Maya's legs.

"You've never had that pain before, that fear." Her voice cracked, and she covered her mouth with her hands, her body shaking. Now the tears ran freely, falling off her chin.

This time, the strength from the Goddess statue slid into

Joseline's body with ease, willing her to stand. Maya was trembling as Joseline knelt, wrapping an arm around her shoulders. The younger girl all but fell into Joseline's arms.

"It's not fair," Maya choked. She gripped Joseline's vest, gasping for breath as the tears continued to fall. "Why did he leave us, why did he force me to face them alone?"

Joseline stoked her hair. "I don't know," she whispered. "I wish I could say something to reassure you, but I don't know."

"My childhood was a nightmare I could never run away from. If I tried, the men would find me and bring me back home and punish me for leaving." Maya sniffed again, straightening a bit. "When Fallon asked me to go with him, my mother was furious."

Keep her talking, Shea said. *She's calming down.*

"What did he say?" Joseline prompted.

"He told me I had a warrior's spirit. Told me he could help me become strong, if I helped him in return. My mother almost convinced me to decline his offer."

"What changed your—"

"Quinn." Maya took a long, shuddered breath, rubbing her eyes, and sat back against the statue. "Quinn saved my life the night before, and when he walked into the room standing beside Fallon, despite all the abuse I'd gone through, I knew in that moment I would follow him to the ends of the earth."

"So, you left everything to go with them?"

Maya stared at her. "Everything? I had nothing to leave." She pulled at the short blonde strands framing her face, tying them back with a scrap of cloth. "Quinn, Jenson, and Fallon were everything I wanted in a family. The way they interacted with one another, with me. They welcomed me with open arms, made me feel like I belonged somewhere."

Joseline smiled. "They bring out the best in each other, don't they?"

Maya nodded. "I was only eight. Quinn was older, stronger, handsome. He was incredible, *is* incredible. Jenson is kind, but Quinn makes me feel like I could be anything, do anything if I believed in myself. After two years, Fallon sent me to train at the Assassins Guild in the southern desert. I trained for five years to become strong enough and confident enough to tell Quinn how I felt. But when I returned, a fierce warrior and a self-assured young woman, he'd already bedded every available woman in the capital."

"But that doesn't change how you feel about him."

"He rejects me without even knowing it, without thinking about the types of memories his actions might bring back. Being ignored. Being unappreciated. It hurts. Gods above, he doesn't even realize how badly it hurts." Shea licked Maya's arm, an attempt to sooth her.

"He...he isn't a bad man, you know." That Goddess strength pulsed within her as she said it, as if she was admitting it to herself as well as Maya. "Can you hate him for feeling differently than you do?"

Maya's head fell into her lap. "All I want is to be loved, cherished, but instead I get that longing tossed in my face. My father, my mother, Quinn, even the village boys I used to play with, I've always been rejected when I need someone most. Is that all I deserve?"

Despite the pain in her muffled voice, Maya squeezed Joseline's hand. It was all the thanks she needed.

"Of course not." Maya sat up at that, their hands still clasped. "I may not have the same past as you, but I know a good amount about rejection. I was never the heir my mother wanted, not really. I know she favors my sister, though she'll never tell me. No matter how much I succeed, it isn't enough for her. I'll never compare to the perfection that Julia is in my mother's eyes."

She'd never admitted that to herself. It felt nice to say.

Maya sniffed. "Really?"

Joseline gave her a thin smile. "She always hovered over my lessons. We argue and butt heads. When Julia was born, my mother just took to her so much easier, even as a baby. She was my mother's sweet angel child. After Julia was born, our relationship drifted as far apart as it could. I have too much of my father in me, too much defiance. My mother doesn't think it's becoming of a lady, much less a future queen."

"I don't think you have enough sass. Especially not toward

Quinn." They laughed, the genuine sound echoing through the room.

"I'll have to keep that in mind." It was silent for a moment. "For the record, I cherish you, Maya." The younger girl blinked at her. "I've never had a true friend before. I had a few girls I could talk to, and we were close, but even they could never truly be my friends, not when their responsibilities called them elsewhere. You were the first person to ever make me feel like I could be myself. I won't forget that."

Maya stood, holding out a hand.

Joseline took it.

"You know, I've never had a friend before either. Not a female one anyway." She gave Joseline's hand a squeeze. "It'll be a change I could get used to, I think."

Joseline didn't object as Maya pulled her up the stairs, twining their fingers. Shea trotted after them in her usual silence.

Once outside, Joseline's chest fluttered and she glanced back, finding Quinn where he stood in the shadowed alcove near the door. He gave a brief nod, smiled, and vanished into the woods.

Joseline quickened her pace so she wouldn't stumble as Maya pulled her toward the tavern, their hands still clasped tightly.

forty-two

Julia trusted Niven when he said she was safe here. But that didn't ease the fear racing beneath her flesh at the shadows she knew followed her.

They lingered within her subconscious every time she so much as closed her eyes, the inky tendrils reaching for her through the security of the castle walls. They watched her, waiting like they would steal her away if they touched her. She found herself avoiding the windows. Even in the rays of summer sun she saw them, the shadows dancing within the corners of her vision.

But here in the library, no windows could pull her attention toward the eerie darkness only she could see, could show her the ruins of the capital city still breaking around her. She could escape wherever she wanted, opening the pages of the ancient tomes; at least for the hour of free time she had a day from her lessons with Master Eldridge and Master Kasia.

The stories of myth and magic were her favorite. Mystical faeries, the white Aonani foxes of the Goddess, witch queens with lilac eyes, and pirates covered in jewels from head to toe. A different time. A time where magic ruled Navarre within every country more than the simplicity of mortal healers.

Something crashed deep within the library, sending Julia

tumbling to the ground as she jumped. The book she'd been holding toppled from the table. Her eyes darted toward the darkened bookshelves, fighting to stop her racing pulse. The candle enclosed within the glass orb beside her shuttered, the flames flickering.

But the library was silent.

Julia clutched the jet pendant. She was safe here, protected. Shaking her head, she stood, brushing off her skirts. *Come on, Julia. You're being ridiculous.* She cleared her throat, running a hand over the leather binding of the book.

A gust of wind hissed from the shelves behind her. Julia whirled, her grip tightening on the pendant. "Hello?" Her back pushed against the long wooden table. "Hello, is someone there?"

Again, silence.

Julia gulped, reaching behind her for the book and the light, and began walking toward the door Niven had left cracked open. It took all her will not to look behind her, not to search the dark shelves for the eyes she felt along her skin.

Niven stood outside the doors, a hand on his sword hilt. She nearly collided with him. "Your Highness, are you alright?" His deep voice was filled with concern.

She nodded, forcing her pulse to calm.

Niven frowned, his chocolatey eyes shifting toward the dark library. The grip on the eagle pommel tightened. "Are you sure?"

"Yes, I...I'm sure." she replied weakly.

He raised an eyebrow. "You would tell me if you weren't, right? You know you can tell me."

She tried a smile. "I know." She glanced back into the darkness, unable to shake the feeling of unseeing eyes watching her. She gripped Niven's fingers. "Let's go. Master Kasia will be angry if I'm late for my next lesson."

Niven laughed, letting her pull him down the hall. "I don't think anyone could be angry with you, little one."

Julia giggled, blocking the dark tendrils from her mind as best she could. *I'm safe.* She glanced up at Niven, his jade cloak billowing behind him. *Nothing can harm me.*

The tendrils reached toward her, hissing and mocking as she walked further from their grasp. Their presence sent a shiver down her spine.

forty-three

The midday sun shimmered like molten gold through the trees and onto the forest floor.

Quinn was still adjusting to the constant clear air. The cramped, bustling city would always be home, but there was something soothing, something surreal about the forest that made him feel at ease. It was vastly different from the film of smoke that clung to city air.

A meditative calm enveloped his body. They'd been in Rivedas a month and still he couldn't stop thinking about what Gavin mentioned that first night, what the shadow being had taunted in the catacombs.

The Elirona children, the Fae royals, were butchered a century ago. What Gavin said was impossible. But if he were Fae it would explain so many questions...

No. He couldn't be.

Fallon would have told him. Besides, he had other things to worry about.

After the battle, after the injured were seen to by Nora and the other healers and he permitted the elder to tend to him, Jenson had entered his rooms, a rare frown coating his expression.

The shadow creatures, he'd said, vanished into thin air. Not even a footprint or trace of their black blood remained. They'd disappeared not long after Quinn ran off to find Joseline. Kellen was gone as well, and they hadn't been seen again in the month since.

It worried him. Grunting, Quinn shifted in the grass, tucking his arm behind his head. He tossed a pebble into the air, catching it smoothly between his thumb and pointer finger.

There was so much they didn't know. If Aeron was growing an army somehow, they needed to work faster. Raenya was still half a continent away, and despite her progress, Joseline was nowhere near ready to defeat the demon king.

"I was wondering where you'd gone." Quinn bolted upright at the sound of Fallon's voice. "Always so paranoid." Quinn flashed him an exasperated look, and the older man chuckled. "What's bothering you, boy?"

Curse his mentor for knowing him so well. "Nothing," he lied.

"If you think I'm going to believe that, you really are the idiot the princess claims."

Quinn couldn't hide the smile. "She's a handful, isn't she?"

Fallon barely made a sound as he moved. "You only disappear on your own when something's bothering you."

Quinn lay back in the grass again, the breeze dancing over his skin.

The forest was alive. Birds chirped from the trees and squirrels scuffled amongst the underbrush lining the clearing. Even the soft rush of water was audible from the stream several feet away. With each breath, his fears ebbed from his body, slithering in the wind. It gave him the strength to dare asking that first question he couldn't ignore.

"You've always been a father to me. I owe you my life a million times over. You taught me everything I know."

Fallon bowed his head. "The honor was mine, and I would do it again. But that still doesn't answer my question."

Quinn watched his mentor. The long silvery hair that danced in the wind beside him, the elegant grace in which he sat despite his age, the beautiful, unwrinkled skin, aside from the scar accenting his chin, and the wise, ever-knowing silver gaze.

"Will you answer me honestly?" Another graceful bow of his head. "Am I Fae." Not a question, but a realization he wasn't prepared to admit. Quinn had been pondering how to word it all day.

For the first time in his life, he saw Fallon sigh in acceptance. Part of him wanted Fallon to deny it, but he'd already concluded the truth.

"Yes."

A shuddered breath slid through Quinn's lips and he gnawed on the bottom one anxiously. "Demi-Fae, or..." he couldn't form the words, his throat bobbing.

Fallon closed his eyes. "You're pure Fae."

Quinn pulled his knees up into his chest, clinging to them as if they could keep him from shaking. He wasn't sure what to feel, wasn't sure how to handle the truth now that he knew. He was Fae. Fae warriors were legendary, mythical immortals the human world didn't think existed. Yet here he was.

Pain flashed in his eyes as he turned to his mentor. "Why didn't you tell me?"

"I wanted to." Fallon opened his eyes. "Gods above, I wanted to every single day."

Quinn didn't wipe at the tear as it fell from his chin, gritting his teeth. "But you never did." Fallon shook his head. "Why not?"

"To protect you. I thought if I kept it from you, if I concealed what I could of your true power, you would be safer." He pointed to the pendant. "It's enchanted to conceal your true form. It's also enchanted so you won't think about it."

"So I would never take it off, you mean."

Fallon nodded. "Do you want to?"

"No." Quinn shook his head. "No, I don't. I need time to..." he wiped a hand over his face.

His body radiated with the internal fire, a newfound discovery. He wanted to be angry at Fallon, but relief and acceptance flooded through him. They coursed through his blood, whispering promises. He breathed deeply, opening his mind and soul to the power now fully awakened within him.

But he wasn't afraid.

It was different than losing control and meeting the burnout. The flames soothed him, acknowledged his superiority.

"Quinn."

He blinked at Fallon, letting go of the pendant he didn't remember gripping in his palm. His skin glowed with blue green-light; turquoise wildfire shimmered around him, dancing along his flesh, and vanished.

"I'm sorry I didn't tell you the truth sooner," Fallon whispered. "I didn't want to lie to you."

Quinn only smiled, pushing the other thought from his mind. He would think about the royalty notion later. That was the dangerous concept, the one he couldn't accept the possibility of. For now, knowing this was enough.

As if satisfied with his response, Fallon ran a hand through his hair. "I must teach you more. I taught you everything I know of control, but it's essential you learn to utilize your skills more than the basics."

"Is that something you're capable of teaching me?" Quinn gripped his arms, still in awe of the sheer magic force.

Fallon gave a half-laugh and Quinn shot him an inquisitive look. "Jenson will be relieved I've told you at last."

Quinn furrowed his brows. "He knows?"

"He's one of the only Demi-Fae who avoided capture on the southern continent, of course he knows. He knew the moment he laid eyes on you."

But he never said a thing, not once. Even when I asked him what to do about Fallon, he said nothing.

"Jenson is a good man, Quinn, a good friend. A loyal friend. You couldn't ask for a better *sielapora*. So is Maya. Loyalty like theirs can be hard to come by."

"I know that," he said, smiling. "I'm glad Jenson doesn't have to keep your secrets anymore, old man."

Fallon shoved him, sending him toppling face-first into the grass.

"You have no idea how old I am, *boy*."

"How old, two hundred?"

He'd meant it as a joke, but Fallon's grin was merciless. "Not even close."

As a child, Quinn barely measured up to Fallon's hips. Now, they stood eye to eye, their stares both carefree and challenging. "Well then, *grandpa,* why don't you give me a taste of that ancient superiority of yours? I think some training will do me good right now."

A force like a strong gust of wind billowed into his chest. Quinn twisted in the air, landing on his back several feet away, Fallon looming over him. "Boy, you've got a lot to learn before you go around demanding things like that." He held out a hand, helping Quinn to his feet. "I've had centuries to hone my magic. You are at my mercy."

Quinn didn't say another word, only listened as Fallon taught, guiding him through several exercises on controlling the power dancing through his veins. The clearing filled with his calm voice, the light shimmering with Quinn's turquoise flames and Fallon's own silver wind. They were one—their magic syncing as Quinn's control grew to meet his mentor's.

They were still training when the moon rose to kiss the stars.

forty-four

He wasn't sure how long it had been.

Hours, days, years. It was all the same to the darkness.

He was blind, immobile.

He tried again to scream, his throat raw from the useless effort. Pain engulfed him, mixing with the shadows. Blood coated his tongue, the taste metallic. Had he been hurt again? He wasn't sure.

His back was numb. The ruined flesh no longer ached when he moved.

Not that it mattered anyway.

A door creaked open. He twisted his head as if that would help him see, and his body shrieked in protest.

No light flowed in the dark, only the stench of something foul.

"This is the right place?" someone hissed. "There's another prisoner in here."

"It is."

The faint sound of chains rattled beside him, but the blackness was so thick nothing was certain.

"The Master will be pleased."

A wicked, hissing laugh. "Pleased? This one has failed the Master one too many times. There's nothing pleasing about what awaits him."

The Master? Who was the Master? Did they mean Dax?

"Water…I need water…" He could barely make out the third voice. It was deep, rasped, and tired.

The chains rattled, and someone grunted. The sound of water splashed onto the floor, echoing through the darkness, followed by a bout of vicious coughing and that hissing laugh again.

"You don't get to make demands around here, you lost that privilege."

A snicker. "He never deserved that privilege to begin with. He's nothing more than a broken toy the Master has lost interest in."

More rattling chains. "We're just to leave him?"

"Those were the orders."

Footsteps echoed, then halted.

He held his breath as footsteps resumed, moving closer to him. Pressure gripped his chin, cutting off his air. He coughed, the bitter blood swelling in his mouth, the suffocating feeling touched with vague familiarity.

"Who do you suppose this one is? I haven't seen another of his race amongst the slaves."

Pain lanced through him as something sharp tore through his back, but he had no energy left to cry out.

"No idea. Probably an unlucky slave who stepped out of line. The Dwarfs were dealt with centuries ago." The pressure on his chin released, but the pain along his spine continued.

"Come on then, we don't want to upset the others by being late. I hear the pretty pirate lord has a temper as nasty as Aeron himself." The door swung open, then shut with a groan.

The other prisoner shifted, chains rattling. "Is there someone else in here?"

He tried to speak but his throat was so dry no sound emerged.

"Hello?" the other voice asked. "I heard that, are you there? It's so dark, I can't see anything."

He gritted his teeth, swallowing the salty blood coating his tongue. "Yes," he managed. "It's pointless to waste energy. Nobody is coming for us."

A whispered chuckle in reply. "I wasn't expecting anyone to come for me." A moment of silence before he added, "At least I know I'm not alone. I'm going to die, but I don't want to be alone when I do."

He took a breath, his spine shivering in protest. The darkness was consuming him again, drowning out the other voice. The eternal cold returned.

"What's your name?"

He gulped, the bile in his throat threatening to make him vomit, but he replied, "Elyon." He hadn't said it aloud in so long he was surprised he remembered it. "You?"

There was silence. For a moment, he thought the other man might have fainted, but the rasp came at last.

"Kellen," he said. "My name is Kellen."

The days continued to blur together and Elyon grew numb to the hunger and the blinding darkness. Kellen's presence was a minor comfort, but still, he longed to do something. Anything but sit and wait to die.

"Do you think we could...get out somehow?" Kellen asked, his words echoing Elyon's desires.

But the Dwarf boy only laughed, wincing in pain from the action. "I thought you didn't care about that," he replied. "I thought you knew you were dying here."

Kellen was silent for a moment before he whispered, "I don't." A pause. "I don't care about myself. But you...you're innocent. I failed to protect the innocent one too many times. If there's a chance I could save you, I would give my life to save yours."

A sniff echoed through the dark, but Elyon didn't comment on it. He rolled his shoulders slightly against the chains. "You don't know me. You don't owe me anything."

"It doesn't matter," Kellen whispered. "I'm a knight of Rathal. It was my duty to protect. I want a chance to make it right." More silence. "So," Kellen said, the tremor gone from his voice. "Do you think we have a chance?"

Elyon gulped. He'd never thought about escape. Never

considered it. With Evalyn gone, it had seemed pointless to think about. But now... "I don't know," he admitted. "But I suppose it wouldn't hurt to try."

forty-five

The sheets beside her were cold when she rose. She rolled over, clinging to the quilt where Dax's scent lingered. A crumbled piece of paper caught her eye, tucked under the tarnished brass candle holder.

Early meeting.

We have things to discuss later.

Don't be difficult.

Dax

So, it hadn't been a dream. She was worried it would be.

Crossing the cold floor, Evalyn tossed a few thin sticks and several bigger logs into the embers of the dying hearth, the note shriveling atop fresh wood as she began her exercises. With more space to alter the movements, her muscles savored each action, bare chest bobbing as she dipped to the ground.

She'd been wrong about him. The shock still consumed her.

She spent eighteen years building walls against the pirate captain who saved her from death only to shove her toward a worse fate. She used every waking moment to plan the revenge she would repay him with. The agony of her brother's disappearance and her mother's brutal death had been too much to bear. She'd needed someone to hate, something to justify any horrid thoughts running wild in her imagination.

Dax had been that someone for eighteen years.

But that was before the constant smiles, the kindness, the various conversations reawakening the doubts she tried to forget, doubts that made her a weak, whimpering child once more.

He saved her life. He brought her here, to this monstrous hellhole, and left her. She'd never forgiven him.

If he was telling the truth, there was nothing he could have done to get her out and watch over her. Here was his home, the one place he could try to keep her safe.

Dax wasn't in charge here, not in the way she once thought. The Shadow Beasts were, their decisions made without his knowledge. Yet he had authority over the foreman, whom he never allowed to harm her no matter the trouble she caused.

When her magic exploded, the foreman wanted to kill her, or dump her in the cellars for the shadow beings to *play* with. But it was Dax who suggested an equally horrible alternative, to tie her, naked, to the fortress turrets with no food or water, and Dax who chained her in the irons.

I can only try to keep you safe in so many ways.

He might have taken her into his bed sooner. But his reputation with women was well-known. Some women would vanish for a night, returning dreamy eyed and giggling whenever they caught sight of him. Others would disappear for weeks, returning with the same girlish actions.

But not her, never her.

My biggest regret, after all these years, is that I couldn't think of a better excuse to keep them from enslaving you.

That one sentence had broken her.

Everyone she cared about abandoned her or died before her eyes. Her brother, her mother, the father she had no recollection of. The kind woman, the sick old man, Elyon, even Dax.

But Dax regretted letting her go.

He hadn't wanted to let her go.

His regret meant more than he could ever know.

She didn't hear the door open. A startled gasp snagged her

attention, and she met Naomi's wide eyes. She gnawed on the inside of her cheek, wondering what caused the response, then blushed deeply and draped her thick hair over her exposed breasts, covering the rest of herself with her hands. "You're here early," she said.

Naomi's cheeks flushed beet red. "The captain, um...Captain Dax told me to bring you fresh clothing and help you bathe." She turned away, clinging to the gowns in her arms. "I'm so sorry, I meant no breach of your privacy in staring."

Evalyn raised an eyebrow at the flustered girl, tilted her head toward the ceiling, and laughed. Tears leaked down her face, and her stomach clenched. When Evalyn at last wiped her eyes, the girl was still red. "I'm sorry," she chortled. "Decency has never been a concern of mine."

She walked into the bathing room. Naomi hurried after her clumsily, struggling not to drop the gowns as she hung them over a dressing screen in the corner. "I see that." She started the bath, hot steam filling the room. "Do you do that every morning?"

Evalyn nodded, inspecting several vials lined along the side of the tub. Opening one, her nose wrinkled in disgust, and she replaced the cork. "For about six years now." She opened and sniffed another bottle, replacing that cork as well.

"Even in the cells?"

"Yes." Evalyn opened a third one, smiling at the pleasant fragrance. "What are these?"

Naomi laughed. "Dax doesn't like smelling of ash when he has important meetings." She turned the knob off on the tub. "Would you like me to add one to your bath?"

"I don't know the first thing about what smells nice," Evalyn said. "I hardly remember life outside this foul-smelling mountain."

"You seemed to like that one well enough." She took the bottle from Evalyn's fingers and poured a splash into the steaming water before Evalyn could protest. "There, too late now."

The scalding water burned and soothed her all at once. The fire pulsing through her veins hummed at the heat, welcoming it. "What smell is that anyway?"

"Citrus and sea salt," Naomi fiddled with her apron. "Dax's favorite."

"Of course it is," she mumbled, dunking her head underwater. She emerged moments later, gasping for breath as she pushed wet hair from her eyes.

Naomi was still staring at her. Evalyn raised an eyebrow.

Waking from the trance, the girl stood, slipping where water had splashed on the wide stone steps. She wiped it up, blustering apologies, and hurried out of the room, stuttering something about calling her when she was ready to dress.

Evalyn sank back into the tub, resting her head against the edge. She stared out the large bay window making up the wall to her right. The stone lip of the tub was level enough for Evalyn to rest her chin along the ledge, keeping her lower body submerged.

Deep indigo curtains pulled back from thick glass, the height of Dax's chambers so high even the mountain peaks were barely visible. The ocean view was clearest from this side of the fortress, the peaks less jagged, and the crashing waves visible along the shoreline made her smile. There was something soothing, peaceful about the sight.

By the time she picked up the cloth rag, the water was no longer steaming. She washed her body and hair, then toweled dry before calling Naomi back in.

She smiled meekly at Evalyn before sitting beside her on the wide steps and brushing her hair. She worked in silence until she was halfway done. "I always wished I had hair like yours. It's so long and thick, you could do anything you wanted with it."

Evalyn glanced over her shoulder at the girl. "You can style it if you want."

"May I?" Awe filled Naomi's voice.

Evalyn laughed. "I don't see why not." She held up a fistful of damp silver strands. "I wouldn't know the first thing to do with all this. It's hard enough to manage a braid."

Thin fingers ran along her scalp. "It just takes practice."

Evalyn snorted. "I never cared much. It was more a nuisance. I debated hacking it off with my pickaxe for years."

224

Naomi gasped as she reached into her deep apron pocket, producing a pouch of pins. "But it's so beautiful."

Evalyn only shrugged, glancing toward the gowns. "What's the occasion?"

"Dax is hosting dinner for the Shadow Commanders this evening. I don't know much, only whispers from other servants. They don't tell me anything. Apparently, Dax is furious he wasn't informed sooner. He's been stomping around the fortress all morning."

The thought of sitting through another dinner with those monsters made Evalyn roll her eyes. "I take it my attendance is required?"

"As Dax's current lady, you are expected to look presentable when he has company."

Naomi tugged and pulled on her hair with gentle efficiency. When she was done, she led Evalyn to the brass oval mirror hanging on the wall near the door. Loose braids framed the crown of her head, swooping backward and into a larger twirl of silver at the nape of her neck. Two strands framed her face, accenting the pointed ears. Despite its dampness, her hair shimmered in the light seeping in the window.

"It looks lovely," she said. "Thank you."

Naomi blushed, motioning for Evalyn to follow her to the dressing screen. "It was no trouble at all."

The gowns were exquisite. Billowing skirts of silk, satin, and lace. Corsets beaded with jewels and embellished swirls. Layered underskirts, extravagant jackets, and delicate embroidery. Vibrant colors and soft pastels, fabrics worth more gold than she would ever lay eyes on anywhere else.

Garments fit for a princess, not an insignificant slave girl.

She'd never seen anything so beautiful. She felt unworthy of wearing them.

"This blue one would accent your eyes beautifully," Naomi was saying. "But I have several for you to—"

"The silver one," Evalyn said, running gentle fingers along the shimmering fabric.

It looked like molten moonlight. Not the blood red moonlight that bathed the island, but true, pure moonlight, just as she remembered it. "The silver one."

fORty-six

Dax was seething by the time he started up the spiral staircase. His boots echoed off stone, resonating in every dark corner.

He was tired of their games.

He was tired of playing the pawn.

They brought more slaves every day without his consent, though the cells were packed to discomfort. Already he piled three or four per cell and even that was too many. Toren, his damned foreman, continued pushing his temper, challenging every decision in favor of the monster's preferences. Everywhere he turned he was undermined, most of those loyal to him either in hiding or an ocean away. It was infuriating.

How was he supposed to protect them all if he couldn't even protect himself in the process?

But at least Evalyn was safe...safe as she could be, anyway.

After all she'd seen and been through, she had every right not to believe him. Of all people, he would have understood if she hadn't. But she had, and that surprised him most of all.

He'd slept with so many women—an attempt to find someone, something, to make sense of the horrible things he had watched happen. To make his inability to save any of the innocents around him seem less infuriating.

But it never worked. He never cared about pleasing anyone. He knew it made him selfish.

Until a stormy night eighteen years ago.

For some ungodly reason, he'd saved the damned girl from her inevitable death, and she'd been the death of him ever since.

Every fiber of his being had screamed to protect her, cherish her, and he hadn't, not as well as he could have. Something pulled him to her, something he couldn't explain, something he knew she felt too. But he fought it against his will because, deep down, he feared the shadow's wrath. By fighting for the child's safety after disobeying orders not to bring his own hostages, he would have forfeited both their lives and quite possibly the lives of all the other slaves on the island.

Maybe he was a selfish coward.

Dax opened the door, ready to apologize, and froze.

She leaned over the table piled with old books she could barely read, looking like something out of a fairy tale.

She'd chosen the silver gown. He knew she would.

Layers of silver and ivory silks billowed around her narrow waist, beaded pearls and gems shimmering like starlight in the flickering fire. The ivory corset, covered in whorls of silver lace, accentuated her chest. Fabric like iridescent moonlight hugged her arms loosely, flowing out around her elbows, twirling about her forearms when she moved.

That silvery hair twisted together just behind her right ear, several stands hanging free to frame her face, accenting the delicate Fae ears. Hands planted firmly on her hips, she glared down at the words, her small feet barefoot.

She turned to him then, smiling that wicked little smile of hers that made his body shiver with unexplainable delight. Those turquoise eyes pierced straight through him, a spitting image of the clear seas he longed for.

The words lodged in his throat as he crossed the room to her, wood crackling in the hearth.

She frowned, button nose wrinkling. "What's the matter?"

"You...you look like a goddess." He couldn't hold the words back. "If Nova or Ywone were mortal, you would match their beauty."

Evalyn bit her lip, her cheeks reddening. "What?" Those piercing eyes met his, long lashes fluttering. "The Moon Goddess and the Goddess of Beauty? Don't be silly."

He swore aloud that time. "You do, you look beautiful."

She shoved at his chest. "Oh, stop it. You think just because I cried last night I'm going to let you get all starstruck on me?"

"No, I..." She was grinning at him. "Damn you, woman." He walked into the bedroom to change before their company arrived.

The aroma hit him as he passed her.

He studied her, eyes narrowed.

She raised an eyebrow. "Yes?" she asked, her melodic voice sweet.

Of course she had. "The smell suits you. Free and spirited. It suits you well, little dove."

Evalyn bit her lip again, following him as he stripped off the sweaty tunic. "I think I startled Naomi today."

He removed his belt, stripping down to his undergarments. "Why is that?"

She laughed. "I exercise in the mornings when you leave. I'm usually dressed by the time she comes, but today..." Her voice trailed off and she laughed again. "She came early to help me dress for this lovely dinner—"

"I don't like it any more than you, trust me," he tugged on ivory pants, sending her a wary look.

She held up her hands. "That isn't what I was going to say."

Dax frowned at the tunics he held up, deciding on the ivory to match his pants. Then he approached the closet for an overcoat. "What's the problem with her seeing you exercise?"

"Nothing, I suppose. I just exercise naked."

He froze again, trying not to picture her unclothed. "I see." He shoved his arms through the long coat, adjusting the collar flaps and fiddling with silver clasps, the sea dragon on his left breast a patronage of his beloved ship, *Seraphina*. The only act of defiance he was still capable of making without risking innocent lives.

"You would think she's never seen herself naked."

He turned toward her, forcing himself to look at her face and not let his gaze slip lower. "Maybe she's never seen someone else so exposed."

With a shrug, Evalyn looked him over. Her eyes flashed with admiration as she took in the subtle beauty of his clothes. "Aren't we a stunning pair."

He took a step, half expecting her to back away, but she remained in the doorway. "Evalyn, I—" Voices echoed from the stairwell, he swore. "Try not to sass anyone, no matter what you hear."

She growled. "How can you expect me to remain silent?"

"I don't...I can't. But I need you to try. I'll discuss everything with you when they're gone. I want no more secrets between us." He walked back into the other room, preparing to greet them.

"Dax." She gripped his hand.

He shook his head in warning. "I want to share things with you, Evalyn, and I promise I'm going to. But speaking of it now is dangerous, for both of us. You don't know what they're capable of, and this fortress has eyes and ears everywhere. I promise to do everything in my power to keep you safe, but you must listen to me."

They were entering the room now.

The firelight dimmed as the Shadow Beasts approached.

Dax held his breath, waiting for her response. He could feel their wary, soulless eyes watching. He forced himself not to tense, not to turn and face them.

But Evalyn just took another step toward him, smiling wickedly.

The air in the room relaxed as she stood on her toes, gripped his collar, and whispered into his ear, "Anything you say, Dax."

He loosed the breath.

Evalyn brushed a finger along his chest and sauntered to the table. His eyes trailed after her, fixing her with that ravenous smile he used only when the monsters were near.

The suspicion faded.

He might hate the games, but the two of them were learning to play rather well. Maintaining their façade in public, never speaking the unspoken.

Ringing for the meal, Dax took a seat between the commanders and Evalyn. Seconds later, servants entered with trays of food. Sizzling fish garnished with herbs and a savory, spicy sauce surrounded by steaming vegetables, salad dressed with fresh berries and honey-glazed nuts, and toasted breads.

Evalyn, despite her lack of courtship knowledge, was a complete lady. She had a knack for table manners, though he'd never taught her himself. Something he appreciated just now.

When they finished off a tray of blueberry and lemon sweet cakes, the commander turned to Evalyn. "So," he hissed. "You decided to keep the Fae girl around. More trouble than she's worth in my opinion."

The others, even Toren, chuckled. Dax kept his expression blank and Evalyn blushed, studying the table.

"I have to agree, Captain," Toren said. "She always was a pain in my ass."

"Who I choose to share my bed with is none of your concern. I've done what was asked of me, haven't I?"

Toren snorted. "I suppose, but can she be trusted?"

Evalyn's blush deepened, ever innocent. "I won't be any trouble, sir, I promise." She fluttered those lashes at him, biting her lip. "If...if you want me to go, I don't want to be in the way if you have important..."

"She's staying."

Toren's grin made his round, stubbled cleft chin appear even uglier. "You train your women well, don't you? So obedient, you wouldn't know she was once a sassy little bitch, would you?"

A challenge.

"Watch your mouth when you speak about her."

"Or what, *Captain*?" Toren spat the words through brown, crooked teeth, several drops of spit hitting his cheek.

Dax wiped saliva away with the back of his hand, flashing Toren a warning look. "Or I will punish you for your inability to watch your tongue by removing it."

"If you're done bickering, *mortals*, we have business to discuss," the Shadow Commander hissed.

Resigned, Dax nodded.

"Good. We need to discuss the obsidian mining and how to speed it up."

Dax didn't think he would ever get used to those voices. "Speed it up?"

"Is that a problem, *mortal*?"

Dax shook his head. "No, but it will take consideration. We already loose at least three slaves a week to sickness or exhaustion, and even more are whipped to death." He shot Toren a glare.

"I hear nothing but excuses."

One of the other Shadow Beasts added, "If you need more slaves, that can be arranged."

No, Dax wanted to cry. *No more slaves.* But instead he said, "If you think that would be the best solution."

Another creature turned to Toren. "You, foreman, will stop whipping slaves to uselessness, understood?"

Toren gave a curt nod in response.

"Why the sudden demand after twenty-five years?" Dax almost didn't ask the question for fear of the answer.

The commander turned to him, those gnarled, oozing lips curving into a smile. "Our plans have changed. We must begin our obsidian testing on the magic wielders as soon as possible."

"Why is that?" He couldn't stop asking now. His knee bumped against Evalyn's beneath the table, steadying him.

The commander leaned forward, their faces inches apart. "It doesn't matter why, Captain. If you want your island back, if you want to protect those you care so much for, you will obey our commands without question. That is the arrangement."

Dax met his stare evenly. "Our agreement, *Commander*, was thirty years of service. If you are asking me to quicken the pace or divert from our original time frame, which you are, you owe me an explanation. I am not some mere mortal for you to throw demands at. Do not forget the power I still have over you. The seas and those who sail them obey my orders."

"Barely," Toren snorted.

None of them seemed to hear.

"You have no right to talk to us that way, *mortal*," one of the Shadow Beasts hissed. He leaned forward, several others following in his wake. But the commander held up a hand, shaking his head.

He kept his focus on Dax. "The Fae King's precious Order has the mortal princess in custody and are making their way to Raenya as we speak. Aeron's broken little pet failed twice to retrieve her and is no longer useful. We must harvest the obsidian's magic power to begin our tests, hunt them down, and kill the Fae bastards before they can destroy everything we've worked toward."

forty-seven

It was nonsense.

Evalyn clenched shaking fists beneath the table, unable to comprehend what she was hearing.

Fae Kings, an ancient Order, Raenya. All mystical stories her mother told her as a child when she couldn't sleep at night.

But for the stories to be reality?

Dax's knee pressed against hers, the only comfort keeping her fear invisible. She clutched her napkin in an attempt to keep her nails from digging into her palm.

Dax was furious.

Tension radiated from him in violent waves. The same tension she was trying to keep from radiating off herself.

She thought this time would be different, the utter dread within her awoken by the shadow creatures easier to handle. But having the secret knowledge about the truth Dax hid only made it worse. Knowledge that could be used against both of them.

The information Dax requested did nothing to ease that.

She didn't understand any of it. The obsidian's magical properties were being harvested only to be filled with a different, darker power. They were draining magic wielders, dumping the decaying, lifeless corpses into mass graves beneath the fortress or into the sea. Slave intake was increased daily to make the magic force stronger, and all in the name of Aeron. A demon king? Why was the mortal princess they spoke of so important?

The conversation continued for hours.

She didn't want to understand.

"Well, girl?" She blinked, realizing the foreman—what was his name? Toren—had spoken to her.

"Your thoughts on the increase of slaves to increase overall power? We were discussing it yesterday."

Dax's voice, calm, lazy, and slightly bored, beside her.

She tried not to let her relief flicker. "I'm just a slave, what does my opinion matter to you?"

Tension crept into the room as the Shadow Beast frowned, but no one moved. "It doesn't," the commander replied. "I'm merely curious to know your insignificant opinion."

Evalyn focused on keeping her face blank as they watched her with those hollow, lifeless eyes. "I believe it's silly to harvest the power over time. I mean, if you need it so badly, and you don't care about the death of innocents, why not just drain all magic at once or in large groups?"

"We need the slaves alive to test them. Or, mostly alive." The commander smiled. "But it's an interesting notion. Perhaps we can gather larger groups for testing rather than picking off the weaker slaves as they fall."

She shrugged, sipping her honeyed wine to settle her nerves. "I'm afraid being a slave all my life I don't know much about plans and schemes."

"What of your life before you were enslaved? If I recall correctly, Dax saved you from drowning as a child and brought you here despite our strict orders not to."

Evalyn kept her expression neutral. "I don't see how that has anything to do with the current issue."

"Where did you come from?" the Shadow Commander pried.

"I don't remember." It wasn't quite a lie—she'd long blocked out the memory of her mother and the brother she lost. But even if she hadn't, she would never share those precious memories with the likes of them.

"We have ways of recalling forgotten information." The creature looked as though he might reach for her, but Dax shielded her.

"You will not touch her."

The creature lifted its head, glaring down a thin, pointed nose at Dax. It took everything Evalyn had to conceal her terror.

Toren cleared his throat. "It's getting late. I'm afraid I have other business to attend to down at the ports." He bowed mockingly to Dax. "By your leave, Captain."

Dax returned the gesture and Toren left.

The creatures stood as well, the dark shadows at their feet churning, floating them over the ground. The commander fixed her with a vicious stare. "Once we begin gathering slaves for a more thorough extraction process, we will drain everyone, including your Fae pet, *Captain*." Then he was gone.

Dax locked the door and eased her to her feet, her legs heavy, body vibrating with fear. "If they do that, it will kill everyone," she breathed.

Dax put cool, callused fingers beneath her chin. Pain filled his eyes. "They know, but they don't care."

Internal flames snapped against iron, struggling to break free, to fight the inevitable. "A magic wielder can't survive that sort of ritual. One's magic essence is tethered to the soul. A body without a soul is no more than an empty shell."

"I've also heard them whispering about binding shadow magic to the wielder's soul, forcing their magic to fuse with the darkness so it can control their actions," Dax murmured. "I think that's what they mean to use the obsidian to harness."

Evalyn let out a choked laugh. "That makes it even worse. Being trapped within one's own body..."

Dax pulled her close, momentarily calming the fury pulsing through her. "I wish I could do something, to search for a way the slaves might escape. But I can't, not if I want to remain alive and attempt to help the others held captive here."

She gripped his collar, looking hopefully up at him. "There's a way to escape?"

Dax shook his head. "The Shadow Beasts replaced my men at the mine entrances. They monitor the ports on and off the island and regulate any trade over my shoulder. Swimming is useless. Creatures of darkness lurk in even the shallowest ocean crevices. No one sees them and survives."

"Do the Shadow Beasts ever leave?"

There had to be something, some way.

"When they bring the new slaves or supplies, but those trips are only once every two weeks." He walked into the bedroom as he spoke, Evalyn following behind him. "At least five of my men run the crew, but they have little to no say in decisions."

She braced a hand against the dresser and motioned for him to undo the suffocating corset laces. He obeyed. "So, if a stowaway were to slip onto a ship, they could get off the island."

His hands froze on her waist. "Whatever you're thinking, stop."

There was a way, then.

A risk, and probably a foolish one, but still hope.

She said nothing, and Dax sighed, continuing to loosen the laces. She laid the corset over the chair, doing the same with the flowing silks and underskirts. Then, she pulled the pins free from her hair, silver tumbling around her, and walked to the bed, reaching for the nightgown discarded there that morning.

Only then did she turn back to him and the gape she knew would be on his face. She flashed a wicked little smirk.

"No modesty," Dax breathed.

"There's none in those mines, it means nothing to me." She paused. "I might have been afraid once, to be like this with you. But I'm not anymore. I don't know what that means." The feeling flickered as Evalyn walked to him, running a hand along his jaw and through the dark, well-groomed beard. "I'm going to get off this island. I refuse to die here."

He gripped her waist when she tried to walk away. "I can't let you forfeit your life trying to sneak onto one of those ships. I'd never forgive myself."

She met his eyes, tangling her fingers in that wavy, unbound raven hair. "Then help me," she whispered. "Dax, we could do it, together."

She wasn't sure why she said it. Her heart fluttered at the thought of not being alone. But it was foolish to ask of him.

Still, she could sense his hesitation. "I can't. There are spies everywhere, I could be recognized. Being seen with me would put you in even greater danger."

Evalyn smiled lightly, touching his hand. "That's a risk I would be willing to take."

He said nothing, and she pulled her hand away.

"Then at least help me," she repeated, her voice stronger despite the pain filling her chest at his rejection. "Help me leave before it's too late."

From the look in Dax's eyes, she thought he might kiss her. But he only sighed, stroking her cheek. "No more pretending, no more lies. I failed to protect my own people, but I will do whatever I can to keep you safe, even if it costs me my life."

"I don't want it to cost you your life." It was a realization, a truth she needed him to hear, even if he didn't know what it meant.

He put a finger to her lips, smiling thinly. "In the morning, we'll discuss everything. You'll tell me what you're planning inside that whirling brain of yours. Until then, I don't want to hear another word about it."

forty-eight

Quinn knew.

He knew, and Jenson felt as though a weight had been lifted from his shoulders.

When he arrived in Orira, an orphan immigrant from the enslaved southern continent, no one wanted to help him. A Demi-Fae who didn't know his own strength. The Fae people were so detached from the mortal parts of the world that rumors and gossip about their lifestyle spread like wildfire. So harboring an orphaned Demi-Fae fugitive and angering a merciless dictator was the last thing anyone in the peaceful port city wanted.

He'd been homeless and starving for over a year before Fallon found him.

He'd known exactly who Fallon was.

The storytellers of his hometown favored tales of the Fae kingdom, Dorwynn, and their ageless line of just and noble rulers. King Reul Elirona and his most trusted friend and advisor, Fallon, were two of the greatest Fae warriors in history. Many of King Reul's relatives had high seats of honor on his royal council or served within his personal cadre.

The thought of ever laying eyes on one of the legendary warriors was nothing more than an orphan's wildest dreams.

Until Fallon had walked right up to him in that trash-filled alley of Orira and called him by name like an old friend.

Jenson fainted.

When he awoke, Fallon told him of The Order and its purpose.

The plans Aeron built and left behind so he might to rise to power once more, the slaughter of the royal Fae children, the purpose of Kynire and why he and King Reul created it.

Centuries of royal secrets confided to a half-dead orphan. The Order created to fight against the anticipated return of the Demon King and his forces, the three hundred years he'd spent scouring Navarre for worthy warriors to join the resistance and fight beside him.

He told Jenson of the pure Fae also under his protection, only two years younger. A comrade and a friend whose Fae identity and true strength were unknown to him. Jenson and Quinn met when he and Fallon returned to Kynire's Rathal headquarters. The two were near inseparable.

The legends of King Reul's cadre and Aeron's looming threat were a faded memory. Most mortals thought the Fae people were extinct or some sort of Gods.

Yet here he was, training with not one, but *two* pure Fae.

Hiding Quinn's identity from him became harder as they got older—Quinn's natural Fae speed and reflexes exceeded even Maya's, who had returned from five years of training with the Assassin's Guild in The Redlands as a swift, lethal weapon. Jenson weighed the pros and cons of defying Fallon and telling Quinn the truth, but always decided against it. No one else knew the truth of Quinn's heritage.

So when Fallon slipped into Jenson's rooms to tell him Quinn had learned his heritage, Jenson slept like a baby. The relief was one of the most wonderful feelings he'd ever experienced.

That was a week ago.

When they traveled, Maya took evening watches with him, while Quinn rose early to train and take the morning watch with the princess. He wanted to approach Quinn, if for nothing else but the ability to share the truth. But the moment hadn't come.

Jenson pulled the thick wool cloak more firmly around his shoulders, shivering as the brisk morning wind kissed his skin, whipping ebony strands of hair about his face.

"I don't think I've seen you this silent since the year Fallon thought you caught the red plague from eating foul meat." Quinn had a habit of sneaking up on people, another benefit of that cat-like Fae grace.

Jenson gave him a thin smile. "Just thinking about a lot."

Quinn ran a hand through his hair. Jenson always wondered what Quinn would look like with the silvery hair of the Children of Dorwynn. Fallon had given Quinn the enchanted pendant before they'd met, the charm blocking his Fae appearance. Only pure Fae were born with moon-kissed hair, the trait a clear symbol of their race.

"We should cross the border soon. Fallon is worried about where the shadow beings disappeared to in Rivedas. They could be lurking anywhere. At least Joseline is getting stronger, and Maya's been less of a pain since the two of them talked." He turned back to see the two girls giggling like old friends. "I'm glad, Maya needs a friend."

He was rambling. He never rambled to anyone else, and he only did it at all when he was unsure how to confront a topic.

Jenson sighed, giving him a long, hard stare. "Quinn, I know."

Quinn let out the breath he'd been holding. "Fallon told me."

More silence.

"I wanted to tell you. Every day I wanted to tell you, but the thought of seeing Fallon angry still terrifies me."

Quinn's lips twitched slightly into a smirk. "Jenson, it's alright." Another moment of silence. "I'm more upset with him for not telling me to begin with, but I'm glad you didn't tell me. I wouldn't have believed it anyway."

Jenson laughed. "Yeah, you're an idiot like that." Quinn joined in the laughter.

"It doesn't change anything. You're still my *sielapora*, the brother I never had, and I still trust you with my life."

"As do I," Jenson replied, grasping his friend's outstretched hand.

Quinn flashed that crooked smirk again. "I know. Now I'd better get back to the princess before Fallon notices. I just wanted to make sure you were alright."

A few feet ahead, Fallon called out, "I notice everything, Quinn. You two whisper like a pair of gossiping old crones." Jenson stifled a chuckle. "Oh, and if we get ambushed, it'll be your fault."

Quinn rode off without another word. Jenson watched him, smiling.

forty-nine

Dax ran a hand through disheveled hair as the Shadow Commander spoke, forcing his breath to remain steady amidst the tedious discussion.

The air in the circular room was stale, reeking of pain and suffering. The pewter gray stone walls and domed ceiling lacked vibrance, radiating that same unwelcoming staleness.

The waves beat against the rocks through the open window at his back, their beautiful rhythm taunting.

They knew it tortured him to listen. They knew he longed to feel the wind on his face, to taste the salty sea as it kissed his skin.

It tortured him almost as much as the fool's hope to save the innocent people suffering around him, to get Evalyn off this island. A fool's hope he would make a reality nonetheless.

He'd failed once, years ago, to save the people he loved.

He wouldn't fail again.

He would give anything to keep her safe.

But there was no way to fulfill that dream. Not without consequence, without sacrifice.

The thoughts of what he had to do, what he *would* do, to get her away from the monsters haunted his subconscious, petrified him. As much as he longed to go with her, he couldn't. Her chances of survival were better if she left alone. But they would know he helped her, they would know he'd allowed her to escape, and they would harm the others to punish him. He couldn't stand it, couldn't take that chance. It left only one feasible alternative.

Death.

He wasn't afraid of death, not really. A pirate's life revolved around the Lady of Death's foreplay, every minute at sea potentially their last.

But despite planning the possibility of his own end for eighteen years, it had never truly become a reality. He'd never cared, but he'd never had something to live for until now.

Dax scratched at the dark, untrimmed scruff tickling his jaw. He hadn't slept in days. The thought of leaving her again, of breaking her again, was unbearable.

"Well, *Captain*?"

Dax blinked, staring into the soulless black eyes of the monster across the table. "I beg your pardon?"

Torn and oozing lips peeled back into a silent snarl. "You seem...distant. Your Fae whore tiring you so that you can no longer uphold your obligations? She can be disposed of to prevent that."

Dax clenched his fists beneath the table, refusing to let his anger flicker to his face. "No."

"No?" An evil smile followed.

"She is not a distraction."

"If you insist." The commander hissed, lowering his head once more to the paper-covered table.

Damn them.

Damn them all to the mercy of The Twelve. May Syvi drown them within her depths without pity.

The meeting continued without conflict, the usual tired topics of obsidian counts and trips to the mainland port in Easthaven for supplies.

But Dax knew they watched him.

They always watched him. In the halls, in the mines, in his rooms.

No place was safe in the Shadow Beasts' presence.

No place would be safe for Evalyn while he was alive either. They would use him to harm her. Even if everything went according to plan and she somehow managed to escape, they would know he helped her. They would know, and torture him for information until he broke. They all broke, the ones the shadows kept in the dungeons, it was only a matter of time.

He knew that. He knew his death was the only true way to give her a chance at freedom, a chance to escape. He'd never been able to give any of the innocents around him that chance, but now he could. At a price he knew would destroy her. He hated himself for it.

But if that was the only way for her to truly be free, so be it.

fifty

After a week of traveling, Joseline began to doubt the woods would ever end.

They left Rivedas, moving off the Northern Road, traveling along less-used paths in search of another branch of Kynire, whom Fallon claimed dwelled within the seclusion of Farowa Forest. He trusted those in charge, but they hadn't been in contact for a hundred years, too worried about the attention it might draw, and every day they traveled was a day closer to the Rekiv border.

Joseline huffed out a sigh, wrinkling her nose.

Whining about it will do you no good, Shea's proper and sophisticated voice echoed in her head.

Joseline turned to glare at the Aonani fox sprawled on Bellona's rear. "I'm not whining."

Shea raised her eyes sarcastically, her tail flicking with lazy boredom. *You could have fooled me.*

Joseline opened her mouth to send the fox a smart reply, but closed it when Jenson halted, swinging to the ground. "Is everything alright?"

He walked over, taking Bellona's reins as she dismounted. "There's a river crossing about a half a day's ride ahead, marking the border. Fallon wants to stop here instead of risking it in the dark."

She pulled Shea into her arms. "That's probably for the best."

Maya approached, flashing a little grin. "So, you've been training every day with Quinn for well over a month. How about a little duel?"

Joseline's pulse quickened. "You wish to challenge me?"

Maya nodded. "Quinn is an excellent fighter, his dagger skills the best I've ever seen. I'm curious how he instructs. He's never been patient with me."

Joseline twisted a scarlet curl around her finger. "I suppose."

Challenge flashed in Maya's light green eyes.

"Just try not to kill my student, please? She's important."

Joseline turned to where Quinn stood beside a thick oak tree, hands shoved into his pockets, and glared at him. "You spend all this time praising me about my progress, yet you have no faith in me?"

"Little Yaya is one of the swiftest warriors I know." Quinn smirked at Maya, walking toward her to catch the younger girl in a headlock and ruffle short blonde hair.

She squealed, trying to twist away from him. "Oh, would you knock it off?"

Quinn chuckled, letting Maya go before meeting Joseline's eyes. "Do not underestimate her."

It was that teacher-to-pupil calm he spoke with. An instruction, not a jest.

She nodded, following Maya. Her heart beat so violently she thought it would burst.

She hadn't attempted any form of real combat since the Goddess's power all but consumed her will, driving her actions. She'd killed the shadow creature by pure luck and didn't remember any of it.

The Goddess power had awoken several times since, but she didn't understand it, and it had never been in combat.

Quinn also started practicing knife and staff fighting with her, but she could barely keep up. She was slow and clumsy, useless against his inhuman speed.

A few days ago, Quinn gave her a small ornate dagger. A beautifully feminine weapon, the silver blade delicately carved with flowers to match the pommel, the hilt encrusted with vibrant shades of pink gems. He'd purchased from a merchant in Rivedas so when she was ready for her own weapon, she wouldn't have to steal his, he'd mocked.

She reached for it now, but Maya shook her head, hefting the long, makeshift staff of a fallen tree limb against her hip. The length was similar to the tree limbs Quinn used for their training. Joseline held back a sigh of relief.

"I know Quinn taught you some staff fighting. I figured this would be safer than sharp steel." Maya winked, tossing her the stick.

Joseline caught it with both hands, taking a step back from the impact. The wood was fairly smooth, thick enough for her fingers to encircle comfortably. She tried to recall all Quinn taught her within the past few weeks, to focus. But her mind swam.

"Your Highness?" Maya held her own stick with both hands, one end pointed toward Joseline's chest. "Shall we?"

Joseline took a breath. She'd started working on awakening that ancient power when she trained, using it to keep her focused.

Now, it seemed to yawn upon her request, soothing her racing heart.

She stepped forward with one foot, chin high as she crossed her stick with Maya's. Her eyes filled with determination. "Yes, we shall."

Joseline swung her makeshift staff toward the younger girl.

Wood clicked together, and Maya batted her attack away.

Maya moved, Joseline blocking her as their sticks clicked again.

Her feet shifted as she attempted to swing one end of the stick up and under Joseline's chin.

Joseline stepped to the side, knocking it out of the way.

Maya narrowed her eyes, wiping at a strand of hair that fell loose from the tight ribbon holding them back.

They repeated the same round of movements several times. Joseline kept her focus on the position of her hands and the timing as she swung the staff.

The sun was just beginning to set, blinding as it shone in bright, splotchy patches through the thin canopy above when Maya aimed the staff suddenly at her side, almost knocking her to the ground as she blocked and stumbled.

"If you're forced on the defensive, worry less about your feet and more about blocking your opponent's attacks." Maya barely sounded out of breath.

Joseline nodded, her own breath quickening as she started to tire. But the power within her was steady, fueling her movements.

Maya was swift, as Quinn said, but Joseline remained calm as their staffs met again and again.

Twirling her makeshift staff over her head in a wide arc Maya lunged as if to crack the wood over Joseline's skull.

She adjusted her grip in preparation, holding her own stick in defense.

Then she was falling.

Joseline's back slammed into the ground with a loud thud, and an airy huff slipped through her lips as the breath left her body.

Maya pointed one end of her makeshift staff at her throat.

Joseline blinked.

"If your opponent makes an obvious show of movement, never assume they're going to follow through with it. Chances are, you'll fall right into their trap, dead." Maya twirled the stick with one hand, holding it vertically against her side behind her shoulder. Smiling, she held out the other hand.

Joseline took it, Maya yanking her up. Shea was at her ankles, fluffy white tail curling around her.

The younger girl grinned. "Well fought, Josie. Very well fought!" Maya gave a little squeak and threw her arms around Joseline's shoulders. "I have to say, I'm impressed."

"My sister is the only one who's ever called me Josie before," Joseline mused.

"I like it," Maya replied, pulling away from Joseline to favor her right hip. "If you don't mind?"

Joseline shook her head. "No, I like it a lot."

Maya's gapped teeth showed when she smiled. "Good."

"Your Highness." It was Fallon. Joseline turned to see him

leaning against a tree trunk, Jenson and Quinn at his sides. "You did well."

Something fluttered in her chest. She was grateful to have them at her side. "Thank you."

Fallon dipped his head in a slight bow and walked away with Jenson at his heels. Maya, exchanging a look with Jenson, jogged after them, laughing at something he said.

Quinn tossed a water skin to her. That blank stare faltered as he gave her a close-lipped smile. "You should be proud. How do you feel?"

She wiped at her forehead as sweat dripped into her eyes. "Like I finally accomplished something."

You have. Your training shows that every day, Shea purred.

Quinn gave her a strange look.

She blushed, fiddling with a scarlet curl as the ancient calm began to fade, replaced by nerves.

Joseline didn't expect the firm hug that followed.

Quinn pulled her toward him, squeezing her shoulders. Strong, muscular arms encircled her, as secure and safe as the smell of pine and frankincense that enveloped her senses. She became all too aware of how tiny she was, her eyes barely level with his chest as she lifted her chin.

"You have...you've accomplished so much," Quinn whispered into her hair. He stroked a hand over her curls, her back, but she didn't shy away.

Security enveloped her. She never would have believed that feeling was possible around him of all people two months ago.

She smiled, snuggling against him, the leather vest he wore warm against her cheek as her eyes trailed along the tattoo poking out from beneath his tunic. Quinn's cloak draped over her shoulder, his chest rumbling as he chuckled.

After a moment he released her, staring into her eyes.

She didn't know why the tears fell, but Joseline couldn't stop them as they spilled down her face.

Quinn frowned, the grip on her arms gentle. "Joseline, why are you crying?"

She shook her head. "I...I don't know," she blubbered, scrubbing at her cheeks with a sniff.

Quinn laughed, the sound pure and happy.

She glared at him, shoving him away. "It's not funny, you idiot."

He bit his lip, the playful look still in his eyes, but he didn't touch her again. Instead, he bowed, his hand sweeping out to the side. "My most humble apologies, Your Highness. You're right, it isn't funny."

Joseline snorted. "Now you're milking it. Leave the dramatics to Jenson." She started to walk away but turned back. He raised an eyebrow. "By the way. It isn't anything urgent, but I like it when you call me Joseline."

She continued walking, Quinn a comforting presence beside her. "Joseline it is then."

They'd almost reached the others when Quinn put a hand on her arm. She looked up at him expectantly. "Yes?"

"I..." Quinn bit his lip. "I really am proud of you."

Joseline raised an eyebrow, smiling. "You mentioned that."

Quinn huffed out a breath. "No, I..." he turned away, groaning. "No forget about the rest of them. *I'm* proud of you."

Now, he blushed. Joseline's pulse hammered in her throat as she waited for him to continue.

"Not...not as a warrior, or a protector, or any of that. Just...just as me. As Quinn."

Her breath hitched, but she allowed her hand to slid down his arm until it found his larger one and she squeezed his fingers. "As Quinn," she repeated softly. "As a friend?"

"As whatever you'd like, Joseline." He met her eyes then, something shimmering in them she didn't quite understand, and she fought to look away. "You have no idea how far you've come. And I...I'm glad I've been by your side to watch you grow."

Joseline eyed him slyly. "You don't do this admitting how you feel thing often, do you?"

Quinn opened his mouth then closed it, pursing his lips. "It's that obvious, huh?"

She laughed, tugging him toward the others. "Don't worry, I won't tell Jenson." Her voice softened before she added, "and thank you."

He only nodded in response, the fingers sliding apart as they approached the others. Joseline took a seat beside Maya, who passed her a water skin, linking their arms and resting her head on Joseline's shoulder. The men sat together, whispering and laughing. Shea's soft purr echoed from where she lay curled by the low fire. The golden-orange sunset peeked through the trees, a beaming, vibrant ray. The wind whispered amongst the leaves above, several floating to the ground.

She always felt welcome in the palace. And she loved and missed Julia fiercely, but something about the freedom of the forest and the company around her made Joseline feel more at home than she ever had before.

Once, the thought might have frightened her. But now, she only smiled with content.

fifty-one

A week and a half came and went, and by sundown, Evalyn was too exhausted to focus on anything.

After an evening of heated arguing, Dax agreed to spend an hour at dawn teaching her hand to hand combat skills. Her personal training could only get her so far. Her lessons with Naomi continued during the day, and when Dax returned sweaty, muttering, and covered in volcanic ash, he spent yet another hour lecturing about the realm so foreign to her. He showed her maps of the continent and sea, constantly praising her ability to learn.

Since Dax completely opened up to her, he was a different person. Just the sight of her put his tension at ease. His actions were always gentle, as if a weight that he'd held over himself for years had at last been lifted away.

Evalyn almost felt loved in his company.

Her constant fears of abandonment hardened her, but Dax made the shell she'd built feel unnecessary. She liked him, this man revealed beneath the public façade, and often found herself smiling at the thought of him.

He believed in her, trusted her enough to share secret information when they were alone, though he always kept his voice hushed for fear of unwanted listeners. This fortress, he claimed, had eyes and ears everywhere.

They'd been discussing such secrets this evening, before Dax stopped to tell one of his numerous pirate tales, bored of solemn topics. The food was long removed from the table now littered with sea charts and maps. A tray of half eaten cheeses and fruits lay next to an empty flagon of honeyed wine, the remnants filling the glass dangling from Evalyn's fingers.

They sat before the hearth, firelight dancing around the room in burnt orange shadows. She leaned on one arm, her legs sprawled to the side, her head tingling slightly from the sweet wine. Dax lay beside her on the carpet, eyes closed, his hands folded behind his head.

Evalyn laughed, giddy at the thought of a young Dax caught in a storm, navigating uncharted waters, with a crew of blubbering, superstitious fools.

She loved listening to him talk, that deep, silky voice rising and falling with the intensity of his tale. The sea echoed through the open window, burgundy curtains blowing in the breeze.

By the time he finished, her glass was empty.

She watched him, flustered and wide-eyed, as he sat to cross long legs, pushing up the sleeve of his dark navy tunic. Wavy onyx hair fell just passed his collarbones, the bearded jaw and upper lip in desperate need of a trim. His eyes were so dark a blue they were almost black.

Once, she said he might have been handsome if he weren't such a pig. Now, she saw only the beauty.

Evalyn fiddled with the golden cords running down her sides, the lilac fabric of her gown soft beneath her fingers.

Dax fixed her with that curious look, eyes slightly narrowed, one corner of his mouth tugging upward in a crooked smile. "Eva, what's the matter?"

She sucked in a breath, heart fluttering at the nickname as she tucked a silver strand behind her ear, sticking her chin out, lips pursing together. "Nothing," she said, her voice much quieter than she hoped.

Dax laughed. "Don't play dumb, I know that look by now."

She tried to ignore the racing nerves. "I don't have a look."

She gasped as long, gentle fingers gripped her chin. "That look, right there."

"It's nothing," she mumbled.

Dax shrugged, dropping his hand. "If you say so." He started to stand, but she grabbed his wrist. He raised an eyebrow.

"It's just...are you sure you can't come with me?" Evalyn didn't realize how badly she'd begun to want him with her when she left.

Grief flashed across his face. "Eva, we've talked about this. You know why I can't."

Giving a resigned nod, she rested her head in his lap, curling her knees into her chest. Dax ran his fingers through her hair. They sat like that, listening to the distant waves and the crackling fire for a long time. Evalyn drifted off to sleep until Dax spoke.

"They aren't going to extract all the magic at once like you suggested, but they are going to start their testing soon."

Evalyn bolted upright. "When?"

He ran a hand through his own hair. "I'm not sure exactly. I've been trying to push the date back, but..." his voice trailed off.

Evalyn put a hand on his chest, smiling weakly. "Dax, we both know you don't have control over this."

His smile didn't reach his eyes. "Eva, I...I do wish I could..."

She pressed a finger to his lips, shaking her head. "Don't get all sappy on me now, it isn't at all becoming on you."

Dax laughed bitterly. "I'm going to miss that sass of yours."

Evalyn wasn't sure when they got so close, but she couldn't move away. Her heart thumped so rapidly against her chest she was sure he could hear it, her breath caught in her throat.

Dax's eyes flickered down to her mouth, then up again.

Her thoughts flashed to that first night in these rooms, a slightly different, darker man masking the gentle one beneath, blurring eighteen years of her vision. Kinder than she'd expected but misunderstood all the same. A pirate captain patiently playing a losing game, covered by a lie to keep himself alive, to keep them both alive.

Those dark eyes flickered down to her mouth again, asking.

Dax had never actually kissed her. The thought of it now sent a wild chill down her spine.

"Dax, I—"

The words tumbled out of her head as a calloused hand cupped her face, his thumb brushing in soft strokes across her skin. He inched closer still, his eyes never leaving hers.

The door opened, and Dax jerked his hand away. Whatever spell had been cast before Naomi entered was broken.

The girl blushed, twiddling her thumbs before bowing and dashing to the tray of uneaten food. She tripped halfway, sliding across the wooden floor with a squeak. She lay there for a moment, and Evalyn's eyes flicked to Dax, who stood with a resigned sigh. Naomi took his outstretched hand, blustering apologies, and sprinted from the room.

He smiled at Evalyn. "Syvi's breath, I don't know why I keep her around, she's so clumsy."

Evalyn shrugged. "Why do you keep me around? I'm so sassy."

Dax rolled his eyes, motioning for her to follow. Evalyn regretted standing as she swayed and nearly toppled over. But Dax was there, a steady arm around her waist.

"Thanks," she muttered, all too aware of the flush in her cheeks.

"I want to show you something," he whispered into her hair. They walked into the bedroom, turning toward the closet.

Evalyn flashed him a wry look. "Ooh, take the drunk woman into your closet to seduce her, how classy and considerate of you."

He chuckled as they entered, candlelight from the room behind them illuminating faint silhouettes against walls lined with elegant garments. He halted, shoving aside hangers draped with fine jackets to reveal an iron door.

One side was lined with a multitude of locks, all clicked shut. It was smaller than average, but not so short that much crouching would be required to use it, wherever it led to. It had an ancient, secret feel to it, something long-forgotten.

Dax twisted the locks and gave the iron a swift tug.

It made no sound as it opened.

The passage beyond was dark as night. The flickering candlelight allowed no more than a foot of visibility into the darkness, the light veering to the left as stairs spiraled downward. A soft, cold draft wafted toward them. It smelled of the sea, the breeze enticing.

"What is that?" Her voice was hushed.

"That," he whispered, closing, locking, and concealing the door once more, "is how you escape, little dove."

Her head spun, from the wine or the thought of escape, she wasn't sure.

"It leads under the mountains to cliffs facing the sea. You can climb along the ledges if you're careful, though I'm afraid there's no real path. Stay to the left, and it'll lead you to the port."

She all but fell onto the bed, the wine's grip growing stronger. "After I reach the port, how will I get onto the ship?"

She was vaguely aware of Dax sitting beside her. He eased her up and held a glass of water to her lips. She drank, murmuring thanks.

"We can discuss this in the morning," he said.

She shook her head, moaning at the movement and motioning for him to bring more water.

When he returned, he said, "You'll know the ship when you see her. *Seraphina* demands attention."

"Her?"

"Yes, her. Beautiful, gold and black with a sea dragon decorating the bow."

"She was yours." Not a question, an acknowledgement.

"Yes," his voice was touched with sadness. "Find her, and sneak on, either on foot or in a barrel near the boarding docks. Those always go aboard the ship. Get down below deck. You'll be safe then."

"Aye, Captain, Sir." Her eyelids drooped, and she laid back on the pillows, not bothering to remove her gown.

Dax chuckled, draping an arm over her. "Eva," he cooed, pulling her close. "If you're sick in my bed, I'll kill you myself." She waved a heavy hand, muttering something about useless worries before sleep consumed her.

fifty-two

It was all Dax could do not to race through the fortress halls. Running would only draw unwanted attention.

The urgent meeting amongst the commanders just past midnight had been sudden and unpleasant. Mercifully, Evalyn had remained asleep despite the frantic knocking; he only hoped he'd be able to wake her now.

The monsters had decided to start their testing today.

They were selecting slaves at random, but the commander had made it clear Evalyn would be amongst those in the first group of subjects.

He had to get her out, ensure her safety. He couldn't fail again. Dax would do whatever it took to keep her safe, even if that meant giving her a reason to leave—even if it meant breaking her completely. She was strong, he knew she was, and he knew she would go on without him to be free of this wretched place. He just needed to give her a reason to go, give her a reason to believe she couldn't help him by staying behind and sacrificing herself.

He only hoped she could find it in her heart to forgive him somehow.

He clenched already aching fists, closing the door before he sprinted for the bedchamber.

Evalyn was still as he'd left her. Silvery-white hair shimmered across silky sheets in the moonlight like stars.

She looked so young when she slept, so peaceful.

He sat beside her, tucking a strand of silver behind her ear. She stirred, smiling and curling into his hand. He fought to contain the sigh.

He didn't know how much time they had. The Shadow Beasts hadn't said *when* they would begin. There wasn't a second to lose.

He gripped her shoulders, shaking her as he leaned down to whisper in her ear. "You need to leave, little dove, now."

Evalyn's eyes fluttered, and she yawned, rubbing groggy eyes. "Right now?"

Anxious, he glanced toward the door, half-expecting them to burst in and snatch her away at any moment. "Yes," he pulled her from the bed.

She stumbled along, still half asleep.

Almost frantic, he yanked a black pair of loose pants and a long-sleeved black tunic from the dresser. "I just came from a meeting with the Shadow Commanders. They're starting to select test subjects today."

That seemed to wake her up. She helped him pull the cotton gown over her head, replacing it with the tunic. "I thought you said soon?" she whispered.

Dax glanced to the door again. "I did."

The pants fit simply at her hips, flaring around her thighs and calves. Her feet slid into already-laced black boots. "Today is not the same thing as soon, Dax."

"I *know* that. This is the first I've heard of it as well." She was shaking, but he gave her an approving nod and gripped her arms, meeting the fear in her eyes. "Look at me." He unfastened his dark navy cloak, twirling it around her shoulders and hooking the silver clasp.

"I can't take this," she hissed, following him to the bed.

He tried not to let his fear show on his face. "You can, and you will. I don't need it anyway. Not anymore."

259

She narrowed her eyes, frowning as she sat beside him. "Not anymore, what do you mean?"

His gut clenched. He'd been thinking of the best way to tell her for weeks now. But in the end, bluntness was the best method, the knowledge would hurt either way.

Dax smiled, her clear eyes piercing through him. Then, he took a deep breath, and said, "You don't need to face any setbacks my torture might cause. You don't need to stay here and ruin your only chance to leave because you want to be with me. I don't need the cloak, because you're going to kill me."

Evalyn stared at him, wide-eyed.

"What?" she whispered hoarsely.

She couldn't form the words, her throat too raw.

No, she wanted to say, but no sound emerged.

She shook her head fiercely, as if that would change his mind.

Dax was still smiling at her with that calm, beautifully crooked smile. "It's the only way, the best way. If I'm alive when you leave, they *will* use me to find you. I can't let that happen. I cannot let myself be the reason you want to stay, the reason you suffer. I've put you through enough suffering already."

Gods, how was he so calm? She shook in violent pulses now, all fears resurfacing. Not this, not again.

But it was worse, this was so much worse.

"No, Dax. I can't do that. I *won't* do that. Not to you. I wanted to once, but not anymore." The breath caught in her throat.

She could not do what he was asking, not this.

He loosened the dagger from his belt, forcing it into her hand. She tried to pull away, but he gripped her hand and the hilt in his.

"It..." he choked, the calm slipping. "Eva, my dear, sweet Eva." He brushed a calloused thumb across her cheek with the other hand. "Please, this is the only way for you. I will not be your downfall."

Evalyn pressed her forehead against his, their hands still clasped around the dagger between them as she closed her eyes. The tears spilled down her face. "And I will not be yours." Her chest tightened. "Dax, please," she begged, opening her eyes to look at him. "Do not ask me to do this."

But his eyes were clear. "I'm not asking you. I need...I need your strength."

Her chin trembled, and he wiped at the tears. "When it's done, take the candle and open the door. There's a torch along the wall. Follow the stairs to the cliff and keep left. There are guards at the port, but they won't be expecting anything, you can slip by if you're careful. Get onto that ship."

She listened, paralyzed as the tears fell.

She couldn't move, numb with the terror of words consuming her.

Her fault.

This abandonment would be her fault. The man she had grown to care for so much would be gone, forever.

"Eva." He ran his hand through her hair, forcing himself to smile. "I know you can do this."

"I can't," she whimpered.

"Yes, you can. You will." He adjusted the blade against his abdomen and shuddered a breath, wincing. "Promise...promise me you'll get on that ship."

Evalyn choked on the tears that almost blinded her. "Dax, I...I think we could have..." She couldn't finish the words.

Dax silenced her with a finger over trembling lips. "I know, little dove."

They sat there, gripping the dagger together, holding it unmoving against his abdomen. "Dax, it can't end this way. There's so much I..."

Blood flowered his tunic as the sharp steel bit into his flesh. She tried to pull away, but again his hand gripped hers firmly, only drawing more blood. "In another life, another time, I will find you. But in this one, I will do whatever I can to protect you from harm. I will do this for you."

"I wanted you to come with me. To be safe, with me."

"In another life." He tucked a silver strand behind her ear, his voice faint. "Now, promise me you will get on that ship."

"I promise," she whispered.

He touched soft lips to her forehead. They lingered, sealing all the unspoken feelings within that one touch as if that would somehow keep them safe until they could be unlocked once more.

"Together," He released a steady breath, placing his hand on hers. "Together."

She nodded, reaching into herself to find the strength he believed she had, fixating on it. "Dax, in another life—"

"I will find you again, Eva. I will find you, and I promise I will never abandon you again."

That was the last thing he said before Dax pulled her against his chest, hugging her with a fierce longing as he thrust their conjoined hands into his abdomen and bit back a cry of agony.

Glossary

<u>Words</u>

Sielapora- (say-LAH-pour-AH): ancient Dorwynnian term for kindred souls or warrior soul mates, a unique, non-romantic bond between fighting companions.

The Shadowplains- the demon realm
Narcio- (Nar-SEE-oh)
Dorwynn- (DOOr-win)
Rekiv- (Rah-KEH-v)
Rathal- (Rah-thAH-l)
Ebondenn- (Ebb-OHN-den)
Chiron- (Ch-ih-ROne)
Raenya- (RAY-een-yah)

Joseline- (JAHss-eh-LYN)
Evalyn- (Eh-VAH-lyn)

<u>The Twelve (Navarre's Gods, also the names of the months)</u>

Noria- (no-REE-ah): Goddess of Healing
Eona- (ee-OH-nah): Goddess of Love and Desire
Rinoa- (rih-NO-ah): Goddess of Life, the Sun and Precious Minerals
Syvi- (sIH-vee): Goddess of the Sea
Ywone- (yih-WOE-n): Goddess of Beauty, Morality, and Fertility
Ryenas- (riy-NEE-ahs): God of Trade, Agriculture, and Wine
Malous- (MAL-oh-oos): God of Wealth
Kyaos- (kiy-AH-ohs): God of Wisdom
Nova- (NO-vah): Goddess of the Moon
Era- (ERR-ah): Goddess of War and the Hunt
Yvaos- (YAH-voh-s): God of Strength
Sauda- (SA-ou-da): the Goddess of Death

Acknowledgments

Long ago and far away there lived a small girl with a wild imagination. It grew with her, yearning to touch the lives of those around it with fantastical stories. She was blessed with love and showered with praises by those who loved her. But not all did. And those who did not sought to ruin her spirit. They teased and tormented her with cruel tricks and games until she found herself defeated, withering, and broken beneath their doubts.

Even so, a small sliver of hope remained. And from that hope, so her courage grew again, giving her the power to do what all heroes do: rise from the ashes.

This is my excessive and dramatic attempt at explaining how Awakening Shadows came into being for ten-year-old Sydney. I was extremely bullied as a child. I didn't have many close friends when I was little. And the ones I did have, I never quite felt I could be myself with. I was constantly ridiculed for the smallest things, mocked, laughed at, and too sweet to stand up for myself.

So, I created a fantasy world where I could be whoever I wanted without fear of anyone's mockery. Max Porter came into existence as my imaginary friend and partner in crime. His story was similar to mine; sob story of a misunderstood child with no friends to rely on. He grew as I grew, and by the time I was ten, his world and his story had blossomed into a beautiful realm with endless perils.

And thus, Navarre was born.

That seems like eons ago. Eons since that spark first ignited within me craving to be told. Max has since transformed into my beautifully annoying Quinn, and Navarre is a much, MUCH darker place than originally planned. But I'm not complaining, not when I have so many wonderful people to thank for joining me on this journey.

First and foremost, I need to thank my Nana. She was my light. My rock in so many things. Even though she's gone, I've never felt like she truly was; her presence is always within my heart and soul, braving the doubts each time I face them.

To my parents. Mom and Dad, thank you for never doubting me. For showing me every day the beauty that is our imagination, and for never trying to crush mine no matter how old I got. Even though I refused to tell them when I was being bullied, their love and pride in my dreams was never ending and for that, I will forever be grateful. And to my mother, who single handedly made my book map possible, best birthday present EVER.

To Laura, the first friend who truly believed in me. My alpha reader who isn't a writer. My writing wing woman. Girl, you have been there from the very beginning. From the time when Max was accused of murder and going to a magic school to solve his problems. Gods, talk about Harry Potter wannabe...yeesh. You've never failed to support me and be there to read my work with endless praise, even in the beginning when I knew it was awful. The sleepovers staying up late to bounce around ideas, and the endurance through the darkness. Honestly, I would be completely lost without you, and I cannot thank you enough for your friendship. <3

To Aunt Dana, who first pushed me to really publish. You stood by my side, helped me create an account, and handed me the opportunity to jump off the ledge. I'm glad now that I didn't take the leap back then, but I'm still grateful to you for showing me the way to the top of the hill without ever letting go of my hand.

To David, who despite being a non-reader, has never failed to love me unconditionally and support me as I pursue my writing dreams.

To Andie, for being the best Instagram friend a girl could ask for. We are half a world away, literally, yet I feel like we were meant to be friends. You were my first social media friend, my first creative cohort, and my OG critique partner. It seems like forever ago that we sent each other those care packages for the holidays, and I can't believe how far we've come since then. You've been by my side cheering me on for several years now. Several years of crazy long emails sobbing over the cruel yet satisfying plot twists we have planned, gushing over our precious babies and their relationships, over the endless flow of worldbuilding. The interior of AS even looks flawless because of you. I know I wouldn't be half the writer I am today without your support. So thank you, for being by my side. <3

To Lina, my dearest partner in crime. My soul sister. Where to begin? If we lived closer, we'd be inseparable, that's all there is to that. I get the sappy feeling that the beginning of Navarre would have started out a lot differently if I'd grown up with more friends like you. I remember making the decision rather timidly to ask if you wanted to be CPs, and I couldn't imagine this journey with anyone else as a staple by my side. I mean, who just randomly offers to draw family crests for you for free because they have nothing better to do and know you're tight on money? Nobody. <3 You are a beautiful, kind, exquisite soul, and I am so grateful for your friendship.

To Katie, the queen of romance and another one of my lovely CPs who has believed in my characters and their relationships from the very beginning. Your squeals of excitement over their actions never ceases to make my heart swell.

To my Beta Readers. Dani, I have no one to thank but you for originally suggesting I change around the ending. Your endless support of my random "oooo, oooo, what about this way?" messages is unequal. Savannah, your support and pride in my characters is a gift I will always cherish! Kristen, Rae, Lauren, all of you. Thank you, from the bottom of my heart for all your help and motivation and for loving my world even in its more primitive stages.

To my editors. Camilla, thank you for editing my baby and making yet another beautifully flawless suggestion to the plot. And Renee, my love for you knows no bounds. Not only did you edit Awakening Shadows for me with love and squeals of excitement, but your knowledge and help along this path to publishing and your willingness to answer all my questions about this crazy indie world has been so precious to me I still want to cry from your kindness.

To Mrs. Franks and Mrs. Chernick, my favorite high school English teachers, who never stopped believing me and helping me to continue believing in myself.

To Jess from Lizard Ink Maps for helping me bring Navarre to life. Literally. I still can't believe how absolutely STUNNING that map is! I will be forever grateful that I got the chance to work with you. <3

To Celin (@celingraphics) my cover designer, for bringing my imagination to life when I was struggling. I am so blown away by your talents. I cannot believe that you took the concepts I was drowning in and made them flesh so effortlessly.

To all the authors who sparked the excited look in my eye every time I picked up a fantasy book and made me want to pursue those dreams myself. Tamora Pierce, J.R.R. Tolkien, J.K. Rowling, C.S. Lewis, Holly Black, Sarah J. Maas, Leigh Bardugo, I am forever grateful for the beautiful worlds you created, thus inspiring me to create my own.

To my fabulous street team and ARC team for helping me bring the magic of Navarre into the world by storm! For your beautiful reviews and endless excitement. I can guarantee you I would not be here without them. I cannot thank you lovely humans enough!

And to you, my lovely gemstones, my magical readers. Thank you for believing in me and my realm. For cherishing my characters the same way I do. For spreading the word about my books to other future readers. For your love. For your undying support. For making my dreams a reality. Your support is worth more than any precious gem in this world.

About the Author

Sydney has been devouring fantasy for as long as she can remember. She dabbles in theater, crafting, and cosplaying or cooking (badly) when her free time isn't consumed with reading or writing. She's the oldest of three and co-parent to two precious kitties, (Pandora and Panther Lily) and enjoys discussing the struggles of life with them whenever she can. After five years of nursing school failures, Sydney finally has her Associate of Arts and is currently dancing through life with her soulmate and partner-in-crime.

For more information on her journey, her work, or simply to fangirl over fictional characters, feel free to follow her on Instagram—@sydneysbookshelf or Tiktok—@faeriequeensydney, check out #thelilacbookblog for book reviews, and sign up for her newsletter, The Lilac Letter! (**www.worldofsydneyhawthorn.com**)

the story continues!

Anxious to know what happens next?

Follow me on Instagram (@sydneysbookshelf), visit my website and subscribe to my newsletter for updates and behind-the-scenes goodies, or visit my shop for signed copies, merchandise, and more!

Made in the USA
Middletown, DE
03 April 2021